THE COMPLETE TALES OF SHERIFF HENRY, VOLUME 5

W. C. Tuttle

HENRY PLAYS A HUNCH

THE COMPLETE TALES OF SHERIFF HENRY, VOLUME 5

W.C. TUTTLE

COVER BY

EMMETT WATSON

ILLUSTRATIONS BY

SAMUEL CAHAN

STEEGER BOOKS • 2021

PUBLISHING HISTORY

"Henry Plays a Hunch" originally appeared in the October 9–30, 1937 issues of *Argosy* magazine (Vol. 276, No. 4–Vol. 277, No. 1). Copyright © 1937 by The Frank A. Munsey Company. Copyright renewed © 1964 and assigned to Steeger Properties, LLC. All rights reserved.

"Henry Hits the Warpath" originally appeared in the December 24, 1938 issue of *Argosy* magazine (Vol. 287, No. 1). Copyright © 1938 by The Frank A. Munsey Company. Copyright renewed © 1966 and assigned to Steeger Properties, LLC. All rights reserved.

TABLE OF CONTENTS

HENRY PLAYS A HUNCH

*That amazing, red-nosed, bespatted lawman, Sheriff
Henry Harrison Conroy of Tonto, is back again with
a fresh gallon of prune juice and a job to tackle as
tough as any Wild Horse Valley has ever offered him*

CHAPTER I

DUSTY PROPOSES

SANDY CRANE HUNCHED dolefully on the top pole of the Bar M corral, his eyes centered on the front door of the ranch house. Sandy, whose nickname had been shortened from Sandhill, was tall and gaunt and gangly. His face was deeply lined, his eyes sad brown, and he boasted the widest mouth in Wild Horse Valley. With muffled voice he sang:

> If m' darlin's dead jist show the red,
> But if she's better-r-r-r, show the blue.

But Sandy's mind was not on his song. It was a subconscious action, even if he did hang onto some of the notes with a coyote wail. He was watching that front door, waiting for Dusty Cole to appear. Dusty was on a dangerous mission. At least, Sandy thought so. He knew Peter—known locally as Peter the Great—Morris very well indeed. Peter had tremendous strength and a hair-trigger temper.

Sandy had warned Dusty of this, but the warning went unheeded, because Dusty Cole, reckless and young, was in love with Laura Morris. Sandy did not blame him for that. Nearly every cowboy from Scorpion Bend to Tonto Town was in love with Laura Morris. Dusty had, to outward appearance at least, rather the better of it, because he worked on the Morris ranch, the Bar M.

"I seen it comin' on," remarked Sandy, when Dusty told him.

"I've seen the same expression in the eyes of a bogged-down calf."

And now Dusty Cole was in the main room of the ranch house, telling Peter the Great that he, Dusty Cole, was in love with Laura and wished to marry her. Dusty had his speech all rehearsed.

Sandy, his voice still muffled, sang:

> Ta-a-ake back your gold,
> For gold will never buy me-e-e-e....

And then the front door banged open, propelled by the hurtling body of Dusty Cole. There was a rather flimsy railing around the porch, and this proved but little obstruction to the body. Dusty Cole ended in a sitting position in the dirt about six feet from the edge of the porch.

For almost a minute he sat there, as though trying to puzzle out just what had happened. The door had shut behind him. Down at the corral, Sandy Crane's sombrero bobbed a trifle, due to the quizzical lifting of his brows. Then Sandy softly cleared his throat, and it seemed that a ripple of mirth jiggled his belt-buckle.

Dusty got slowly to his feet, felt himself over painfully. Then

he limped down to the corral fence. He paused there to look sourly at Sandy. Dusty was barely past his majority, well built, good-looking. A long lock of curly brown hair straggled down over one eye, and he shifted it with a gusty blow of his lips.

"Well, Romeo," remarked Sandy, "it kinda looks to me like yore balcony done busted."

"My what?" asked Dusty blankly.

Sandy sighed and rubbed his nose. "When you leave a place, yuh shore do leave it, Dusty."

"Oh, yeah," agreed Dusty, looking back at the porch. "If anybody ever tells me that Peter Morris is the strongest man in the whole danged world, I'm goin' to nod my head."

"Come up here and set down," invited Sandy.

"Yo're crazy," declared Dusty. "I've done too much settin'."

He sighed dismally, shrugged his shoulders, then added:

"Well, we might as well pack our plunder, Sandy. We're fired."

Sandy removed his sombrero, looking wide-eyed at Dusty.

"*We're* fired?" he gasped. "Was that what yuh said, Dusty?"

"Both of us," agreed Dusty.

"Well, holy smoke, I didn't ask him for his daughter's hand!"

"That's exactly what I told him," declared Dusty. "He said, 'The next thing I know that saw-faced, two-by-four pardner of yours will want to marry her.'"

"I said, 'Yo're wrong, Mr. Morris. He told me he wouldn't have her as a gift, if he had to have you for a daddy-in-law.'"

"You told him that, Dusty? Why, dang yore hide, I'll—"

"Wait a minute! He said you was saw-faced, didn't he? Heck, I won't let anybody slander you, Sandy. Anyway, I was the one that wanted her."

"Well, ain't that wonderful!" exclaimed Sandy. "You ask a man for his daughter's hand—and I get fired"

"Me, too," sighed Dusty. "But I told him a few things, y'betcha."

"Yeah, I'll bet you did! Well, I'm goin' up there and tell him I never said I wouldn't have her. Why wouldn't I have her? She's the prettiest girl in Wild Horse Valley."

Sandy got off the fence and tightened up his belt. Dusty looked him over sadly, and held out his right hand.

"Good-by, Sandy," he said, a sob in his voice. "I'll wait in Tonto City for the coroner to bring in yore remains."

Sandy shook hands solemnly with him, adjusted his sombrero, and looked thoughtfully at the house. But he seemed then to hesitate.

"After all," he said finally, "forty a month ain't worth fightin' over. But what about our money?"

"He said it would be at the bank for us."

"Uh-huh. Well, I don't reckon there's anything to keep us here. It's a lucky thing we own our own horses. But you ain't givin' up Laura without a struggle, are yuh—or do yuh figure you've just had one?"

"When Peter the Great gets hold of yuh—struggle and be danged. But I'm not givin' up Laura, and I'm not leavin' the country. Peter Morris is goin' to find out that I'm one cow-waddy he can't handle."

"Yuh better try out—guessin' him, Dusty," grinned Sandy.

"I s'pose," sighed Dusty. "But love or no love, if he ever puts a hand on me again—or before he does—"

"I wouldn't think about anything like that," said Sandy quietly.

Dusty changed the subject.

"Let's go up to the bunk-house and collect our stuff," he said, "before I get so stiff I can't walk. Man, I shore set down a long ways."

FROM A window of the big ranch house Peter Morris watched the two cowboys leave the ranch. Morris was a huge man, bearded, powerful as a bull, and not lacking in arrogance. Peter Morris had nothing against Dusty Cole as a hand. To him, Dusty was a run-of-the-mill cowboy, capable of earning forty dollars a month, inclined to be as wild as a hawk, and not at all a suitable husband for Laura.

As he turned from the window Laura came down the stairs. Laura had inherited none of her father's likeness or traits. She was small and slender, with brown hair and gray eyes. But in spite of her size and beauty, there was nothing of the clinging-vine in her makeup. There was a defiant blaze in her eyes as she looked at her father.

"Dusty Cole," he said laconically, "had the nerve to ask me to let you marry him."

"I saw your answer from my window," she answered coldly.

"You saw it, did yuh?" Peter Morris chuckled.

"I saw you throw him out."

A shadow of surprise crossed his face. "Well, what could he expect?" he demanded.

"Civil treatment—at least."

"Huh?" Peter Morris stared at her. "You don't mean to stand there and intimate that you'd marry *him*, do yuh?"

"I told him I would. Maybe he didn't tell you what I said."

Peter Morris turned slowly to the window again.

"Well, yeah, he did mention it. But what of it? He hasn't

anything. I owe him about six dollars, and I'll bet he hasn't got another cent. Marriage! You'd starve with Dusty Cole."

"Did mother starve, when she married you?" asked Laura.

Peter Morris turned quickly. "No, you can't use that as an example. Things was different in them days. Why, we—stop that danged grinnin', will yuh?"

"I am not grinning—I'm showing my teeth," retorted Laura. "If I know Dusty Cole, he hasn't started fighting yet."

"Stubborn, eh—along with his other bad habits. Drinks whisky, smokes cigarettes and plays poker."

"So do you—and in addition, you chew."

"You let my personal habits alone, young lady."

"Then you stop defaming Dusty Cole," she snapped. "He doesn't chew—and that's a lot in his favor."

"Prob'ly make him sick—and that's why he don't. Anyway, I fired him and Sandy Crane today, and they're off the ranch for good."

"Why did you fire Sandy Crane?" asked Laura.

"Why? Because he told Dusty he wouldn't have you as a gift, if he had to have me for a father-in-law."

Laura's gray eyes were dancing, but her face was sober as she said: "That would be quite a responsibility, I suppose."

Peter Morris ignored the jibe. He picked up his hat.

"I'm goin' to town," he told her. "I've got to pay the boys off, this afternoon, 'cause they'll all want to go to town tonight."

"I believe I'll go to town, too," remarked Laura.

"You will, eh?" growled her father. "Well, you keep away from Dusty Cole. I won't have it. I tell yuh. You'll obey my orders, or I'll lock yuh up."

Laura laughed at his threat. "You'll be there to watch me, won't you?"

"I will not, because I have to meet a man here tonight."

"Well, I'll try and get along alone," said Laura soberly. "I might go out and have a visit with Molly Hope."

"Yeah!" snorted Peter Morris. "There's an example for yuh. She married in haste, and look what she got. Oh, I don't care if she is Judge Myers' daughter. If I had a son-in-law like Sam Hope, I'd trade him for a sidewinder."

"Molly is the sweetest girl on earth," declared Laura warmly.

"Sure," agreed her father. "But she was bull-headed. The judge didn't want her to marry Sam—but she knew best, and look at the cripple-brain she got."

"She loves him, Dad."

"Love!" Peter Morris laughed harshly. "There's no accountin' for taste, as the prospector said when he kissed his burro. But I sure ain't goin' to let you make the same mistake Molly Myers made."

CHAPTER II

PRUNE JUICE AND CHICKENS

HENRY HARRISON CONROY had been born back-stage in a theater, and all his life had been spent behind the foot-lights, until he came to Tonto City. When vaudeville waned, his contract had been cancelled. Soon after that an aged uncle died and willed Henry the JHC Ranch in Wild Horse Valley, Arizona. Up to that time Henry's knowledge of the West had been gained by watching a stage production of *The Squaw Man*.

Henry was short and very fat, with a moon-like face, squinty, blue eyes and a huge red nose, which had been featured in vaude-ville from coast to coast for years. Tonto City and Wild Horse Valley, intrigued and amused by this red-nosed, derby-hatted, white-spatted and gold-caned personage, welcomed him as an innovation, and in a spirit of fun elected him sheriff of the county.

Henry accepted the honor in the same spirit by appointing "Judge" Van Treece as his deputy, and Oscar Johnson as his jailer. Judge was sixty years of age, tall and gaunt, had managed to drink himself out of the limelight as a criminal lawyer, and was more or less of a derelict when Henry appointed him. Oscar Johnson, a giant of a Swede, whom Judge nicknamed "The Vitrified Viking," had been a horse-wrangler on the JHC until Henry made him jailer. But in spite of their combined eccen-tricities, the sheriff's office at Tonto managed to function with reasonable efficiency.

Just now the three peace officers were in the office, with

Henry at his desk. Judge tilted back against the wall, his heels hooked over the top rung of his chair, while Oscar sprawled on a cot, clad in a badly-wrinkled, sickly-green suit of clothes, his once-white collar hiked up around his big ears.

"Sifting your rambling statement to plain facts," Judge was remarking soberly to Oscar, "you hired a horse and buggy here last evening, with the intention of taking Josephine Swensen to a dance last night at the city of Scorpion Bend. During the evening you, as usual, drank too much whisky, became exasperated at Josephine and drove home, taking the wrong horse and buggy. Am I right, Oscar?"

"Ay yust got de wrong hurse and boggy," nodded Oscar.

"And smashed the buggy wheels against the first obstacle you saw," added Henry dryly. "I understand that you drove into the livery stable at some ungodly hour this morning, with both the wheels on one side of the buggy ground down to the hubs."

"Ay t'ought de road vars high on vone side," grinned Oscar. "But Ay am t'rough vit Yosephine, you bat you. She can't make no fule out of me—sometime."

"I suppose it was Olaf again," said Henry.

Olaf was a huge Norwegian who had tried to take Josephine away from Oscar, but with no physical success.

"It vars not," declared Oscar indignantly. "It vars a shiph-order from Black River City, named Nels Yensen. Yust a damn shiphorder."

Henry blinked back some riotous tears. "What started the trouble, Oscar?"

"Va'al, it vars like dis," began Oscar, enumerating on his huge, cucumber-like fingers, as though counting. "Nels Yensen gave Yosephine a ring, and she shows it to me. Ay made her give it back, and Ay said to him, 'If you give yewelry to my girl again Ay vill knock your ears off.'

"Nels he say to me, 'Ay yust gave it to her so she vould remember me.'

"Ay said to him, 'She don't need it, because every time she sees a yackass she vill remamber you.'"

"And so you fought with him, eh?" queried Judge.

"To ha'al *vit* him!" snorted Oscar. "Ay fought *against* him, Yudge."

"Who won the fight?" choked Henry.

Oscar grinned sourly. "Yosephine," he admitted.

"How on earth did Josephine get into the brawl?"

"It vars in de holl, vere dey serve de sopper. Yosephine had small piece two-by-four. Ven Ay voke up dey vars taking Nels out. Yosephine vars dere, and she says, 'What in de ha'al are you vaiting for?' Ay yust vent out oll by myself.

"Ay vent to de Scorpion Saloon. Nels vars dere and he says, 'Yudas Priest, you hit me so quick I never see it.' Ay says to him, 'You bat you, Ay am great fighter. Ay can vip anybody in de vorld.'

"And den he hit me right on de nose. Ve busted up all de furniture in de saloon before Ay got sqvare poke at him. Ay knock him as cold as Norvegian iceborg. Den Ay take him outside, put him in boggy, untie de hurse and give him de lines. Dat vars de end of it."

"You put him in your own buggy, didn't you?" queried Judge.

"By yeeminee, Ay bet Ay did!" snorted Oscar.

Judge shook his head sadly.

"You're a fine example of law and order. Drunken jailer fights with a sheepherder. Henry, is it any wonder that they call us the Shame of Arizona? Is it any wonder that they point the finger of shame at your regime?"

"Have I ever denied the allegation, Judge?" asked Henry.

"Confound it, sir, we should have a little dignity!"

Oscar was peering out the door. "Ha'ar comes Free-holey," he announced. "Yust about time."

FRIJOLE BILL CULLISON was the cook at the JHC. He was past sixty years of age, a little, skinny rawhider, with a peaked face and long mustaches. When he wasn't cooking food or clean-ing house, he was distilling prunes—and there was little cooking or housekeeping to do these days.

Frijole had a gallon jug, all wrapped up in a burlap sack, which he carefully placed on the cot beside Oscar.

"And that," he declared, "will whip anything ever made in Kentucky. Twenty years old, if it's a day, and it was made yester-day. That stuff ages so fast that if yuh left it alone for a week, it'd turn into a mummy."

"I give you good afternoon, Frijole," said Henry soberly.

"I'll take it—and thank yuh, Sheriff," said Frijole. "Everything is fine at the rancho—except Bill Shakespeare, the rooster."

"What happened to Bill?" asked Judge. "Now, don't lie about him."

"I hope t' die sometime, if I ever lied about him, Judge. Yuh know how Bill's allus been about my prune mash. Him fillin' up on it and goin' out to pick a fight with a wildcat. Well, sir, Old Bill finally jist about cleaned all the wildcats out of that coun-try. When he fanned them two lions out of Jawbone Canyon, I figured he'd gnawed off a chunk, but he got rid of 'em awful quick.

"Yesterday, when I dumped my mash, I noticed that Bill was kinda shinin' up to a red hen I named Emmelina. Well, he started bowin' and scrapin' beside the mash-pile; so she comes over and starts eatin' of it. Old Bill, with sort of a grin on his face, digs into it himself. Well, sir, inside of ten minutes them two are fightin'. I'll tell yuh this much, Old Bill ain't no gentleman. Him havin' spurs and a five, six pound advantage. So I separates 'em, catches the hen, and I wires a couple ten-penny spikes on her legs. Whooee-e-e-e!

"Well, to make a long story short, Old Bill's up on the ridge-pole of the house. Been up there since yesterday afternoon, and danged if he'll come down. All he's got left in the feather line is his wings and one tail feather."

"And where, if I may be so bold as to ask, is Emmelina?" asked Henry.

"Oh, her," said Frijole, a faraway look in his eyes. "Well, sir, she pulled off what a Frenchman would call a *fox pass*. There's a coyote been hangin' around the ranch, aimin' to have a chicken dinner. When he made his visit last evenin', he didn't see Emmelina on the top pole of the corral fence. She landed plumb straddle of him. Then she socked them ten-penny spurs into him, and away they went.

"I've been doin' a heap of thinkin' about it since then. Yuh see, she ain't had much experience with spurs, and I figured she's done mastered the art of sockin' 'em in, but she didn't know how to yank 'em out. Anyway, she ain't such a loss; bein' as she ain't layed any eggs for months."

"I don't believe a word of it!" snorted Judge.

"Why, Judge!" exclaimed Frijole. "Wouldn't I *know* if she laid any eggs?"

Henry wiped the tears away and rubbed his waistline, while Judge rumbled and mumbled, deep in his skinny throat.

"I rode in with Dusty Cole and Sandy Crane," remarked Frijole. No one seemed interested, so Frijole continued: "Peter the Great fired both of 'em today."

"Why?" asked Henry.

"Love—they told me."

"Love?"

"Yeah. Dusty asked Peter the Great for the hand of his daughter, and Peter threw Dusty out of the house. Then he tied a can on both of 'em."

"Well, my goodness!" exclaimed Judge. "Dusty is a nice boy."

"Laura Morris is a nice girl, too," added Henry. "Love seemed doomed to setbacks in Wild Horse Valley. Look at Oscar."

"What went wrong with the big Swede?" asked Frijole.

"Ay have bruk off vit Yosephine."

"Well, I dunno," sighed Frijole. "After what I seen Old Bill do to Emmelina, I'll—"

"Don't!" interrupted Judge. "You told that once, Frijole."

"Ay vould like to try dis prune yuice," remarked Oscar.

"On top of the hangover you already have?" queried Judge. "Don't do it, Oscar."

"His love has been shattered, Judge," reminded Henry dryly.

"Well," declared Judge, "there is no use of dynamiting the remains. My advice is to keep that stuff corked."

Frijole shook his head vehemently.

"I wouldn't," he said. "Yuh notice I've got a string tied to the cork, in case she blows. I dunno how many corks I've lost. I done tried standin' a jug on the cork; but it blowed the jug through the roof. That happened 'bout nine o'clock at night, and next mornin' that cork was still bouncin' around the room."

"Of all the confounded liars," wailed Judge.

"Yea-a-ah?" queried Frijole. "Well, you come out and I'll prove it."

"How can you prove it?" demanded Judge.

"I'll show yuh the cork."

Henry reached for his hat and went waddling out of the office, his expansive equator jerking from internal convulsions.

THERE WAS nothing dry nor dull about Tonto City. When Henry had been elected sheriff Tonto was strictly a cowtown, but the discovery of gold had made it both cowtown and mining camp. Muck-covered miners just off shift, burro-punching prospectors, cowboys, gamblers and the usual riff-raff of a mining town rubbed elbows together in the saloons and gambling houses.

The town smiled at Henry Harrison Conroy and his misfit helpers—and Henry smiled back at them. Part of the time he wore high-heel boots, huge Stetson sombrero and a holstered gun; and sometimes he appeared in a pastel-gray suit, gray derby—and spats. At those times he also carried a gold-headed cane. But at all times his nose had the color and sheen of a polished beet.

Henry was wearing his Western outfit this day, as he strolled up to the weathered old building which housed the county offices. He saw Judge Myers, the Superior Court justice, motioning to him from an office window. Nodding, he entered the building.

Judge Myers was decidedly of the Abraham Lincoln type, tall and awkward, thin-faced, sharp of eye, and with a sense of humor. As he motioned Henry to a seat, it was evident that he was disturbed. Henry sat down, folded his fat hands and squinted quizzically at the judge.

"Judge," he said, "after looking at you I would decide that all is not beer and skittles. May I ask what is on your mind?"

Judge Myers sat down at his desk. For several moments he nervously shuffled some papers. Finally he asked:

"Has Peter Morris said anything to you about—er—Sam Hope?"

"No, Judge—not of late."

"He promised he wouldn't."

"Sam in trouble again, Judge?"

"He was," sighed the judge.

"By the way, you started Sam in the cattle business a few months ago, Judge. Bought out that Bar N brand, I understood."

"It wasn't much, Henry—but I had to dig into my savings. Confound it, I didn't do it for Sam—I did it for Molly. Sam isn't worth the price of the dynamite it would take to blow his head off. Oh, he was grateful and all that. Promised to reform, of course. And it made Molly very happy."

"Too bad about Sam," sighed Henry. "Molly is as sweet as any woman on earth. Damn it, Judge. I don't know why sweet women cling to no-good folks like Sam Hope. But what was the trouble?"

"The trouble," explained the judge grimly, "was the fact that Peter Morris caught Sam herding a Bar M calf with a Bar N cow. Whether he intended altering the calf to a Bar N—I do not know. Peter drew a gun on Sam, and took the calf. He came to see me today. Because of Molly he did not have Sam arrested."

"What did Morris want?" asked Henry curiously.

"He asked me to have that Bar N brand cancelled and register another mark. He thought that the similarity of brands might influence my dear son-in-law. Henry, I believe I am the only Superior Court judge in the world whose son-in-law is a protected cattle rustler."

"A doubtful honor, I am obliged to admit," said Henry gravely. "Does Molly know this?"

"Not unless Sam has told her. I haven't talked with Sam. Don't believe I shall. Confound it, Henry, the young man hasn't a single redeeming feature."

"He has a winning smile—and an uncanny ability at throwing a knife," remarked Henry.

"Yes, he has that ability."

"But he doesn't carry his liquor well, Judge."

"Not well—but often, Henry. Oh, I've talked things over with Molly many times, and begged her to divorce Sam. But she only smiles and says that Sam needs her. Needs her!"

"I suppose he was indignant at Peter Morris."

"Of course. Oh, he has plenty of nerve. I believe he told Peter Morris that some day he would make him eat his gun."

"Rather a hard dish," mused Henry. "Even with such jaws as his. I misdoubt that Peter could masticate it entirely. Well, I suppose there is nothing to be done about it, Judge. I believe there is a saying that if you give a calf enough rope, he will hang himself."

"That is exactly what I am afraid might happen, Henry."

"Worry will not help matters, Judge. I suggest that we advance on that pool of iniquity known as the Tonto, and indulge in the cup that cheers. I am several minutes past my drinking time."

"And mine, too," agreed the judge, reaching for his hat. "We must look on the bright side of things, I suppose"

THEY FOUND Sandy Crane at the bar in the Tonto Saloon. Sandy was still able to stay upright—but with an effort.

"Misser Conroy," he said expansively, "you are jus' 'n time to shettle grave debate. Me and the barten'er has problem. Take look at me, will yuh. Conshider me from every angle. Tha's right. All right. To the bes' of your ability and judgment, would you shay I'm drunk?"

"My dear Mr. Crane!" exclaimed Henry.

"Then I win!" exploded Sandy triumphantly. "Gimme that four-bits, barten'er."

"Aw, he didn't say yuh ain't drunk."

"I believe," smiled Henry, "that Mr. Crane is in the same position as the traveler who stops a few rods out of town and asks someone if he is headed in the general direction of Tonto City."

"How's that?" queried Sandy.

"Well, he is headed right and has only a short distance to go."

"I shee," grinned Sandy. "But in order to be real good 'n drunk, I've still got a ways to go, eh?"

"After all," smiled Henry, "I am not able to state the degree of sobriety or intoxication which you are enjoying. I would declare the bet a draw."

"Tha's shenshible," agreed Sandy. "Will you and Judge honor me?"

Of course they would, they assured him. And they did. Henry inquired about Dusty Cole.

Sandy chuckled over his glass. "Dusty's gone out to Sam Hope's ranch," he told them confidently—in a loud voice. "Peter the Great kicked us both off the ranch t'day. But Dusty knowed that a shertain lady was goin' to Hope's ranch; so Dusty went there."

"Have you seen Sam Hope in town today, Sandy?" asked the judge.

" 'Bout an hour ago," nodded Sandy. "And was he pickled! Had hard time gettin' on his horsh."

"Nothing unusual about that," sighed Judge Myers.

"Jus' a little stiffer 'n usual," remarked Sandy Crane.

CHAPTER III

LIGHTNING TESTIFIES

OUT AT THE JHC Ranch, Thunder and Lightning Mendoza prepared to go visiting. They were a pair of undersized and over-fat, half-Mexican, half-Yaqui breeds whom Henry had hired, more because of their misuse of the English language than any ability with cows.

Juan Mendoza, cook at the Morris ranch, was their uncle, and it was to visit Juan that they were all dressed up that Saturday evening. Lightning was smooth of face, while Thunder boasted a six-hair mustache which he nursed carefully.

"Madre de Dios!" exclaimed Thunder. "Those stove polish make theese boot shine like neeger's hill."

"She's shine like hell," agreed Lightning admiringly. "But w'at ees a neeger's hill?"

"Por Dios, I am ashame from my own ignorance," declared Thunder. "You know w'at ees a toe?"

"Sure. I'm got me t'ree, four, myself."

"Well, theese hill I'm spik 'bout is the firs' bend—"

"Oh, sure! You mean hill. Like theese hill of a boot. You spik Englis' like a shipherder."

"Leesten!" exploded Thunder. "Leesten, my leetle brodder! W'ere you get those rad necktie?"

"You like heem, eh?" smiled Lightning proudly. "I buy heem from Frijole for twenty-five *centavos.* W'en he ees ver' young he ees four-handed, but Frijole cut heem off and he mak' ver' nice bow, eh? He say he cut off the soup ends."

18

"Frijole, eh? That son-of-a-gonn! Twenty-five *centavos* for my rad necktie. That mak' me very seek."

"How long you have rad necktie?" asked Lightning.

"How long? That necktie ees almos' new. I bet I don' have heem over seek year—that's all I hope."

"Well," remarked Lightning, "she look damn good on me. How we go see Juan?"

"Everybodee ees gone to Tonto Ceety. There ees team in the stable, and bockboard in the yard."

"That team from 'orses ees not broke ver' well."

"Are you scare from 'orses? Bah! I drove worse 'orse than this all your life. Señor 'Enry hees saying I am worse driver than Ben Hur. He say I can do more dang' theeng weeth 'orse and boggy than Oscar Johnson, who ees the worl' champinn. W'at you theenk of those?"

"That sound damn good," agreed Lightning. "But after I am dead, w'at ees the use of leestening to you. Sure, I go. You are jus' as crazy as I am."

DUSTY COLE came back to Tonto City about dark, and found Sandy Crane sound asleep in a chair at the Tonto Saloon. Dusty had discovered that he had forgotten his Sunday boots at the Bar M, and wanted Sandy to ride out there with him, but Sandy was in no condition to mount a horse.

Laura Morris had told him that her father would come to take her home about ten o'clock, and urged Dusty in the meanwhile to have another talk with him when he went out to get his boots.

Still, Dusty did not share her optimism when she said that "He might look at things differently now."

Nevertheless, Dusty wanted his boots; so he rode out there alone. There was a light in the ranch house. When he arrived Laura had mentioned something about her father having an appointment, but she did not know who was coming out to see him. Dusty rode quietly up near the bunk-house. He could go into the bunk-house, secure his boots, and ride away, without disturbing anyone.

He dismounted beside the bunk-house and walked to the door. He opened it and stepped inside. In the darkness he started to the rear, where he knew there would be a lamp on the table. Halfway across the room he tripped over something and went to his knees.

His groping hand touched a thing that yielded, and he jerked back quickly. Carefully he reached out again, running his fingers over the object. It was a man's face, sticky with blood.

Dusty jerked his hand away, got slowly to his feet, reaching around for the table. With shaking fingers he took a match from his pocket and lighted the lamp.

In the middle of the floor lay Juan Mendoza, the Mexican cook, flat on his back, apparently dead.

Dusty's eyes circled the room, his face grim in the lamplight. What on earth had happened to Juan, he wondered? And where was Peter the Great Morris?

At a sound from outside, Dusty jerked up his head.

From out in the yard came the thudding of hoofs, the rattle and squeak of a wheeled vehicle. Dusty ran to the doorway. At that moment a crash shook the bunk-house. A heavy body hurtled into him, hurled him back against a bunk. His head collided with the wall, and consciousness disappeared in a flash of light.

BUSINESS WAS good that evening at the Tonto Saloon and Gambling Palace. It was payday at the ranches and the mines, and the main idea seemed to get rid of the money as quickly as possible. Henry and Judge were at the bar, talking with Jim McDonald, one of Morris' cowboys. When a very disheveled Lightning Mendoza staggered into the place. Lightning's nose was skinned, and the blood had not improved his appearance in the least.

"Madre de Dios!" he howled. "Dusty Cole hees keel our onkle!"

Henry grasped Lightning by the arm and shook him violently.

"Take a deep breath and count ten," advised Henry.

"No can count," panted Lightning. "Spik damn good, but no count."

"What happened?" queried Henry.

"Our onkle—he's dead."

"Do yuh mean Juan Mendoza?" asked Jim McDonald.

"*Si, si!* He ees dead on hees back, flat."

"Wait a minute," said Judge. "You are excited, Lightning."

"Sure," agreed Lightning. "Dosty keel heem."

"Where is this dead man?" asked someone in the crowd.

"In de bonk-house, on de floor!" snorted Lightning. "Can't you onnerstand United States?"

"In our bunk-house?" asked McDonald.

"Eef that ees where you leeve—sure. My onkle ees Juan Mendoza."

"That's the boy. Where is Dusty Cole?"

"Thunder knock heem steef like a post," declared Lightning. "He ees lock up in the bonk-house."

"Did you see Dusty Cole kill Juan Mendoza?" asked Judge.

"W'at you theenk I'm talking 'bout? *Por Dios*—"

A dozen men raced for the hitch-racks. Judge, who detested riding on a horse, halted Henry long enough to say:

"You lead the posse, while I watch the town, Henry."

THEY FOUND the situation exactly as described by Lightning. Dusty was unconscious, his head swollen where it had banged against the bunk. Juan Mendoza was not dead, but unconscious from a blow on the head, which had cut his scalp badly. Henry kept the crowd back until he had studied the situation, and then ordered one of the men to get a doctor. Neither Thunder nor Lightning came along.

While Henry was trying to figure out what had really happened, Jim McDonald came crashing his way through the men.

"This is only part of it!" he roared. "Peter Morris is dead in the main room of the house. C'mon!"

Henry, in spite of his lack of foot-speed, was the first one there.

"Keep the men back, Jim," he ordered. "Let me handle this alone."

He knelt and examined Peter Morris. The big cattleman was dead—and no mistake about that. A bottle of ink had upset on the carpet, and there was a pen sticking point down in the floor. Henry's squinty eyes peered around the room. He was low enough to see an object under an old sofa, but he said nothing. He got to his feet and turned to the men in the doorway.

"Peter Morris is without a doubt dead, gentlemen," he said. "You will please stay out there in the kitchen until after the coroner views the body. McDonald, I deputize you to take care of Dusty Cole."

"Do yuh reckon he killed Morris?" asked McDonald.

"I hope not, Jim," replied Henry.

As soon as the men moved away from the doorway, Henry secured the object from under the sofa, hurriedly wrapped it in his handkerchief, and put it in his pocket. After which he sat down to wait for Doctor Bogart, the coroner, who was now attending the injured.

After the coroner had at last found time to view the tragedy in the main room, Henry was obliged, on the strength of Lightning's direct testimony, to place Dusty Cole under arrest. By the time they arrived in Tonto City, Dusty was conscious, but very vague as to what had happened. Jim McDonald went out to the Hope ranch to break the news to Laura.

"As I viewed the tragedy," Henry explained to Judge when they were gathered again in the sheriff's office, "someone killed Peter Morris, reason unknown. Juan, the cook, possibly recognizing the killer—"

Judge, quite unimpressed, yanked off a shoe. "Marvelous!" he exclaimed.

"Have you a better theory, sir?" asked Henry stiffly.

"Must I remind you that I am not a detective?"

"I see. Merely a first-class sneerologist."

Judge sniffed, continued to undress. "I was merely reminding you," he said, "that your deductions are elemental. A ten-year-old child—"

"I beg your pardon," interrupted Henry.

"Mm-m-m," muttered Judge. "I wonder how much credence we may attach to Thunder and Lightning's statements. And how on earth could either one of them knock Dusty Cole unconscious? Why, he could whip a colony of them, Henry."

"Dusty is still a trifle vague over what happened," replied Henry.

"Perhaps the morrow will bring enlightenment."

Henry nestled back a little in his chair, said soberly: "I hope it may, Judge. If Juan Mendoza lives—he might be able to name the murderer."

"You aren't sure it was Dusty Cole?"

"How on earth could I be sure?"

"Not absolutely, of course, Henry. But there was a motive. Peter Morris kicked him out of the house and discharged him. Why did he go back there tonight—except to do evil?"

"I feel," replied Henry, "that it is a little too soon to try the case, Judge. Try and relax a little. Remember to not get excited. At your advanced age, it might prove fatal."

"Advanced age, indeed!" snorted Judge. "I am in my prime."

"At the moment you are in your shirt-tail, sir; and neither youth nor prime ever had knees like yours. The unmistakable doorknobs of a misspent life."

CHAPTER IV

INQUEST IN EENGLIS'

JOHN CAMPBELL, THE prosecuting attorney, came early next morning to see Henry. He wanted all the facts of the case, wanted to know just how much direct evidence there was against Dusty Cole.

"You will have to keep a close guard on Cole," declared the lawyer. "Peter Morris was one of our best-liked citizens, and some of the folks might try to take the law in their own hands. No doubt Cole killed him in retaliation for kicking him out of the house."

Henry rubbed his nose thoughtfully, his eyes still sleepy.

"Nothing has been established yet."

"Mighty strong circumstantial evidence, it seems to me, Conroy. I have talked already with Laura Morris. Mrs. Hope brought her to town this morning, and they have gone out to the ranch. She is too upset over it to talk to anyone. How soon may I talk with Dusty Cole?"

"Well, I do not know how he feels this morning, John. Let us give him time to gather his wits, at least, before asking questions. Last night he did not know what it was all about."

"Probably shamming," said the lawyer.

"Not with a bump on his head the size of a goose egg."

Campbell grunted, turned toward the door. "I shall be down at the jail in an hour, Conroy," he said. "Bump or no bump, he must talk with me."

Henry sighed and nodded. He stood there a moment, watch–

ing the lawyer hurry away toward his office. Then he himself walked slowly up to the courthouse and entered Judge Myers' office. The judge, looking over some papers, nodded a welcome to Henry.

"It was a terrible thing that happened last night," said the judge. "Peter Morris was a fine man, Henry. Luckily we have his murderer."

"A most brutal murder, Judge," agreed Henry.

The judge shook his head sadly. "I have known Peter Morris for several years," he said. "He was a fine, honorable citizen; too fine to die at the hands of a wild, vindictive young cowboy. My personal feelings are that a sentence of hanging is far too lenient for such a crime. By the way, Henry, was he shot from behind?"

"Judge," replied Henry soberly, "he was not shot."

"Not shot? Why—"

The judge broke off to stare keenly at Henry. The latter was drawing an object from his pocket; an object wrapped in a handkerchief.

Slowly Henry unrolled it and placed it on the judge's desk. It was a knife of the hunting type, bloodstained. On the handle, inlaid in a white metal, were the initials S.H.

"It was under the sofa in the room where Peter Morris died," said Henry. "You and I are the only ones who know about it, Judge."

Judge Myers started to touch the knife, but drew his hand away. He sank back in his chair, staring at Henry. The sheriff wrapped the knife again and put it in his pocket.

"I saw Molly this morning," the judge whispered. "She said that Sam did not come home last night. My God, this will kill her! Henry, don't you realize what this means to her—and to me?"

"I've been thinking about it," nodded Henry. "Dusty Cole is in jail. I am not accusing Sam Hope, Judge."

"But that is Sam's knife. You know how he can throw a knife."

"I have seen him impale a playing card at fifty feet," replied

Henry. "But that doesn't mean he threw the knife that killed Peter."

"There is a motive," whispered the judge. "That trouble about the calf."

"You are trying to convict him, Judge," remarked Henry.

The old judge shut his jaws tightly, and his knuckles were white from his grip on the arms of his chair. After a moment he relaxed.

"I am thinking of Molly," he said wearily.

"I do not believe they can convict Dusty Cole," said Henry with seeming irrelevance. "At the same time, we do not know that he isn't guilty."

The judge leaned forward, sudden hope in his eyes. "You mean—not mention the knife, Henry?" he whispered.

"If worst came to the worst," replied Henry quietly, "it might be that—well, I have never lost a prisoner—before, Judge."

"And he might be proved not guilty," added the judge.

Henry got slowly to his feet and put on his hat.

"The Shame of Arizona," he muttered. "I believe we are a pair of damned conniving old law-breakers, Judge. I give you good morning, sir."

Henry walked out of the office, gently closing the door. Behind him, he left Judge Myers staring into space, blinking thoughtfully.

THE PROSECUTING attorney was waiting at the office for Henry, when he returned. They went at once to Dusty's cell.

They found Dusty clear-minded and indignant. Talk? Certainly!

"But remember," cautioned the lawyer, "that anything you say may be used against you, Cole."

"I'll try and protect myself," said Dusty grimly. "I never shot Peter Morris nor Juan Mendoza. I went out there to get my Sunday boots, and I fell over Juan in the bunk-house. After I lighted the lamp and discovered who I'd fell over, I heard a team comin'; so I went to the doorway, where somethin' landed on me so hard that I went plumb out."

The lawyer looked his unbelief. "You had trouble with Peter Morris yesterday, I understand, Cole," he said.

"Well," Dusty grinned sourly, "he threw me out of the house. It wasn't any trouble for him—and I wasn't hurt any."

"Then you went back last night and shot him, eh?"

"I did?" gasped Dusty in amazement.

"And when Juan Mendoza saw you—you tried to kill him, too."

"Gee, I'm shore a tough vaquero! You ain't been readin' about Billy the Kid, and got yourself all confused, have yuh, Campbell?"

"Being sarcastic will not help your case, Cole," reminded the lawyer warmly.

"Well, you've got my story," replied Dusty. And he refused to talk any more.

The lawyer and Henry went back into the office, sat down. Henry asked Campbell what he thought of the matter.

"I don't believe there is any question that Cole shot Morris."

Henry settled himself in his chair. "I haven't much money," he remarked. "Oh, I might be able to dig up a few hundred. With what I have, I am offering you two-to-one odds that Dusty Cole did not shoot Peter Morris."

Campbell started. "You—you have other information?" he queried.

"Not a scintilla, as you lawyers say."

"Then what are you betting on?"

"On the simple fact that Peter Morris was stabbed—not shot."

"He—he was *stabbed?* Why wasn't I told of this?"

A trace of a smile creased Henry's lips. "You never asked—you merely presumed, my dear attorney at law," he answered.

"In your own mind, it seems, you have already convicted Dusty Cole for shooting Peter Morris."

John Campbell looked balefully at the fat sheriff.

"I suppose," he said harshly, "I am the last one to know how the murder was committed."

Henry smiled—broadly now. "No, I believe Dusty Cole is also ignorant of the weapon used. He thinks that Morris was shot."

"Well," grunted the lawyer, "I'm not so sure of that. However, we will find out a few things at the inquest. You say that those two Mexicans saw Dusty Cole kill Juan Mendoza?"

"I have found their words to be most unreliable, sir," replied Henry. "Their imaginations are boundless—and their English atrocious."

"They are the state's witnesses," reminded the lawyer.

Henry sighed. "God help our state," he said.

DOWN AT the Tonto, Sandy Crane was nearly as indignant as had Dusty Cole. He swore by all the gods and to all present, including Judge Van Treece, that Dusty was innocent.

"Why don't you do something for him?" suggested Judge.

"I am," replied Sandy, leaning heavily on the bar. "I'm drinkin' enough for both of us."

"You'd better sober up for the inquest," advised Judge. "They will want to know what happened yesterday at Morris' ranch. The prosecution will base their case on the fact that Dusty had a motive for the killing."

"You mean—'cause Morris throwed him out of the house?" queried Sandy.

"Exactly. He went back there to get even with Morris."

"The hell he did!" exclaimed Sandy. Then he paused to reconsider. "Well, I do 'member Dusty sayin'—"

"Saying what?" prompted Judge quickly.

"Oh, nothin'. I was thinkin' out loud, Judge. Forget it." And he would say no more.

Back in the sheriff's office a little later, Judge told Henry about Sandy's broken remark.

"It looks as though Dusty had made a threat," remarked Judge.

"Who hasn't?" grunted Henry. "Take Sandy's advice—forget it. Just forget your legal training and remember that the sheriff's office is not rated on convictions. We are merely guardians of the law."

"And that statement, sir," declared Judge soberly, "would bring a smile at any spot in the state, except in this office."

Henry rose from his chair. "I believe," he remarked, "that this is the opportune time to sample Frijole Bill's latest concoction. You are getting dyspeptic."

AS FAR as general opinions were concerned there was no mystery about the murder of Peter Morris. Peter Morris had rejected Dusty Cole as a suitor for Laura Morris, kicked him out of the house and sent him packing off the Circle M. Dusty had returned to the house, continued the argument and finally killed Peter Morris. Fearing that Juan Mendoza, the cook, had recognized him, he had beaten the Mexican over the head with a blunt weapon, presumably a gun, and had left him for dead.

Juan Mendoza, suffering from concussion, was still unconscious when the inquest was held in Tonto City.

Fearing the temper of the crowd, Henry had refused to take Dusty to the inquest. The place was crowded to suffocation. Thunder and Lightning Mendoza were there, important, but a little frightened.

Doctor Bogart stated the cause of death, described the wound, and how the body was lying on the floor. Henry added his testimony. Then Thunder Mendoza was called to the stand and sworn. He eyed the jury of six men, looked apprehensively at the coroner, and swallowed painfully. Then he said:

"My Onkle Juan, hees got confusion from hees head."

"We understand all that," replied the coroner dryly.

"Juan hees not onnerstand anytheeng."

"Please confine your conversation to answering questions," reprimanded the coroner. "You stated last night that Dusty Cole had killed your uncle?"

"*Si, si.*"

"Did you see Dusty Cole strike your uncle?"

"Sure, I'm theenk so."

"You are not sure?"

Thunder looked quizzically at Lightning and said:

"Am I sure?"

Lightning shrugged his shoulders, spread his hands.

"*Dios mio,* how am I from knowing?" he demanded. "I am driving weeth both hands."

"Just a moment," begged the coroner. "You say you were *driving?*"

"Going like devil," nodded Thunder violently.

"This testimony," declared the coroner, "doesn't make sense. Is there someone in the room capable of taking this testimony in Mexican?"

"I'm spik *Mejicano* pretty good," offered Lightning. "I'm spiking pretty dam good *Americano,* too. W'at you want know, Doc?"

"All right—you take the stand, Lightning."

The change was effected, much to the amusement of Henry and Judge.

"Now, Lightning, I want you to tell us exactly what happened last night at the Bar M ranch," stated the coroner.

"Those dang 'orse run away," stated Lightning. "I'm lose one line."

"I am not asking about horses," said the coroner wearily. "What I want to know is this: did you see Dusty Cole strike Juan Mendoza?"

"You theenk I can see een the dark? *Por Dios,* theese dang 'orses run under clothesline, and theese damn line catch me right onder your cheen. I am almos' hong."

The coroner sighed deeply, shoved his hands deep in his pockets and rocked on his feet.

"Did Thunder see Dusty Cole hit Juan Mendoza?" he asked hoarsely.

"W'y don't you ask *heem?*" queried Lightning blandly.

"Pardon me, Doctor," interrupted Henry, "but I may be able to salvage something from this chaotic situation."

"Thank you, Mr. Sheriff," sighed the doctor. "Take the witness."

"Lightning," said Henry, "I know all about those horses and the buckboard. Without my permission, you and Thunder took that team and vehicle last night. The team ran away near the Bar M Ranch. The team deserted the buckboard behind the Bar M ranch house, and it is still there, one front wheel ruined, the other three decidedly in a bowed condition.

"You may forget the runaway, and confine your answers to a few simple questions. Did... you... see... Dusty... Cole... strike... Juan... Mendoza?"

"Thunder see heem."

"Did he tell you he saw Dusty Cole strike Juan Mendoza?"

Lightning scratched his head and looked thoughtfully at the ceiling.

"You wan' know if Dusty Cole hit heem?" he queried.

"W'at ees use of telling heem?" demanded Thunder, getting out of his chair. "I am the one w'at ees doing all the seeing. Lightning has got clothesline under your cheen."

Henry looked around the convulsed crowd; a look which only added to the convulsions. Solemnly he said:

"... to tell the whole truth, so help you God."

"I do," nodded Lightning, holding up his *left* hand.

"Thank you," said Henry dryly. "Now that we have so much settled, perhaps we might try another angle to the matter. Lightning, are we to understand that Thunder knocked out Dusty Cole?"

"Sure," grinned Lightning, "Thonder ees fighting jeeger."

"I see. He saw Dusty Cole knock out Uncle Juan; so he proceeded to knock out Dusty Cole, eh?"

"I'm theenk so."

"You merely think so. Don't you *know* anything?"

"He ees not ver' smart," interrupted Thunder. "Lightning ees mos' always theenking, but from knowing he ees most' always w'at you call—damn domb. I am the smart one—personally."

"Now," remarked Henry, "we are making progress. Thunder, did you knock out Dusty Cole—and how did you knock him out?"

"Sure," grinned Thunder expansively.

"How?" barked Henry in exasperation.

"Easy," replied Thunder.

"Gentlemen! Gentlemen!" wailed Doctor Bogart, trying to still the uproar. "This is serious."

"Damn right," added Lightning.

WHEN ORDER was restored, Henry wiped away his tears and considered the two Mexicans gravely. It was his opinion that neither of them was clear as to whether they saw Dusty Cole strike Juan Mendoza, nor how they knocked out Dusty Cole. The wrecked buckboard in the rear of the ranch house, and the fact that Lightning had been nearly hung on a clothesline, gave him an idea.

"Your team ran away at the Bar M last night," he said to Thunder. "Isn't it a fact that you were thrown through the doorway of the bunk-house and collided with Dusty Cole?"

"Col—what?" queried Thunder.

"You were thrown through the doorway of the bunk-house and bumped into Dusty Cole."

"*Dios mio!*" exclaimed Thunder. "I'll bet that ees w'at 'appened!"

"Su-u-u-ure!" exploded Lightning. "One boggy wheel hit those corner from the bonk-house. Thonder, you know something?"

"Sure," nodded Thunder. "W'at ees eet?"

"Henry ees got 'more brains than both of you put together."

"You are both excused," choked Henry. "Thank you for coming; you have been a great help."

"Somebody ort to wring both their necks," growled a jury-man.

Jim McDonald, acting as foreman for the Bar M, then asked to testify for Laura Morris, who was not present. He was told to come forward.

"Miss Morris," he said, "told me that yesterday, before her father came to town to get his payroll fixed up, he said he would not stay in town last night, because he had an appointment with someone at the ranch. He didn't tell her who the appointment was with. That was why Peter Morris was not in Tonto City last night."

McDonald had no further information to offer, except that he himself knew nothing about any appointment. Nor did anyone else. No murder instrument had been brought forth. The evidence against Dusty Cole, then, was entirely circumstantial. Nonetheless, the coroner's jury decided that the evidence was sufficient to hold Dusty for the murder of Peter Morris.

Back at the jail, Henry detailed the testimony to Dusty.

"It seems," he explained, "that a front wheel of the buggy hit the corner of the bunk-house and catapulted one of the Mexicans into you, as you came to the doorway."

"So that was it, eh?" muttered Dusty. "I knew it was a heavy body, travelin' mighty fast. But the law can't convict me of murder. Heck, I wasn't near the house. In fact, I was goin' to get my boots and get out of there as quiet as possible. When I lit that lamp, I found Juan. He ain't dead, is he, Sheriff?"

"No. He is still alive. Thunder says he's got confusion of the brain."

"I reckon I've got the same thing," sighed Dusty. "Was Laura at the inquest?"

"No, she did not attend, Dusty."

"I wonder if she thinks I killed her father."

"If she doesn't," answered Henry, "she's a novelty in Wild Horse Valley."

"Do you think I did, Sheriff?"

"My dear boy," replied Henry gently, "thinking is something that I put aside years ago. To some it may show a profit, but to me it merely meant a headache. I am merely an instrument of the people—and in most cases, a pretty dull one. However, they can't hang you until after the trial—I hope."

"Why do yuh say—you hope, Sheriff?"

"That was only a slip of the tongue, Dusty. That inquest was rather a farce. Men laughed heartily, but later they might become sober and fill up with virtuous wrath over the murder of Peter Morris."

"Yeah, I see what yuh mean," remarked Dusty.

"And," added Henry, "they are usually the ones who would kill an enemy as quick as they would kill a snake."

CHAPTER V

TRIAL BY JURY

JUDGE MYERS HUNCHED dejectedly at his desk, his arms folded. Slouched against the desk was Sam Hope, his ne'er-do-well son-in-law, handsome in spite of his dissipations, and smelling of whisky.

"I sent for you, Sam," stated the judge, "but I didn't expect you would come."

"I wanted to see yuh myself—or I wouldn't," replied Sam. "Shoot. I suppose yuh called me here to give me another of yore damn fool lectures. Go ahead—for all the good it'll do, Judge."

"Will you give me an honest answer to one question, Sam?"

Sam shrugged his shoulders. "If it suits me—yes."

"Where were you the night Peter Morris was murdered?"

Sam Hope stared intently at the judge, his eyes narrowing. Suddenly he lurched against the desk, shoving a forefinger almost against the judges nose.

"Don't you try to hang that onto me!" he snarled. "Just because Peter Morris called me a rustler, and—what the hell are you talkin' about?"

"I asked you where you were that night, Sam," repeated the judge.

"Damn yuh, I was home!"

"I requested an honest answer, Sam," reminded the judge.

"Oh, so somebody told yuh I wasn't home, eh? Well, yuh might ask 'em where I was—I don't remember. But what has the murder of Morris got to do with me?"

"Peter Morris was killed with a knife, Sam."

Sam Hope's face twisted bitterly. "And because I'm—I'm a knife thrower—why, anybody could use a knife. Who said I done it?"

"Your knife killed him, Sam."

"My knife?" Some of the color drained from Sam's face. "Why, they said—you're lyin' to me! There wasn't any knife found."

The judge shook his head. "There are only two other men beside yourself who know this, Sam—and I am one of them. The knife has your initials on the handle."

Sam brushed his fingers across his mouth. His hand trembled, and there was a furtive expression in his eyes.

"That—that's funny," he said huskily.

"Now," said the judge, "will you tell me where you were that night?"

"I don't know," replied Sam dully. "I tell yuh, I don't. I was too drunk to remember—or too crazy."

"Crazy?" queried the judge.

"We won't talk about that. I told yuh that I didn't know where I was that night."

"Then you don't know that you did not kill Peter Morris?"

"How could I know—if I don't know where I was? You've got Dusty Cole in jail for the murder."

"I know. But Morris was killed with your knife, Sam."

"All right—what if he was. Dusty Cole was out at my place the night Morris was killed. He came out to see Laura Morris. Is there any reason why he couldn't have picked up one of my knives?"

"I suppose not," admitted the judge wearily. And then, "Well, why did you want to see me, Sam?"

Sam Hope laughed harshly. "I wanted to tell yuh somethin' that won't set so good with yuh, Judge. While I've been hellin' around, Mack Taylor has been goin' out to see Molly."

The judge half rose from his chair, glared at Sam.

"That's a lie, Sam."

"Is it? A devil of a lot you know about it."

Mack Taylor and his partner Tuck Nash owned a small gold mine, known as the Spotted Horse, about seven miles from Tonto City. Mack Taylor was tall, good-looking, and seemed to tend strictly to business. Tuck Nash was an inveterate gambler, several years older than Taylor, and was inclined to hit the high spots.

"I don't believe it," declared the judge. "I've tried to get Molly to divorce you, Sam, but she won't do it. If she was in love with Mack Taylor, she wouldn't stick with you."

"I'm just tellin' yuh what I know," said Sam. "And I don't mind tellin' yuh that Mack Taylor won't get her. I'll keep what I've got."

"Have you told Molly about this?" asked the judge.

"You're the only one I've told. What the devil, I'm not shoutin' it to all the world. He goes out there danged near every day. Some day he'll be carried back."

The judge sat staring at his son-in-law. It was plain in that moment that he would have liked to throttle him. But he made no move.

Without another word then, Sam Hope turned and walked out. The judge saw him crossing to the Tonto Saloon. For a long moment Judge Myers stood staring through the dusty window at the street. He had cut heavily into his savings to buy that ranch for Molly and Sam, hoping that Sam would brace up and make a living for Molly—and what a mess they both seemed to be making of things.

Finally he turned away. He locked his office and went down to his little cottage. There he hitched up his horse to an old buggy and started out toward the ranch. He wanted to talk with Molly, to try to get her angle of things. He felt old and tired, and the sun beat harshly on the flapping top of the old buggy.

THE LITTLE ranch house was hidden away in a grove of sycamores, and as the judge came up through the the ancient grove he saw a saddled horse tied beside the porch. He turned off the road and stopped his horse under a tree near the rear of the house. There was no one in sight, but as he walked beside the house he heard voices. Without quite intending to eavesdrop, he stopped for a moment near the corner of the front porch and listened.

"You must not come here any more, Mack," Molly was saying. "Sam isn't responsible for what he might do, if he knew you came here."

"He isn't responsible for anything, Molly," came back the voice of Mack Taylor. "That's exactly why I want you to go with me. You're not safe with him. Any judge in the world would give you a divorce."

"Sam wouldn't harm me," replied Molly.

"Not if he was in his right mind," agreed Mack. "He don't appreciate you, Molly. Even when your father gave him this ranch, he didn't appreciate it. If he did he wouldn't act like he does."

They lowered their voices sufficiently then so that the judge missed most of the rest of conversation, but he heard Molly say:

"Sam needs me more than ever now, Mack. As I told you before, as long as he lives, I must not give him up."

The judge, grim-faced, wishing now that he hadn't passed to listen, backed up to the corner of the house. He went quietly back to his buggy, sat there until he saw Mack Taylor ride off across the hills. After a sufficient length of time the judge drove around to the house.

Molly met him with a smile of welcome. Neither of them mentioned Mack Taylor. Molly's eyes clouded as she spoke about Sam. Obviously, though, no one had told her of trouble between Sam and Peter Morris, and the judge did not tell her now.

"I'm so sorry for Laura Morris," she told him. "Laura loves Dusty Cole. Do you think they will find him guilty, Dad?"

Judge Myers shrugged his shoulders. "Who knows what an Arizona jury might do?" he countered.

"Oh, I hope not. Why, Dad, you would have to sentence him!"

Molly took a quick step forward, then stopped.

"We won't discuss that, Molly. Is Sam doing any work nowadays?"

"He isn't out here—much," she confessed. "Laura wants me to come and stay with her for a while, but I can't leave Sam."

"If he doesn't come home, he wouldn't know you were away, Molly."

"I suppose not. I might stay with her a while. She's so lonesome." Again the judge urged her to get a divorce, but she refused.

"I loved him enough to marry him," Molly said, "and I guess I still love him enough to stay with him, Dad. He isn't all bad."

"I'm afraid there is mighty little good in him," sighed the judge. "I'd advise you to go away and stay with Laura Morris for a while. Let Sam do his own cooking; it might sober him up."

But Molly made no promises.

WHEN THE judge returned to Tonto City, he found Henry Harrison Conroy waiting for him outside his office. They went inside together and sat down.

"Juan Mendoza recovered consciousness a while ago, but has no idea who hit him," Henry announced. "He says that someone came to see Peter Morris. Later he heard loud voices in the house. He went up and stepped inside the kitchen door, and was promptly knocked down by someone he didn't see. Badly dazed, he ran out to get away from his assailant, but evidently the man pursued him into the bunk-house, and there beat Juan into insensibility."

"Thinking that Juan had recognized him, I suppose," sighed the judge. "I'm sorry it was not true, Henry."

"And here is another bit of information," said Henry. "John Reed, the cashier of the Scorpion Bend Bank, was in town today. He said that Peter Morris drew fifteen thousand dollars in cash the day before he was killed. He remarked to the cashier that he was going to make a cash investment.

"I went to the Tonto bank, but they said that Morris had not made a deposit. Unless the money is out at the Bar M, I'm afraid that Peter Morris was robbed of fifteen thousand. Dusty Cole had no money on him. He was knocked out and locked in the bunk-house; so he had no opportunity to hide the money."

The judge shook his head hopelessly. "If we only knew who had that appointment with Peter Morris…" he sighed. "I am afraid of that trial, Henry; afraid that any jury drawn from Wild Horse Valley will convict Dusty Cole. It starts Monday, with everything fresh in the minds of the public. The court will have to appoint an attorney for Cole at once, so that some sort of defense may be worked out. John Campbell says he can get a conviction."

"I am afraid he is right, Judge," nodded Henry soberly.

"I have never hung a man," said the judge. "In all my years on the bench I have never taken a life."

"I hope you never will, sir," declared Henry. "The law has enough blood on its hands, it seems to me. Have you seen Samuel Hope?"

The judge nodded. "He was here at my office today, Henry. He knows about his knife. Yes, I told him. He says he doesn't know where he was the night Peter Morris died."

"Doesn't know where he was, Judge?"

"That was his statement to me."

Henry looked his astonishment. "What on earth," he asked, "was wrong with him that night?"

"I do not know, Henry. He said he was either drunk or crazy."

"Most killers are," said Henry. "I'm afraid that Sam is about as much help to us as Juan Mendoza. I guess I'll go out to the Morris ranch and see if Laura knows anything about the fifteen thousand dollars. Were you out to see Molly?"

The judge nodded. Then he unburdened himself, told Henry

about Sam's visit to his office, during which he had accused Mack Taylor of making love to Molly.

"That is ridiculous!" exploded Henry.

"That was what I thought," sighed the judge.

"You—you mean that it is true, Judge?" asked Henry.

Judge Myers explained what he had heard of Taylor's and Molly's conversation.

"Well," remarked the philosophical Henry, "I—I can not quite blame Mack Taylor—nor Molly. As long as she told him what she did, it may end right there."

"I hope so," sighed the judge. "Time will tell."

HENRY'S TRIP to the Morris ranch proved fruitless. Laura knew nothing about her father drawing money from the Scorpion Bend bank. Laura had hired Sandy Crane back again. She wanted to know all about Dusty, and how Henry felt about the trial. He tried to evade her questions, answered them lamely, if at all.

"You haven't tried to find the right man," she told him. "You are satisfied to crucify Dusty Cole. I know all about the evidence. The law is satisfied to convict anybody, whether he is guilty of murder or not, as the man who killed my father."

"Yes, ma'am," replied Henry weakly, and hurried out to his horse.

"And you can tell Judge Myers that I'm sending him the same message," called Laura.

"I—I'm sure he will appreciate it, Miss Morris," replied Henry.

And Judge Myers did appreciate it. He listened grimly to Henry.

"I don't like it," declared the judge. "I have appointed Frank Haley to defend Dusty Cole, and—and I went so far as to instruct him how to try and rip the devil out of Campbell's prosecution—but I don't know. Perhaps I talked too much."

"You didn't tell him who we suspected, did you, Judge?"

"No, no! But I did say that I was satisfied that Dusty did not kill Morris."

Henry carefully polished his nose.

"Well," he said. "I have a feeling that before this thing is settled, we will both be heading toward Mexico."

"Are you planning something, Henry?" whispered the judge.

"Yes," answered Henry, likewise whispering. "When I leave here I am going to find that jug of Frijole's prune juice, and drink myself into blissful oblivion. Have you any appointments this afternoon?"

"No," replied the judge solemnly. "But it is such a mighty undignified thing to do, Henry."

"We could take the jug out to your house, Judge."

"Yes, yes—we could do that. Well, sir, what are we waiting for?"

Henry went down to the office to get the jug. He found Judge Van Treece there, an expression of satisfaction on his long, lean face.

"Judge," said Henry, "you look like the cat that found the cream. Has anything new developed?"

"A plot has been thwarted, sir," replied Judge.

"Thwarted? I love that word. It sounds like a lisping duck."

"You understand its meaning, I hope, sir."

"Certainly—I hope. What has happened?"

"Observe," replied Judge, pointing at the desk-top. "I found those in Dusty's cell a while ago."

"Hm-m-m," mused Henry. "Four hacksaw blades—nearly new."

"You, sir," declared Judge, "were about to have a jail-break."

"I see-e-e," muttered Henry. "And you—er—thwarted it. Well! Hm-m-m. Frail little things, aren't they? Not much use against the steel bars of that window, my dear Judge."

"Steel bars, indeed," snorted Judge. "So I thought, until I

made a test. Dusty Cole could have sawed his way out in two hours of uninterrupted labor."

"He could?" Henry straightened up and glared at Judge. "And you—stopped him?"

"You seem displeased, sir."

"Why, damn it, I—I wonder where he got these blades. Perhaps a friend."

"One would suppose so," murmured Judge, but added, "except that he might have a queer enemy."

"Thrown through the barred window, eh? Did Dusty make any explanation—er—say anything to throw light on the incident?"

"Well," replied Judge soberly, "he told me to go to hell."

"I see, not realizing, perhaps, that you are quite busy just now. Later, perhaps. Hm-m-m."

Henry walked outside and went around to the barred window, which was about eight feet above the ground level. No doubt the blades had been pitched through the window at night. He went on back to their little stable, where Oscar Johnson usually kept that jug of liquid dynamite known as Frijole's Fermentation. Halting at the stable door he looked back at the jail.

"Damn Judge!" he exclaimed. "An excellent chance— thwarted." As he started to open the stable door, his attention was attracted by a small, tightly-folded piece of paper, lying against the wall. He picked it up, unfolded it and looked closely at the penciled words:

DESTROY THIS NOTE AND COME TO THE MINE.
MACK

Henry rubbed his red nose thoughtfully. He glanced back at the jail, only a short distance away.

"Hm-m-m," he mused. "Come to the mine, eh? That would be Mack Taylor. Well, well. Possibly the note blew away, when he attempted to throw it through the window. Again it is possible that this note has nothing to do with the case. Might have lain there for weeks. Hm-m-m. Still, that word 'destroy' looks suspicious. Damn Judge!"

Henry put the note in his pocket, put the jug into a paper sack, and went strolling up toward Judge Myers' home.

THE TRIAL of Dusty Cole, charged with the wilful murder of Peter Morris, was at an end. It had been one of the quickest trials in the history of the county. Tonto City had closed up and crowded the courtroom to suffocation. Judge Myers, worn and weary, had instructed the jury to weigh the evidence carefully, and because it was purely circumstantial, to give the prisoner the benefit of any doubt in their minds.

The defense was weak. There was only Dusty's unsupported word, and the judge knew that the jury did not believe him. Their faces told the verdict before they came filing in, never looking at the prisoner. Henry and the judge exchanged glances. Henry's face was very red, and he seemed under a strain.

Seated beside him was Dusty Cole, unshackled, cool, but slightly pale. At the same table was Judge Van Treece, slightly drunk, but entirely serious. Henry sat with his fat hands gripped together on the table, studying the jury.

Judge Myers looked old, and his voice was husky, as he asked:

"Gentlemen, have you reached a verdict?"

The foreman arose, a paper in his hand.

"We have, Judge," he said, and handed the paper to the clerk of the court. The clerk adjusted his glasses, glanced at the paper, and then stepped back near the judge's desk. Again he looked at it, this time more carefully. Finally he looked up at the judge.

"Please—read the verdict," said the judge.

There was a moment of silence.

"Guilty of murder in the *first degree*," croaked the clerk.

Dusty Cole jerked forward, his lips shut tightly. The room was as still as a tomb. There was not a sound, except the ticking of a big clock on the wall.

Judge Myers did not look at Dusty, as he said with obvious effort:

"Dusty Cole, stand up."

Slowly the young cowboy got to his feet. Then, suddenly, his body jerked against Henry, knocking him off balance. Another instant and he swiftly stepped aside toward a rear door, Henry's forty-five in his right hand.

"Don't move!" he snapped sharply. "Hold still—all of yuh. I can hit a dime the length of this room—and you know it. Don't move. I'm goin' out—and I'll kill anybody who tries to stop me."

CHAPTER VI

ESCAPE

SWIFTLY DUSTY BACKED toward that rear door, his forty-five menacingly in his hand. There were probably fifty holstered guns in that crowded courtroom, yet not a man moved to bring his forth. When Dusty's hand was fumbling behind him for the doorknob, someone in the far corner started to speak. His nearest neighbor hushed him with a frightened look.

Then Dusty was gone, the door shutting hollowly behind him. Immediately the room was in an uproar. Henry, red-faced, panting, got to his feet.

"Get him!" he shouted hoarsely.

"He can git away, as far as I'm concerned," replied a cowboy near Henry.

Henry and Judge together strove to shove their way through the crowded room. Then someone yelled:

"Why don'tcha go down the way he went, you danged fools!"

Henry seemed to look sheepish. It was true that the door Dusty had fled through opened on a narrow stairway that led to the main entrance. Dusty could make it to that entrance far ahead of anyone going down the usual way.

"We may as well try that, Judge," said Henry, as if the thought had just occurred to him.

"Wasting all this time!" panted Judge.

When Henry and Judge at last reached the bottom of the narrow stairs, the crowd was already surging down the main stairway. A cowboy who had made it early yelled at them:

"Dusty and Sandy jist pulled out, and there ain't a danged saddle horse left at any of the racks. This kid here says that Sandy herded every horse out of town, before Dusty made his break."

"My goodness!" panted Henry. There was seeming concern written all over his face as they surged out into the street to find the cowboy's report confirmed.

"Our horses are still in the stable, Henry!" exclaimed Judge helpfully.

"My goodness!" gasped Henry. "What a day, Judge!" He grabbed Judge's arm as the latter started to run. "Not too fast. I am afraid I pulled a tendon on those devilish stairs."

Nevertheless, they finally reached their stable, followed by part of the crowd. There they brought up short. The door had been locked with a nearly new padlock!

Henry and Judge looked at each other questioningly.

"Well, sir, where are the keys?" gasped Henry at last.

"Keys?" wailed Judge. "Why, damn it, sir, I never saw that lock before in my life!"

"My goodness!" gasped Henry. "Someone has locked our stable door."

He sagged against the door and mopped his perspiring face.

"Well," remarked a cowboy, "it don't look as though Sandy and Dusty overlooked any bets. They shore figured on goin' *alone.*"

"I wonder which way they went," said Judge wearily.

"The kid said they went straight west," offered another cowboy.

"Go west, young man," muttered Henry absently.

"What did you say?" queried Judge.

"Nothing informative, Judge."

John Campbell, the prosecutor, shouldered his way past the crowd and confronted Henry.

"Good afternoon, John," said Henry dryly.

"Good afternoon, be damned!" snorted the lawyer. "Why didn't you have your prisoner handcuffed?"

"Handcuffed?" queried Henry. "Oh, yes—handcuffed. Well, John, he seemed so—er—resigned to his fate, as it were. Humiliation, and all that, you know. My fault, of course—entirely mine. There will be no stigma attached to you, of course. But isn't it human to err? I—I fear that I was mistaken in the young gentleman."

"Henry," declared Campbell, "you have proven to my satisfaction that you are a bungling, incompetent damned old fool."

Henry's eyes screwed up as though on the verge of tears, but a smile slowly creased his face.

"John," he said, "I'm not so *old*."

Mumbling profanity, Campbell then whirled and went back up the street.

BY NOW, the missing horses were slowly being rounded up and brought into town, but Henry and Judge went into their office and closed the door.

"We must prepare a warning to telegraph to all counties in the state, Henry," said Judge. "The murderer must be recaptured."

"Oh, yes—of course," agreed Henry. He eased himself into his chair.

"I shudder to think of public opinion on this, Henry," wailed Judge. "It looks—I mean—well, confound it, sir, they will say that you aided and abetted Dusty Cole in his escape. We shall be lucky if they do not kick us out of office"

"And lucky if they do, Judge," added Henry.

"Why on earth did you forget to handcuff him, Henry?"

"My dear Judge! If I was so absentminded as to forget to place handcuffs on his wrists, how on earth can I tell you how I forgot to do it?"

Temporarily, that silenced Judge. He looked narrowly at Henry for several moments.

"Rather coincidental," he said at last, thoughtfully.

"What was that, Judge?" queried Henry.

"That Sandy Crane should have turned all those horses loose and been ready at exactly the proper time for Dusty to join him."

"Um-m-m—yes," admitted Henry.

"They must have planned it all out, sir."

Henry nodded solemnly. "One would jump at that conclusion," he agreed. "Perhaps they talked the matter over—Sandy and Dusty—and—er—decided."

"Except for one thing, Henry," stated Judge. "Every time Sandy Crane has been here to see Dusty, I have been present. There has been absolutely no chance for them to have made any plans."

"My goodness!" exclaimed Henry innocently. "Do you suppose Sandy is a mind-reader, Judge?"

"Of all the asinine—hmph!" Judge snorted explosively. He whirled and stamped out of the office.

Henry went to the doorway. More of the loose horses were being brought into the street, and knots of men were standing along the wooden sidewalks, discussing the escape. Henry sighed and put on his hat.

"If public taste hadn't changed," he muttered to himself, "I might be still behind the footlights of a three-a-day vaudeville, following the trained dogs, and not be in danger from anything more formidable than an ancient egg. Henry Harrison Conroy, you are about as subtle as a drunken Indian. Damn it, sir, if you make another mistake, I shall be first to ask for your resignation as sheriff of Tonto Town."

Not caring to answer questions nor meet the inquiring glances of the men along the sidewalk, Henry left via the back door of the jail. He circled around to the courthouse, went straight up to Judge Myers' chambers.

The old judge was standing alone in his office, gazing through a window, his hands locked behind him. He turned as Henry came in. They looked keenly at each other.

"I presume he got away, Henry," said the judge quietly.

"Yes, Judge," nodded Henry. "Sorry. He is the first prisoner ever to escape from me."

"You did this for me, Henry," said the judge. "One word from you, and Sam Hope would—you know I am right. You never believed that Dusty Cole—"

"A jury is never wrong, Judge. They found him guilty."

"On the slimmest damned evidence I ever heard, Henry. As I told you before, I have never been obliged to pass a death sentence on any man or woman. It—it was a terrible task. When I saw Sandy Crane taking those horses—"

"My goodness!" interrupted Henry. "You sat there on that platform, where you could look down at the street and see Sandy Crane removing all the horses—and you never spoke?"

"Henry," replied the judge soberly, "my job is to sit here on the bench and *try* to judge my fellowmen—not to act as a dry-nurse to a lot of confounded cow ponies. I understand that someone padlocked your stable, so you could not get your horses, and—" Judge Myers smiled slowly, "and probably threw away the key."

"Ahem!" Henry cleared his throat raspingly. "Judge, I almost forgot the time. It is past my drink time—will you honor me?"

"I shall be pleased to drink with you, Henry. But as far as any honor is concerned—I honestly believe we are a pair of lawless reprobates."

"But able to sleep tonight, Judge."

"That is true. But don't look so devilish self-satisfied, until we hear what the rest of the world has to say about it. I am not asking how you were able to plan all this out, but weren't you taking grave chances—letting Dusty take your gun? He might have shot someone in the courtroom."

"Not with my gun, Judge," assured Henry soberly. "It was loaded with blank ammunition. Shall we advance on those belated drinks?"

FRIJOLE BILL had brought Thunder and Lightning Mendoza to town, but they were too late to see the finish of the trial. They found Oscar Johnson at the office, and the big Swede told them what had happened. Frijole turned to the amazed Mexicans.

"Yuh see, now?" he jeered. "You fellers, with yore cock-eyed testimony, almost hung Dusty Cole. Now he's loose, and I'll betcha he'll slit yore necks for what yuh done agin him."

Frijole knew that their testimony had little to do with the conviction of Dusty—but Lightning and Thunder did not know it. They believed every word of Frijole's dire prophecy. Then Oscar added his bit.

"Yah, su-ure," he agreed. "Dosty vill come back and yerk the leever out of both of you. By yimminy, if Ay vars in your place Ay vould ron like ha'al."

"*Dios mio!*" wailed Lightning. He turned savagely on Thunder.

"You see w'at you do?" he choked. "You say too damn much. Dusty ees *mucho malo hombre*. He ees mad from you, and pretty queek he ees come back and cut off your *cabeza* right behin' my damn ears."

"Aw, heck, you talked as much as Thunder," declared Frijole. "He'll cut off both yore heads. But that won't bother yuh for a couple weeks, 'cause it'll take yuh that long to find it out."

"W'ere you theenk he go?" asked Lightning.

"He's prob'ly hidin' in the brush behind our house," said Frijole soberly. "He'll prob'ly start carvin' yuh tonight."

"*Madre de Dios!*" gasped Lightning. He got Thunder by the sleeve and drew him outside the office. Lightning had a loaded gun concealed on his person. It was a very heavy forty-five, with a barrel only two inches long. Lightning had tied a string to the trigger guard, fastened it to a button on his pants, and lowered the gun inside the waistband. The weight made it difficult for him to keep his pants up.

"Sometheeng mus' be done," he told Thunder.

"W'at you theenk?" queried Thunder.

"Theenk? This ees no time for theenking; it ees time for doing, damn fast. Can't you say sometheeng, excep' jus' looking."

"Sure. Haitch is for hockleberries."

"W'ere the devil you leesten to theeng like that?"

"Oh, I'm hear Henry say that to Judge. Judge ask heem— why you don't say sometheeng, and Henry say haitch ees for hockleberry."

"Leesten," gritted Lightning. "I'm asking you to feeger sometheeng to save your damn life, and you spell hockleberry."

"Don't speet," ordered Thunder. "Can't you say 'Leesten' weethout making heem so wet? I'm leestening."

"We mus' leeve theese co'ntry."

"W'ere we goin' leeve heem?"

"Leeve heem right here."

"That's good place for heem."

"Sure," said Lightning expansively. "I'm goin' buy quart tequila, and then we feeger next theeng for doing. Whoa, Beel! Theese damn gon almost pull my pant off. Leesten! Don't act scare. Act like notheeng ees going on. Wheestle—do someth-eeng."

"W'at you like me to wheestle?"

"*Dios mio!*" grunted Lightning. "Every time I look at you I'm won'er eef I am not losing your mind."

"That ees seench," agreed Thunder brightly. "Go buy tequila."

IT WAS well after dark when the quart of tequila was finished, but that amount of potent juice of the maguey had failed to bolster the nerves of the two Mexicans. There was a night stage for Scorpion Bend, which left Tonto City at seven o'clock, driven by Nick West. They decided to take that stage.

The trip was entirely Lightning's scheme to get away from any possible assault by Dusty Cole. Neither of them had the price of a stage ride to Scorpion Bend, but they hung around until the stage was loaded. Then they managed partly to conceal themselves among some bales and boxes on the boot.

There were no paying passengers on the stage when it finally started. Nick West drove his stage over the long road toward Scorpion Bend, not knowing that he was taking two stowaways who clung to the swaying rear of that lurching old stage.

It was bright moonlight, and the dust, boiling up from behind the rear wheels, almost suffocated the two Mexicans. Otherwise, everything was all right until they reached the grades of Piñon Canyon. There the stage came to an abrupt stop. The heavy vehicle had made so much noise on the rocky road that neither Thunder nor Lightning had heard the sharp warning to stop.

Lightning eased an aching knee from under a tight rope and shifted his position.

"I theenk we meet somebodee," whispered Thunder.

"Sh-h-h-h!" hissed Lightning. "Theenk to myself, biffore somebodee find us."

They could hear voices, as though several men were talking. Slowly Lightning lifted his head above the rear of the stage, that he might get a view of what was going on. The bright moonlight illuminated the scene, showing two masked men, guns in hand, while near the wheel of the stage stood the driver.

"Madre de Dios!" gasped Lightning. With a trembling hand he grasped the string and drew the heavy gun from inside his waistband.

Cocking it carefully, he lifted it over the top, took careful aim at one of the bandits, closed both eyes and pulled the trigger. It might be more correct to say that he yanked the trigger. There was a spurt of flame, and the canyon walls blared back the roaring explosion of the heavy forty-five. The gun bucked out of Lightning's hand, broke the string with its own weight and went into the dirt.

The frightened team lurched ahead, broke into a run. They headed down the grade, tires screeching from the pull of the brakes, with Thunder and Lightning hanging on with both hands and both feet. They negotiated the first turn in safety, but came to grief on the next. There a front wheel crashed into the rocky corner, slewing the stage around. It dislodged both the clinging passengers, and jerked the team to a stop.

Being suddenly bumped on the hard road for several moments, both Mexicans were utterly dazed. Lightning was the first to find his voice, and then it was only a wailing whisper:

"Thonder, are you keeled?"

"Sure," admitted the agreeable Thunder, "W'at in hell ees all the shooting for?"

"Leesten!" ordered Lightning breathlessly. "I jus' keeled Dusty Cole."

"No!"

"You theenk I'm seet here and lie?"

"W'ere ees Dusty Cole, Lightning?"

"I keel heem, I tell you. W'at ees the matter weeth my ears? Can't you hear notheeng? You come weeth me—I show you."

Cautiously they limped back up the grade, around the turn, and onto the straight piece of road where the hold-up had occurred. Not a living soul was in sight, but there was something lying near the road, looking very much like the body of a man.

"You see heem?" breathed Lightning.

Very slowly they approached. It was a body, lying there unmoving. Both of the Mexicans were breathing heavily, as they approached the body. Reaching it, they stopped and stood stock still.

The moonlight slanted down into the pale face of Nick West, the stage-driver.

"Theese Dusty Cole hees get old queek," remarked Thunder.

"Brodder," choked Lightning, "we better go like hell from these places. I'm keel the wrong man."

"Wheech way you like from running?" asked Thunder.

"Tonto Ceety," whispered Lightning. "Nobody ees knowing we come here. *Madre de Dios,* thees ees terrible. They 'ang both of us."

"Together?" asked Thunder blandly.

"Don't stop for talkeeng."

"Sure. But w'y you theenk theese man ees Dusty Cole?"

"Biccause I'm seeing Dusty Cole and Sandy Crane weeth heem."

"Eef we go back, Dusty Cole ees keel hell out of us," protested Thunder.

"Leesten, my leetle brodder," said Lightning ominously, "we are in devil of a feex. If theese law don't 'ang us for morder, Dusty Cole hees keel us. Well? W'y don't you say sometheeng?"

"Haitch ees for hockleberry," replied Thunder.

"Come on," sighed Lightning. "Eet don't make no deeference which way I'm get keeled, biccause you are so dumb I won't feel eet, anyway."

CHAPTER VII

ARIZONA HAPPENSTANCE

HENRY AND JUDGE were snoring heavily at the Tonto Hotel that night when Tom Rickey, the proprietor, hammered loudly on their door. Judge's snore ceased, and he sat up in bed, blinking at the moonlight through the window.

"Is it necessary to knock down the door?" he asked.

"Wake up!" called Rickey. "There's been a hold-up and attempted murder. Hurry up!"

"Did you hear that, Henry?" asked Judge.

"My goodness!" grunted Henry. "Some folks do select the most ungodly hours for their criminal activities. And I was enjoying a most wonderful dream. It seemed that I was—"

"There has been a robbery and attempt to murder!" interrupted Judge. "And you try to tell me about your dream."

Judge was hurrying into his clothes.

"Pants," remarked Henry, "are for the legs. I'm afraid the sleeves of my coat would be a bit short for your shanks."

"Confound it!" snorted Judge. "You put your coat on top of my pants."

"The life of a fireman," sighed Henry, dressing as rapidly as possible. "I wonder who got robbed. However, I suppose we shall find out eventually. Mr. Rickey seemed rather heavy-handed. We'd better examine the hinges on our door in the morning. Ready?"

Already there was a small crowd in the little lobby when the two came out. The crowd hastened to inform Henry that the Scorpion Bend stage had been robbed by two bandits, and Nick West, the driver, had been shot. Two men, driving in from Scorpion Bend, had found the stalled stage. A little later they had come upon Nick West, staggering back toward Tonto City. They had brought him in and left him at Doctor Bogart's house.

Henry went down to see West. He was sitting in the doctor's office, still looking a little dazed, his head bandaged. Doctor Bogart said that a bullet had bounced off Nick's head, but that it was not serious.

"I dunno who shot me," said the driver. "It wasn't neither Dusty nor Sandy, 'cause I was watchin' them."

"Good Lord!" gasped Henry. "Dusty and Sandy—why, what do you mean?"

"They held me up," explained Nick.

"Hell's bells!" gasped Henry. "You—you recognized them?"

"Why, yeah. They wore masks, but that wouldn't keep anybody from recognizin' 'em. I asked Dusty what the heck he was tryin' to do, and he said, 'As long as they want to hang me, I might as well draw some pay for stretchin' their danged rope.'"

"Whimsical rascal," breathed Henry. "But that stage never carries any money, Nick."

"It did last night, Sheriff. There was a sealed box, which would weigh about seventy-five, eighty pounds, shipped by the Yellow Warrior mine."

"And they got it?"

"Yeah, they got it all right."

"My goodness; But you say neither of them shot you, Nick?"

"Couldn't. They was facin' me—and I was hit from behind."

Nick had told the same story to the two men who brought him to town; so the story quickly spread. Henry went to the office, where Judge was waiting for him. He told Judge about the theft.

"Over twenty thousand dollars in gold bullion!" exploded Judge. "So Dusty wants pay for stretching rope, does he?"

"He does seem rather mercenary, Judge," sighed Henry. "But I suppose he considers it the last job he will ever do; so he wants it to be a paying one."

"Your levity is unseemly, sir," declared Judge. "They are saying that you aided and abetted Dusty Cole in his escape. Damme, sir, if that is true you are as guilty as he. You foisted a monster upon Wild Horse Valley."

"Well," sighed Henry, "it—it was a nice night for foisting. Where do you get all those fancy words, Judge? Thwart and foist. If this continues I shall need an interpreter. Why not go back to bed? There is no earthly use of riding out to Piñon Canyon. Certainly, those two bandits are not waiting for us there. In the morning we will ride out and search for clues."

"Clues! Why, the driver recognized Dusty and Sandy. What more evidence do you need, if I may ask, sir?"

"Judge," replied Henry quietly, "I fear that I am becoming a confirmed skeptic."

"I have my own opinions, sir," replied Judge.

"I shall not argue with you, Judge," stated Henry gently. "Any time I desire an argument I shall contact someone whose mind is nearly as flexible as a yard of concrete. Shall we retire?"

DAYLIGHT FOUND Henry and Judge out on the Piñon Canyon grade. Judge had grumbled and growled all the way out there. He hated to ride a horse. But Henry was adamant—so Judge was with him. It was not difficult to find the spot where the hold-up had occurred, because the stage driver had told Henry.

Just beyond the spot on the grade was a small canyon, brushy and concealed by a sprawling sycamore, where the two bandits had left their horses. There was no evidence which way they had gone, but Henry presumed that they had turned back into the valley.

As they mounted their horses to start back home, Henry saw an object in the dusty road. He quickly dismounted and picked up a heavy revolver with a two-inch barrel. Hanging to the trigger guard was a few inches of dirty cord. One chamber had been fired.

Henry handed the gun to Judge. The latter looked it over critically.

"That gun," declared Judge, "looks familiar, Henry. The barrel has been sawed off."

"Yes," nodded Henry. "I sawed it off three months ago. Then I stood ten feet from a five-cannon can, fired six shots and never hit the can once. Then I threw the gun in a dresser drawer at the JHC."

"But," said the puzzled Judge, "how on earth did it get here?"

Henry shook his head slowly.

"And why is there a string attached?" queried Judge.

"Well," replied Henry, "that might have been attached to increase the mystery."

"I wonder if that is the gun with which Nick West was shot."

"It has been fired once, you will observe," said Henry. "Let me concentrate for a moment, Judge. There are Frijole Bill, Thunder and Lightning—they were in town last night, I believe."

"Yes," agreed Judge. "I saw those two impossible Mexicans last night. But Henry, I—I believe we shall have to look further. When Frijole Bill drove back to the ranch, both Mexicans were with him."

"You can vouch for that?"

"Absolutely. I heard Frijole berating them for spending all their money for tequila."

"Hm-m-m. That does complicate things. But who in the devil took my gun away from the ranch, I wonder."

"Possibly those two Mexicans sold or traded it. They have no idea of right or wrong, Henry. We shall question them."

"I hope we have more success than the coroner had, Judge—or the prosecutor."

As they rode back toward Tonto City Judge said:

"Henry, we must capture Dusty Cole. I doubted his criminal tendencies when he was arrested; and my sympathy was with him during the trial—but the man is thoroughly bad. This robbery proves it. And if we don't capture him, we may as well resign. The county will not stand for us any longer."

Henry nodded solemnly. "Perhaps you are right, Judge. We are both growing too old for active service. I mean, collectively. Personally, I am still in the prime of life, but you are—"

"Wait a minute, sir!" interrupted Judge. "I am still on this side of sixty."

"*This side*—yes," admitted Henry. "I have been called an old man, but no one has ever said, as they have of you, that I was an *elderly* man."

"Some day," said Judge ominously, "I hope I catch the editor of the *Scorpion Bend Gazette* hung up in a barbwire fence. He also called you a red-faced nincompoop. Or was it a red-nosed one?"

"I wish they would leave my nose out of it," said Henry. "After all, my nose is not to blame for my failings."

"He said it was so big that it gave you a distorted view of the world, Henry."

"Well," said Henry, "I believe we should concentrate more on the problems at hand, and ignore the sarcasm of a jaundiced editor."

"That is true," agreed Judge. "I suppose it would not be good policy to mention that gun."

"Hardly," replied Henry dryly. "They might accuse one of us of shooting Nick West from behind."

When they got back to town, they found Nick Borden, the superintendent of the Yellow Warrior mine, waiting at the office. He told them that the sealed box had contained eighty pounds of gold bullion.

"As an added precaution," he told Henry, "we brought that shipment in at the last moment and put it on the stage. I can't imagine how on earth they could know about it."

"Possibly they did not know—merely happened to strike it," suggested Henry.

"Well, that is possible. But it seems strange that they should happen to stick up that stage and get the first shipment we ever sent out in that way."

"Anything can happen in Arizona," remarked Henry wearily.

MACK TAYLOR and Tuck Nash rode in from their Spotted Horse mine that afternoon, and Mack Taylor came down to the sheriff's office. They had heard about the stolen shipment of gold, but Taylor wanted more of the details.

Henry explained what they knew about the hold-up. Taylor remarked that Dusty and Sandy had lost no time in picking up some easy money. Without any comments, Henry then handed Mack Taylor the note he had found beside the stable. The good-looking mine operator flushed, laughed shortly and handed the note back to Henry.

"I wrote it," he admitted wryly. "I figured that Dusty was innocent of that crime—and I knew what that jury would do to him. That doggoned note blew away, in the dark, when I tried to put it through the window."

"We found the saws," said Henry. "The note lodged against the front of my stable." And then: "What do you think of Dusty now?"

Mack Taylor shrugged his shoulders. "Well, it kinda looks like he turned wild, Sheriff. Might as well though. A man under sentence of death isn't goin' to Sunday School—not regularly."

"I suppose that is true," sighed Henry.

"I hope yuh won't mention that note, Sheriff," said Taylor. "I never even told Tuck Nash about it. Mebbe I was foolish to do it, but I wanted to help the kid out."

"Oh, it doesn't matter—now," replied Henry. "He never used the saws. How are things at the Spotted Horse?"

"Well, they're lookin' a little better. We've been workin' on a seam of ore that looked like it might develop into somethin'.

Most of our ore is in pockets—but that's all right, if the pockets are rich enough. We're getting' along all right, though."

After Taylor left the office, Judge came in with Edwin Corley, chairman of the mine commissioners. Henry groaned softly. Corley was from Scorpion Bend, a hard-faced, sour-minded person who disliked humor in any form.

"I just came from the prosecutor's office," he told Henry at once. "He is very pointed in his remarks regarding your ability. Personally, I believe you are making a farce out of this office. The people of Wild Horse Valley have been very patient and lenient, it seems to me. Dusty Cole's escape seemed well planned, don't you think?"

"Their timing was excellent, sir," agreed Henry warmly. "One might almost believe that it had been rehearsed. However, it was merely a coincidence, of course."

"Um-m—hah!" snorted Corley. "I suppose it was a coincidence that you did not have handcuffs on the prisoner, Sheriff."

"Exactly," agreed Henry. "Dear me, I regret that oversight. But everyone is prone to make mistakes. The human element again, sir."

"All right!" snapped the commissioner. "We are giving you one week to capture Dusty Cole, Conroy. Unless with one week you can produce that bandit in court, we shall take action against you. You are on probation, sir. I give you good day, sir."

"I take it—and thank you, sir," replied Henry with apparent soberness.

Corley strode noisily out.

"You handled that very well, Henry," said Judge.

"I think so," agreed Henry. "I was gentle, but firm. I suppose he thinks that I am worried about his threats of action."

"Corley will keep his word, Henry."

"I hope you are right, Judge; so few people do. I grow weary of this job. I feel that I am too young to waste the best years of my life. Now, if you had the job, Judge—at your age—"

"You let my age alone!" snapped Judge. "Best years of your

life—indeed! Confound it, will you ever be serious. If you are weary of this job, please consider me—and Oscar."

"I do, Judge—indeed I do. I was joking. But would you have me strike a pose, hammer on my swelling bosom, and proclaim to the world that I am going to capture Dusty Cole, or die in the attempt? I have never played heroic roles, Judge. Mine has always been the sly, subtle humor, invoked by a flaming proboscis and the ability to mis-juggle three billiard balls. A star in my own right—but always spotted so close after a trained dog act that the public thought I was an encore. But I was a free man. My soul was my own—after my third daily appearance."

"I suppose you miss the applause, Henry," said Judge.

"Miss it? Good heavens, I have missed it all my life!"

Judge grinned and tilted his chair against the wall.

"Oscar is drinking heavily," he told Henry. "Love, I suppose."

"I thought he was through with Josephine."

"He was—for an hour or two. Henry, I wish we knew how your gun got out to Piñon Canyon grade."

"Rather puzzling, Judge. No doubt it had assistance in getting out there, because even an Arizona gun is still considered an inanimate object. I believe I shall ride out to the ranch this evening, Want to go along?"

"Yes, I believe I do, Henry. Frijole might have some ideas on that gun question."

CHAPTER VIII

MARIHUANA MADNESS

LIGHTNING AND THUNDER Mendoza rode wearily to the JHC Ranch. They had been on a roundabout trip to Piñon Canyon grade, trying to find that sawed-off six-shooter, but with no success. As they turned their tired horses into the corral, Lightning said:

"Theese ees torrible. Like Frijole say, I am so dang' low I can put on plog-hat and walk over snake's belly. You know w'at I mean, my leetle brodder?"

"Sure," replied Thunder brightly. "I see peecture one time."

"Peecture from what?"

"Saint Patrick. He ees wear plog-hat and step on snake."

"I'm not spik from peectures, leetle *idiota*. Some day I shake you so 'ard my teeth all fall out. You re'lize w'at theese min? W'en those gon ees find by somebodee, Señor 'Enry ees saying, 'Ah-ha, those dawn *Mejicano!*'"

"You theenk he blame us from stealing those gon?"

"*Dios mio!*" exclaimed Lightning. "Who else you theenk steal?"

"Maybe he theenk he lose himself."

"Oh, sure," grunted Lightning, exasperated. "Leesten, my brodder! If Señor 'Enry ees saying, 'Thonder, who steal my gon?' W'at you say?"

"Lightning he steal eet."

"You say those? Yah! You tell heem? Some day I keel you damn dead."

64

"Sure."

"You tell heem you never see those gon. You onnerstand?"

"Sure. Maybe I am saying, 'W'at gon you are spiking of?'"

"You never see any gon!"

"What the heck are you revolutionists talkin' about?" demanded Frijole, who had approached unnoticed. "What gun are yuh yellin' about?"

Lightning drew a deep breath of consternation, but his brain functioned swiftly.

"Thonder ees lying 'bout gun he is seeing een *Mejico*. He say those gun shoot t'ree mile."

"Heck!" snorted Frijole. "I've fired guns that shoot fifty miles."

"Seex-shooter?" queried Thunder.

"No—shotguns, you danged fool! Go wash yore dirty faces— supper's ready. And if yuh don't—well, well! Here comes Henry and Judge!"

"Madre de Dios!" gasped Lightning. "Sometheeng ees goin' 'appen."

Thunder and Lightning hurried up to the back porch, and there proceeded to wash their faces and hands violently. When Henry and Judge rode up, Frijole immediately asked them to stay for supper. They accepted promptly. Then, before the two Mexicans had returned, Henry asked Frijole if he remembered that sawed-off Colt forty-five.

"Shore," replied Frijole. "It's in the top drawer of that bureau in the house."

"It *was*," said Henry. "It is now in my office. I picked it up on Piñon Canyon grade, where it had been dropped during the hold-up. I have reason to believe that it is the gun which shot Nick West."

Frijole scratched his head, staring at Henry, a puzzled frown on his wizened face.

"Heck, that ain't possible!" he exclaimed. "But dang it, you ort to know that gun. You sawed it off yourself."

Henry nodded and looked toward the back porch. Frijole followed his gaze, but turned quickly back to Henry.

"Thinkin' about them two snake-hunters?" he asked. "Well, they went to town with me, got full of tequila, and came home with me."

"Could they have sold or loaned the gun, I wonder?" said Judge.

"Well, that's possible," remarked Frijole, "Why not ask 'em?"

"I will," said Henry.

Frijole laughed and shook his head. "They're scared plenty," he said. "They're afraid that Dusty will cut off their ears for testifyin' against him."

"Somebody should cut off their ears for murdering the King's English," declared Judge. "Their testimony did not help nor harm Dusty Cole, because they never did manage to answer a question."

"You let me handle the questions this time, Judge," said Henry.

"You might do much better with a shotgun," said Judge.

THEY WERE nearly finished with supper, and the early fears of Thunder and Lightning had been banished. Frijole and Judge were beginning to wonder if Henry had changed his mind. Suddenly, then, he leaned across the table, shook a forefinger in Lightning's face and said:

"You stole my gun and shot Nick West!"

Lightning leaned back in his chair, wide-eyed with fright and unable to say anything.

"You!" Henry turned and jabbed the finger at Thunder. "You were with him! Well, well! Why don't you say something?"

"Haitch ees for hockleberry."

Judge choked and Frijole hammered him joyfully on the back. Henry bowed his head, his eyes filled with tears, unable to follow up his third-degree.

"Of w'at gon are you spiking about?" asked Lightning huskily.

"The gun you used to shoot Nick West," wheezed Henry.

"The one weeth the forty-feefth caliber?" asked Thunder.

"The one with the sawed-off barrel," whispered Henry.

"How you know he shoot heem?" asked Thunder.

Henry wiped away his tears and looked keenly at Thunder.

"A man saw him fire the shot," lied Henry.

"Leesten, my leetle brodder," said Lightning. "Every time I open your mouth I put my feet in eet. No man see heem. Dosty Cole and Sandy Crane ees hiding out in the heels. Nobody else ees there for seeing. *Dios Mio!* Eef you have twice so much sense as I am, you are still idiot."

"Sure," agreed Thunder blandly. "Nobody ees seeing you shoot. Anyhow, theese man ees not die. All hees got ees bomp on hees *cabeza*."

"That seems to be settled," said Henry dryly. "Did you see the two men who held up the stage?"

"I see," declared Lightning. "Dosty Cole and Sandy Crane. I'm tak' shot at Dosty, but that gon ees not shoot where I am looking."

"What on earth were you doing on that stage?" asked Judge.

"Hanging on tight," replied Thunder. "We are scare biccause Dosty Cole cut off our ear."

"I see. You believed he would revenge himself upon you for your testimony; so you tried to leave the country."

"I'm 'ave only two ear," said Lightning soberly.

Henry sighed and leaned back in his chair.

"Judge, I'm afraid there is no question as to the identity of the two bandits. Three men have already identified them."

"Try and get 'em," said Frijole. "They know every inch of this valley, and they're both danged good shots. Dusty can shoot the buttons off your vest, as far as he can see 'em—and Sandy's no slouch of a shot. Mebbe you'll get 'em eventually, but I'd hate to think how many cripples you'll have before they're behind the bars."

"Cripples? My goodness!" exclaimed Henry.

"You swore to uphold and enforce the laws, Henry," reminded Judge.

"Eh? Oh, yes—I suppose I did—foolishly. Frijole, that did not happen to be Bill Shakespeare in that stew, did it?"

"No, no, that was Oliver Cromwell. Yuh see, Old Bill's gettin' what they call astigmatism. Yesterday mornin' he chased a skunk down the dry wash—and got too close. All the rest of the chickens are under the stable, and poor old Bill is out there alone, wonderin' what in heck's come over the country. It won't last long, cause he's only got his wing-feathers and one tail-plume left."

"If this wave of crime continues," sighed Henry, "I'm afraid that I will be in much the same condition as Bill Shakespeare."

"Yuh mean—the skunk?" asked Frijole.

"No—the feathers," smiled Henry.

A SHORT time later Henry and Judge rode back to Tonto City and stabled their horses. They were crossing the dimly-lighted street toward the Tonto Saloon, when a lone rider galloped into town. He was sending his mount at top speed straight toward them.

Judge cried out, sprawled in the dirt to escape the animal's flailing hoofs. The horse sped on without swerving, straight toward the Tonto hitch-rack, the rider still spurring viciously.

The animal hit the rack with a terrific crash and went down, flinging its rider over the top pole. The rider lay there, unmoving.

At the sound of the crash men came running from the saloon and across the street. Judge picked himself out of the dust, and he and Henry walked over. Already men were lighting matches above the huddled form there on the ground.

"It's Sam Hope," blurted one of the men. "Good Lord—he must have raced his horse right into the hitch-rack. Somebody get Doc Bogart—quick."

The horse sprawled under the rack, its neck broken. Someone

stripped off the saddle and bridle. Doctor Bogart was on the scene moments later. He directed the bystanders to carry the injured man to his house.

When the doctor had had time to make his examination, Henry followed. Bogart shook his head as Henry entered.

"Collar bone broken, right arm broken, possible internal injuries and concussion," enumerated the doctor.

"It is very strange," said Henry. "Sam Hope knows this town—and yet he rode his horse at full speed into that hitchrack. How do you account for that, Doc?"

"This might be a solution, Henry," replied the doctor.

He pointed to the table on which had been piled the contents of Hope's pockets. Among them was a small, cloth tobacco sack, about half filled. Doctor Bogart opened the sack and sifted some of the contents on a piece of writing paper.

"I still do not understand, Doc," said Henry. "Tobacco, isn't it?"

"Flake cut tobacco, heavily mixed with marihuana."

"My goodness! Why, Doc, he must have crazy with that stuff."

"Speed crazy," said the doctor soberly. "That's the way it affects some people."

"Will he live?" queried Henry.

"It's too early even to guess at that, Henry, too soon to estimate his injuries. He must have been thrown very hard. I'll have to find a nurse for him."

"His wife is out at the Morris ranch, I believe."

"Is she? Well, I suppose you should send someone to notify her."

"Jim McDonald was there at the Tonto. He will tell her. I don't believe she had any suspicions that Sam was smoking marihuana."

"No need of making it public, Henry. After all, it won't help either of them."

"I suppose that is true."

AN HOUR later Henry was crossing the street to his office when he saw the team and buckboard from the Morris ranch pass the lights of the general store and go toward Doctor Bogart's home. It was Jim McDonald, bringing Molly Hope.

Henry hesitated for a moment, then turned and went in the same direction. Judge Myers had heard about the accident, and when Henry arrived at the doctor's house the judge was talking on the porch with McDonald. Molly was in the house with Doctor Bogart.

Judge Myers turned to Henry.

"You saw him ride into the hitch-rack, Henry?" he queried.

"Yes, I did, Judge. In fact, he nearly ran Judge Van Treece down, just before he crashed."

"Mighty queer," muttered the judge. "Badly broken up, too. Might not recover. Feel sorry for Molly. Even after the things Sam has done, she still—well, I never understood women, Henry."

"Does anyone?" queried Henry. "Adam didn't—and he had the only one there was, I believe. What can we poor mortals expect, with millions of them running loose?"

"Not even a Chinaman's chance," declared McDonald.

As the three men stepped into the living-room, Molly and the doctor came out of the bedroom. Molly was pale and distraught, but smiled at Henry.

"Any change, Doc?" asked Henry.

"Not any, Sheriff; he is still unconscious."

"I am going to stay and nurse Sam, Dad," announced Molly.

"It is her idea," stated the doctor.

"Well, I suppose it is all right," said the judge slowly.

"Wonderful," said Henry. "Better than—"

Henry's statement was interrupted sharply. An explosion rattled the windows of the frame cottage, as though a heavy shot had been fired inside the place. Doctor Bogart whirled, stepped quickly across the room and flung open the door of the room where the unconscious man had been placed.

A lamp was lighted on the table, showing the eddying wisps of powder smoke blowing back from an open window.

"Wait!" exclaimed the doctor, backing quickly. "Mrs. Hope, don't go in there. Henry, I'm afraid—"

Henry shoved past the doctor and went quickly to the bed. As he drew the sheet over Sam Hope's face, his usually florid face was very white. Molly was looking at him, a dazed expression in her eyes.

"For God's sake, what happened?" muttered the judge.

"Somebody shot through the window," whispered Henry. "You'd better get Molly away, Judge. Of all the damnable things!"

Henry hurried outside. Of course there was no one in sight, and no chance in the darkness to track the man down. Henry walked on down to his office, found Judge and Oscar there.

Quickly he explained that someone had fired a shot through the window and killed Sam Hope.

"Yumpin' Yudas!" exploded Oscar. "Even a sick man ain't safe in dis ha'ar country."

"Why on earth would anyone shoot Sam Hope?" queried Judge tensely.

"Your guess is as good as mine, Judge," replied Henry.

"Hm-m-m! Still unconscious when killed, eh? Henry, it looks as though somebody did not want him ever to recover consciousness again."

"Isn't that rather elemental, Judge?"

"Can you suggest a deeper motive, sir?"

"I am afraid not, Judge. It is rather puzzling. Why on earth did Sam Hope crash his horse against that hitch-rack? Was he running away from somebody, I wonder—riding blind with fright? Did he have something to tell, or was it a personal matter, involving himself and another party—someone who arrived, found him badly injured, and waited outside that window for a chance to end the feud."

"One solution is as plausible as another, Henry. But no matter what solution—it is cold-blooded murder, sir."

"Yes, that is true. Shooting an unconscious man is about as cold-blooded as any murder can possibly be. There must have been a mighty strong motive, Judge. Men do not kill in that way for amusement. Were you about to speak, Oscar?"

"Ay vars yust going to say that das ha'ar country is getting tough as ha'al," replied Oscar.

"Well, that is worth a thought," agreed Henry dryly. "Have you any suggestions, Oscar?"

"Ay vould say dat de t'ing to do is keep de vindow shut."

"Try matching that one, Judge," said Henry, "while I go to bed and get a little sleep. There is going to be work to do."

"Good! At last you are stirred, Henry. Well, the sovereign State of Arizona will not find us wanting."

"I hope," said Henry, "that the sovereign State of Arizona will find us *getting*. And I also hope that it won't be the worst of it."

CHAPTER IX

OSCAR SORROWS

LIGHTNING MENDOZA CAME to Tonto City next morning to get the mail, loaded his brain with information, and went back to the ranch, swelling with importance.

"*Alto*, look and leesten," he exploded to Frijole Bill and Thunder. "Las' night Sam 'Ope hees try to keeling heemself. I'm theenk he is missing. Then he ees go to slip in Doctor Bogarts' 'ouse, and somebodee ees shooting heem in the head, right behin' my ear."

"Well, I'll be a liar!" exclaimed Frijole.

"Sure," agreed Thunder. "That ees w'at Judge say."

"Judge says what?" demanded Frijole.

"That you are liar."

"Keep yore bill out of this," warned Frijole. "What else happened, Lightning?"

"Well," replied Lightning, swelling importantly, "this morning theese officer against the law 'ave offer two meelion dollar for Dosty Cole, one meelion dollar for Sandy Crane, and for these people wheech keel Sam 'Ope, so much."

"So much what?"

"So much more, I'm theenk."

"Dead or alive?"

"Mus' be alive, or they don't wan' heem."

"Does the reward say 'dead or alive'?"

"I never read heem."

"Who told yuh about it?"

"Oh, I jus' leesten."

"Uh-huh. Didja see Henry or Judge?"

"No. Somebody ees saying they 'ave gone to catch theese keeler from people. Oscar ees ronning the jail."

"Did he tell yuh anything?"

"Sure. He tell me to get to hell out from 'ere."

"Well, I'll be danged!" snorted Frijole. "So Sam Hope tried to kill himself—and missed. Too drunk to shoot straight, eh? Well, I'll believe that."

"He keel hees 'orse," offered Lightning.

"Huh? The heck, he did! Missed himself and hit his horse. But if he missed himself, why did he go to bed at Doc Bogart's place?"

"To sleep, I'm theenk," replied Lightning.

"Yeah! I reckon that's way most folks go to bed. Million dollars reward, eh? Yo're crazy, Lightnin'. Have you any idea how much a million dollars is?"

"*Mucho dinero*," grinned Lightning. "I never see heem."

"I hope to tell yuh—yuh never seen that much. Why, if you had a million silver dollars, you couldn't put 'em in this house."

"Why?"

"Well, yuh jist couldn't—that's why."

"You theenk I geeve damn? Huh! I keep heem in bonk-house."

"Keep it in yore pocket—who the heck cares!" snorted Frijole.

"Tak' theese paper money," suggested Thunder. "He don' weigh so much."

"Yea-a-a-ah!" snorted Frijole. "Is it any wonder I drink prune whisky? If Henry don't git some white men out here to take this here burden off my soul, I'll go crazy as a bedbug in another week."

"You theenk Dosty Cole keel Sam 'Ope?" queried Lightning.

"Heck, yes! He thought Sam was you."

"Dios mio!"

"Yeah, you better git scared enough to talk Mexican. Why, you even had to up and tell Henry that you seen Dusty and Sandy hold up that stage. Golly, yo're shore pilin' up trouble for yourselves."

"You theenk it ees bes' for lying?"

"Well, jist take me for example," replied Frijole. "If I ever told a man the truth, and found it out, I'd come right back and correct m'self. I'm in good health, ain't I? Ain't nobody gunnin' for me. I'll tell yuh this much—I use common sense."

Duly impressed, Lightning said:

"W'at you theenk we should do, Frijole?"

"Do? Why, if I was you fellers I'd try and find Dusty and Sandy—and kinda apologize. Might save yore ears, yuh know."

"Eef we find heem, you theenk he leesten?" asked Thunder.

"Oh, sure. Dusty is a great feller."

"Bueno!" Lightning turned on Thunder. "Leesten, you bongler! W'en we find these Dosty Cole, you let me do the talking, you onnerstan? You are always putting your feet een my mouth. Don't say notheeng."

"Sure," agreed Thunder. "You do the talkeeng, but I tell you theese much—I do my own ronning."

FAR OUT in the hills, where the mercury registered about 110 in the shade, rode Henry and Judge, with Henry in the lead. Heat waves danced across the rocks, and the sun beat mercilessly down upon the two riders.

"I hope you fry in your own grease," groaned Judge.

"Very likely," replied Henry, "but I will not stick to the pan, like you will. In a heat like this, grease is a boon. I may brown, but I doubt if I shall burn."

"This is all so confounded useless, Henry. Riding for miles and miles in the devilish heat, uphill and down. My canteen is boiling. After all, why do you insist on such ridiculous procedure?"

"We, my dear sir, are upholding the law," replied Henry. "We are doing something. After all, the world expects us to act like officers of the law. Criminals will not come to us; so we go to the criminals. Does that enlighten you, Judge?"

"Oh, I see," groaned Judge. "We are going to the criminals. And if I may be so bold as to inquire—when do we get there?"

"That has nothing to do with the case, Judge. Inevitably, I hope, we will run them to earth. We shall ride these hills until our hoofmarks have registered on every pinnacle, and we know every rock by its first name. Two savage old wolves, prowling... prowling..."

"Prowling! Wolves! A pair of blasted old fools, frying their brains out, and not even a will o' the wisp to follow. Do you expect to find Dusty and Sandy sitting out here on a pinnacle, waiting for us?"

"No, I do not expect them, Judge. But if they should be—our chase is ended. I believe in the element of surprise. They expect us to be in the shade of our office. They would feel that we are far too brainy to be doing this. Do you understand my theory?"

"Theory or not, I still think you are crazy, Henry."

They drew up on a pinnacle which overlooked a little valley. Less than a mile way was the Spotted Horse mine, owned by Mack Taylor and Tuck Nash. It had been an abandoned property until Taylor and Nash relocated it and installed a small stamp mill.

"I have been feeling a few pangs of hunger and thirst," declared Henry. "I suggest that we go to the Spotted Horse and see if Messrs. Taylor and Nash have ought to eat and drink."

"Thank Heaven for a bit of normalcy in your mind, sir," sighed Judge.

They found Mack Taylor at the mine cabin, cooking a meal. He welcomed them warmly and invited them to eat. Tuck Nash had gone to Tonto City that morning, but had not come back yet; so the murder of Sam Hope was news to Taylor.

Henry watched Taylor closely, wondering what his reactions

would be, because he remembered what Judge Myers had said about Taylor being in love with Molly Hope. But Taylor's face told him nothing.

"That'll be tough on Hope's wife," he said. "She really cared a lot for Sam, even if he wasn't much good. But who in the devil would shoot him, I wonder?"

"Sam spent quite a little time out here, did he not?" queried Henry.

"Well, he was out here once in a while. As a matter of fact, he was short of money most of the time, and he knew we always kept more or less whisky out here. I never was much of a drinker, but Tuck hits it pretty hard—at times. Sam was a queer duck. Whisky kinda made him crazy. He'd sit here and drink whisky and smoke cigarettes, hardly sayin' a word. I never could quite figure him out."

Tuck Nash came in while they were eating. He was older than Taylor, slightly gray, hard-faced, with sharp eyes. Dissipation had left its mark on him, but he seemed hard as nails. He brought all the information about Sam Hope, which Mack Taylor already had.

"They're sayin' that Dusty Cole shot him," said Nash. "Heck, I suppose they'll blame everything on Dusty Cole from now on. There's never been any bad blood between Dusty and Sam, as far as I've heard."

"I believe they were friendly enough," agreed Henry.

"I wonder if Nick West wasn't workin' his imagination, when he said that Dusty and Sandy held up that stage," said Taylor.

"I am afraid not," replied Henry.

"You never believed that Dusty killed Peter Morris."

"No, I did not," Henry assured him. "As a matter of fact, gentlemen, I still do not believe it, regardless of the fact that Dusty turned highwayman."

"Funny about them gettin' the shipment from the Yellow Warrior," said Tuck Nash. "Like hittin' the OO in roulette, I reckon. Nobody knew about that gold bein' shipped."

"How is your gold vein coming along?" asked Judge.

"Kinda slow," replied Nash. "But one of these days we'll hit a pocket and be on easy street for a while. We're lucky to make wages, I reckon, This mine always was a pocket proposition. Rich today, broke tomorrow."

AFTER THEIR meal Henry and Judge rode on to the Bar M Ranch. They found Laura Morris there, but Molly Hope was still in town. Laura had buried her own troubles in sympathy for Molly Hope. Still, she could not forbear questioning Henry about Dusty Cole and about the hold-up.

"Miss Morris," Henry answered, "I'm afraid we must face the facts. Three men have identified Dusty and Sandy as the two men who robbed the stage."

"I can't believe it," she said. "Dusty was always honest."

"There is always a first time for a man to go bad," remarked Judge soberly.

"That must be a lot of satisfaction to Miss Morris," said Henry.

"What is the good of subterfuge?" asked Judge. "Three men identified Dusty and Sandy as the hold-up men."

"One frightened stage driver and two ignorant Mexicans," corrected Henry.

"The driver stated that Dusty talked with him, didn't he?" asked Laura.

"Yes, he did," nodded Henry. "I asked him if he identified Dusty's voice, and he said, 'It sounded like Dusty.' I asked him if he could give me any idea how Dusty 'sounded,' and he could not."

"That was not a fair test, Henry," protested Judge. "Suppose someone asked you how I sounded. How could you describe it?"

"I would merely say that it was terrible, and in most cases not fit for publication, Judge. That would be definite evidence to anyone who knew you at all."

"Thank you, sir," said Judge dryly.

Henry turned again to Laura.

"If there were only some way of finding out who had the appointment that night with your father," he said, "and why he drew fifteen thousand dollars from the bank at Scorpion Bend…. Unless he hid that money, the man who killed him also stole the money. And if the man who had the appointment with him did not keep it, why doesn't he come forth and tell us? Dusty Cole did not have the money."

"I am sure it was a terrible mistake—Dusty's conviction," said Laura. Bitterly she added. "The law convicted an innocent man, and made an outlaw of him. I'm as sure as anything that Judge Myers did not believe Dusty was guilty. And now they're saying that Henry Conroy turned Dusty loose. Why, that's ridiculous."

"Thank you so much, my dear young lady," said Henry warmly. "That warms the cockles of my heart."

"And extends to the end of your nose," added Judge. "The glow is evident."

In spite of her troubles Laura laughed.

"Juan Mendoza is back in the kitchen," she told him. "Won't you stay for supper? I need someone to talk with, and I'm afraid Molly won't be back tonight. We're having enchiladas—and there is lots of red wine."

"*Viva la Juan Mendoza!*" cheered Henry. "I have tasted the results of his culinary skill—and it is magnificent."

"Requiring, if I remember correctly," said Judge, "at least half a package of baking soda. As for me, I can digest rusty nails."

"Ah-ha!" exclaimed Henry. "At last I have found out what ails you, Judge. Iron and rust! Your system does not digest them—it merely absorbes them. Thank you, Miss Laura—we are honored by your invitation."

IT WAS after dark that evening, when Frijole Bill, Thunder and Lightning came to Tonto City in the buckboard. They tied the team in front of the sheriff's office, took a jug of prune liquor and walked into the office. Oscar was there alone, slumped on the cot. He squinted up at them disconsolately.

"Hyah, Square-head," said Frijole. Frijole had been dallying with his own distillations before leaving the ranch. "Where-at is Henry and Judge?"

"Ay don't know, and Ay don't give dang," said Oscar.

"Feller, you look low," declared Frijole. "I'll betcha you'd have to climb thirty feet up a ladder to rub a snake's belly. What's ailin' yuh?"

"Ay have been yilted," declared Oscar.

"Jilted, eh? Left at the altar. Well, well!"

"Who de ha'al said anyt'ing about a halter."

"Excuse me," chuckled Frijole. "How about a snifter of the prune?"

"Ay could drink nitric acid and like it."

Oscar secured two cups. Thunder and Lightning always reserved their thirst for tequila, and refused prune whisky.

After the second cupful Oscar said:

"Ay am hortsick, Ay ta'al you, Free-holey. Ay yust paid sixty dollar for busting a boggy. Ay am t'rough. Love is not vort' it."

"I hope to tell yuh it ain't. I know *all* about it. Did I ever tell yuh about the time I almost married an Arapajo squaw? Talk about hard luck. Her old man wanted twenty-five ponies for her; so I got the twenty-five ponies and was all ready to make the trade, when her old man discovered that he already owned the twenty-five ponies. I never was worth a dang on readin' Injun brands.

"Well, sir, my dream of love was busted—along with all world records for about six miles. Fill up them cups, comrade. When I git to talkin' about love, it makes me dry."

Oscar blinked.

"Nels Swenson is ha'ar," stated Oscar. "He come to see Yose-phine."

"Oh, oh! So that's the place where it squeaks, eh? Well, what are you moonin' for? You said you was through with her. Can't yuh never make up your mind, Oscar? Let her have Nels. I'd hate to see you marry a woman like her. Why, she's liable to take a hunk of wood and knock you cold any minute. I like the clingin' kind, myself."

"Yosephine is hord to beat," sighed Oscar.

"You mean she's hard to whip, don'tcha?"

"Yah, su-ure. Why you bring those dang Mexican vit you, Free-holey?"

"They're scared to stay home alone," chuckled Frijole. "Where is this Nels person?"

"In de hotal, Free-holey, courtin' vit Yosephine. Ay bet dey are in de oopstairs parlor."

"Well, I'm shore surprised at you," declared Frijole. "Why don't yuh go up there and throw him out?"

"Ay vill ta'al you, Free-holey. Dis ha'ar yigger who owns de hotal told me that if Ay tried to dule around dere, he vill take his shotgun to me."

"Well, yuh can't blame him—much, Oscar. You've done busted up his hotel a couple times. When'd he tell yuh all this?"

"Yust a little vile ago."

"Oh, I see—yuh already had ideas. But—wait a minute! Yuh say the parlor is on that second floor? Huh! Well, why not climb right up them back steps onto that there balcony and take him."

Oscar's eyes opened wide. "Yumpin' Yudas! Pour out some more of dat prune yuice, Free-holey."

"I hope Mr. Rickey, who owns that hotel, keeps on watchin' the front door," chuckled Frijole. "More'n one way to skin a cat."

"Oscar ees going fight a cat?"

"Ay am going fight Norvegian shiphorder," declared Oscar, swelling his mighty chest. "When Ay get t'rough vit him, every ship in Black River Flats vill be vearin' crape. Anodder drink, Free-holey."

"My leetle brodder," whispered Lightning, "theese ees no place for ver' peaceful *Mejicanos*. I'm theenk we better mak' snick in the dark."

"No, yuh don't sneak in no dark," growled Frijole. "We're the moral support and audience for the big Swede. Heck, yuh can't git hurt, jist watchin' a fight."

"Va'al," said, Oscar, flinging his empty cup aside, "vat in ha'al are ve vaiting for? Ay feel for fight."

CHAPTER X

BANDITS!

IT WAS WELL after dark when Henry and Judge left the Bar M ranch, well filled with good food and red wine, and singing the praises of Juan Mendoza. As they jogged along on the outskirts of Tonto City, they passed the home of Frank Beeman, new manager and cashier of the Tonto City Bank. Beeman had only been in charge of the bank about two months.

Some distance from the road, and beyond the house, were several sycamore trees along the fence. Henry drew up and looked over there. In the moonlight, and just out of the heavy shadow of the trees, was what appeared to be a gray horse.

"What do you see, Henry?" asked Judge. But Henry had already reined over in that direction, and Judge followed.

Tied in the shadow of the trees were two horses—a gray and a blue-roan, with three white feet.

"Dusty Cole's and Sandy Crane's horses!" exclaimed Judge.

"Hm-m-m!" muttered Henry. "They made the mistake of tying the gray too long, and he swung around into the moonlight. Criminals, my dear Judge, always make mistakes."

"Which officers rarely do, I suppose," remarked Judge.

"Sarcasm on a filled stomach is unbecoming to you, sir," declared Henry. "Instead of indulging in repartee we must devise ways and means of capturing the gentlemen, when they return."

"I believe," said Judge, "that we should seek reinforcements. We might get enough men to surround the—er—trees and horses, so there would be no possible chance of escape, once they were within our lines."

"I suppose you learned that in the Civil War," said Henry.

"Common sense will tell you that these men are dangerous, Henry."

Henry chuckled. "That is the first time you have credited me with having common sense. Thank you very much, sir. But I believe we will tie our horses out beyond the fence, come back here and take the miscreants into custody, when they return."

Judge grumbled and prophesied dire results for such fool-hardy actions, but followed Henry. They tied their horses and came back to the sycamores. They stood there in the shadow, waiting.

"I am afraid I am going to have trouble with my goose-pimples, Henry," whispered Judge. "Not fear, but suspense. My hand is as steady as a rock, sir, but—it may be those last two enchiladas, trying to keep drowning in that red wine. They have come up twice."

"I—I feel a certain qualm, myself," admitted Henry, "but I—I keep swallowing it, as fast as it comes up."

Suddenly Judge grabbed Henry by the arm. "Good Lord, what was that?" he gasped.

From somewhere in the town had come a wild yell, like the sound of a soul in mortal terror. Both men strained their ears. In a few moments they heard the *thump, thump, thump* of what seemed to be revolver shots. Henry jerked away from Judge.

"Watch the horses!" he snapped. "I've got to see what that was."

And Henry went galloping toward the main street, leaving Judge to lean against the bole of a sycamore, groaning painfully.

THOSE FOUR conspirators against the peaceful love affair of Josephine and Nels used the back yards for their approach. They stumbled past the back of the bank, crossed the narrow alley between it and the hotel. At the bottom of the stairs which

led up to the wide veranda at the second story of the hotel, they stopped.

"Theese ees dang fool theeng for doing," declared Lightning.

"This," corrected Frijole, "is that there Battle of Army-gideon yuh hear about. Keep yore mouth shut, will yuh?"

The four men prowled up the stairs, with Oscar in the lead. There was moonlight, but the rear of the hotel lay in the heavy shadow. The old stairs creaked under their combined weight. Halfway up, Oscar stopped their advance with a wave of his hand.

"Ay am yust about to knock ha'al out from Nels," he announced, lowering his voice until it would only carry about two blocks. "You fallers stay on de porch and vatch me. Coom on."

A moment later something *swooshed* out of the shadows above them. It crashed into Oscar with terrific force, sent him sprawling back into Frijole and the two frightened Mexicans.

The stairs were sharply pitched, and there was no chance for any of them to regain their balance. Oscar Johnson let out a yell that could have been heard a mile away as the four tangled men went rolling and bumping down the stairs. Then they hit in a heap.

Dazed and frightened, Frijole staggered to his feet—only to have a flailing fist knock him spinning. He got up again, saw a huge form bearing down upon him. This time he whirled just in time and went galloping for safety, with the form close behind him.

An open doorway—and Frijole dived for safety. But the big man dived in right after him. Frijole stumbled over a chair, sprawled, and landed on the back of his neck. A gun flashed in his face, and he seemed to hear a lot of guns going off, but for the moment Frijole didn't quite know nor care.

Lightning and Thunder went down the sidewalk and headed for the Tonto Saloon. Men were running out into the street. Then someone yelled:

"The bank's been robbed!"

From the saloon side of the street could be seen the flashes of revolvers. The men were running toward the bank, drawing their guns. One cowboy saw the outline of a huge man close to the front door and took a shot at him, smashing out a large pane of glass. From inside the bank came a howl of fear. While others crowded in, trying to get a shot at somebody, the cowboy sent two more bullets through the broken window.

At that juncture Henry Harrison Conroy arrived, panting heavily.

"Robbers in the bank, Sheriff!" yelled someone.

"My goodness!" gasped Henry, grabbing a porch post. "Still there?"

"I reckon they are."

"Is—is anyone guarding the back entrance?"

There was a general rush down the little alley, only to find the back door closed and locked.

"We've got 'em trapped!" someone yelled triumphantly.

"What in ha'al is going on around ha're?" asked a voice from inside the broken window.

"Oscar!" cried Henry. "What are you doing in there, Oscar?"

"By Yudas, Ay don't know," wailed Oscar. "Ay came ha're during de var. Ay vant to know vat is going on myself."

"Are you alone in there?"

"Ay can't see damn t'ing."

"Hey!" yelled a voice at the rear just then. "Here's Frijole Bill!"

Frijole, his senses returned, managed to unfasten the spring lock on the back door and some of the men entered. They lighted a lamp in the bank. Oscar, one eye swelled shut and the rest of his features more or less skinned and bruised, leaned dejectedly against the wall.

Seated in his desk-chair, bound tightly and gagged with an old towel, was Frank Beeman, manager of the bank. He stared up wide-eyed at the crowd of men. Henry removed the gag, while one of the cowboys untied the ropes. Beeman was unhurt, but excited.

"They never got any money!" he exclaimed. "They came to my home and forced me to come up here to the bank. Then they tied me to the chair. They were afraid to light a lamp. My, what a night! They threatened to kill me, unless I gave them the combination of the vault.

"I'm afraid they were as frightened as I was, because they kept going out to the front, peering through the windows. Then one of them said he was sure that someone was at the back door; so they both went back there. I heard a terrific racket, and I heard one of the men say:

" 'Look out!' Then there was a crash at the back door, and a lot of shooting. I couldn't see anything that was going on, because I couldn't turn around. Then I heard more shots, and glass break-ing. But they never got any money! My, what a night!"

"My goodness!" exclaimed Henry as a sudden thought struck him. "Oh, my!"

He shoved his way hurriedly out of the bank and broke into a galloping run up the street. Bank robbers they were—and he had forgotten Judge and the two horses.

HE FOUND Judge sitting on the ground under the sycamore. Both horses were gone. Henry lighted a match and looked Judge over. He had a purple swelling at his right temple, which he caressed very tenderly, swearing volubly under his breath.

"They—they took the horses, Judge?" queried Henry huskily.

"Yes… they took them."

"You were to guard them, you know, Judge."

"Henry, I—" Judge choked, sighed and swallowed heavily. "Henry, right at the last moment I remembered."

"Oh, I see—you remembered. May I ask what you remembered?"

"I—I remembered that I forgot to take a gun with me this morning."

"My goodness!" gasped Henry. "You—a deputy sheriff."

"I am sorry, Henry. But what had happened?"

"The bank was robbed—or they tried to rob it. I do not know all the story yet. In some strange way Oscar and Frijole were mixed up in the deal. Accidentally ran into the bank, or something."

"Was—was it Dusty and Sandy?"

"I forgot to ask Mr. Beeman. If you feel like moving, I will get the horses. By the way, did the robbers recognize you, Judge?"

"I—er—believe they did, sir. One of them said, 'Well, look what we have here!' And the other one, I believe, struck me with the butt of a loaded quirt. It was very confusing."

SOME OF the excitement had died down when the two got back to town. And fortunately, the crowd had been too excited to notice Henry's hurried fadeaway. Leaving the much subdued Judge at the office, Henry went on to the Tonto. There Rickey, the owner of the hotel, handed him a black sombrero. It was surmounted with a silver studded band that bore the initials D.C.

"It was on the floor of the bank," said Rickey. "I picked it up myself. Can I have a word with you, Henry?"

Not without some trepidation, Henry nodded. They walked outside.

"Henry," Rickey announced promptly, "you must do something about that Swede. Big Nels came over from Black River City to see Josephine, and registered at the hotel. Oscar found out about it and came up there, but I told him to keep away and let Nels alone.

"A while ago, according to Josephine, while she and Nels were sitting on that back veranda, Oscar and some of his friends came up the back stairs. Oscar told them he was going to beat up Nels; so Nels threw a heavy rocking-chair down the stairs, and swept them all down to the bottom."

"My goodness!" choked Henry. "I—I shall speak to Oscar."

"I wish you would, Henry. If Josephine doesn't want to be annoyed by him, he'd better keep away from the hotel."

Henry went worriedly back to the office. Seated there in a subdued circle with Judge he found Oscar, Frijole and the two Mexicans. All four of them showed marks of conflict, but Oscar had the most. Henry looked him over carefully.

"So Nels flung a rocking-chair on your head, did he?"

"Go ahead and give him the devil," urged Frijole. "The big square-head thought I was Nels; so he climbed all over me. Golly, he must have been hit hard to mistake me for Nels."

"Chased you into the bank?" queried Judge.

"I reckon he did. I didn't know it was the back door of the bank—it was jist an open door to me."

"Well," sighed Henry, "with all your mistakes, you saved the bank from being robbed. Oscar, I suppose you took Frijole, Thunder and Lightning along with you to see you whip Nels, eh? As usual, you talked too loud. From now on, you keep away from Josephine."

"Ay don't vant to even hear her name," sighed Oscar. "She can't yilt Oscar Yohnson more den vonce. Ay am going to find Nels."

"And beat him all up, I suppose," said Judge.

"Vorse den that," declared Oscar. "Ay am going to ta'al him he can have Yosephine, vit my blessing."

"Josephine," said Henry, "will probably appreciate you giving her away."

He turned to Lightning. "What part did you have in the recent war?" he asked.

Lightning winced. "I'm got t'ree, four bomp on the *cabeza*," he said. "These big Swid ees make me and Thonder come along. I'm wan' all the time for ronning, but thees big Swid ees saying we mus' see the beeg fight. *Dios mio*, for thees I am shame for yourself."

"That is very good," said Henry soberly. Then he turned to Thunder.

"Well, what have you to say? What is your excuse? Haven't you anything to say?"

"Haitch ees for—"

"Huckleberry," added Henry. "That is very good. Frijole, you will please take these two boys home with you, and use the horse-liniment judiciously on all three of you. Judge, you'd better go down to Doc Bogart's place and take Oscar with you. You both need patching. I am going out to find Frank Beeman and see if he has any clues as to the identity of the two bandits—who almost got his money."

"I wonder where they had their horses staked out," said Frijole.

"That," replied Henry, "is of no consequence now, because they likely took them along when they left town."

"Your trouble, Frijole," said Judge, "is that you think of a thing like that too late."

"They're ridin' a gray horse and a blue-roan, with three white feet," said Frijole. "That's what everybody says."

"Well," remarked Henry, "*everybody* can not be wrong."

CHAPTER XI

HENRY TAKES THE TRAIL

IF THERE HAD been any doubts in the minds of Tonto City folks regarding the guilt of Dusty Cole, the finding of his hat at the scene of the attempted robbery settled the question. So Henry found from everyone he met as next morning he wended his weary way up to Judge Myers' office. The judge was at his desk. He nodded soberly, and sadly Henry sat down.

"I know just how you feel, Henry," said the judge. "Dusty Cole is heaping coals of fire upon your head. To save my daughter and me, you loosed a—a—Frankenstein upon Wild Horse Valley."

"Well, Judge, I would hardly call him that—yet," was Henry's rueful answer. "Frankenstein was sort of a monster, I believe. Dusty has hardly assumed such proportions. I suppose I am finished as sheriff of this county. Unless I can soon produce the body of Dusty Cole, I shall be obliged to resign—and I haven't the slightest idea where that body lies."

"Mr. Corley and John Campbell were up here," sighed the Judge. "I defended you to them. It was the least I could do. The funeral of Sam Hope, by the way, is this afternoon. Molly is very brave over it all. Mack Taylor came to her and offered his assistance in any way possible. I suppose he means well, Henry. After all, who am I to say?"

"That is true. In matters of that kind, you are not the judge."

"Queer about that interrupted bank robbery," remarked the Judge. "I understand they found Dusty's hat in the bank, where it had been knocked from his head."

"I have it," replied Henry. "Everyone identifies it."

AFTER THE funeral that afternoon Henry walked back to town with Jim McDonald, who was acting as foreman for the Bar M.

"I figure that Mack Taylor is crazy about Molly Hope," Jim told Henry. "I've known it for quite a while—but it wasn't none of my business. Mack's a decent feller—worth a million Sam Hopes, if yuh ask me."

"I believe that Taylor and Nash are doing well enough with their mine," said Henry.

"Yeah, I reckon so. Peter Morris always said that they'd strike rich ore on that Spotted Horse some day. I reckon Morris was always kinda disappointed that he didn't locate that mine himself."

"I didn't suppose he was ever interested in mines, Jim."

"Well, he wasn't interested, as a general thing. But he always did say that Taylor and Nash could make a good thing out of the Spotted Horse, if they had enough money to put in a decent stamp-mill. They can't handle the lower grade stuff with that little mill."

"Speaking of Peter Morris, Jim," said Henry, "did you ever know that there was bad blood between Morris and Sam Hope?"

"Yuh mean—about that calf? Shore, I knew about that. Morris was sore as the devil. If it hadn't been for Judge Myers, Morris would've had Sam arrested. Course, Sam threatened to get even with Morris, and when I found out that Morris had been knifed—well, I didn't talk about it. We all knew that Sam was handy with his knives. It wouldn't be like Dusty Cole to use a knife, but yuh couldn't make a jury see it that way."

"What do you think about these hold-ups, Jim?"

"Well, I dunno. Dusty and Sandy are a couple of pretty wild young hellions. Dusty is a convicted murderer, with nothin' to lose; and Sandy would foller Dusty through hell. They're kinda makin' yore office look bad, Henry."

"Worse than that," sighed Henry. "But they will make a mistake some day. They almost made it last night. But by the time they do make that mistake, I shall probably be a private citizen, entitled to make nasty remarks about the inefficiency of the sheriff's office. No doubt I shall do just that, because it seems to be the popular pastime—and I'd like to be popular for a change."

NEXT MORNING much to Judge's discomfort and disgust, Henry routed him out of bed early, and they rode into the hills again. This time they headed for Jawbone Canyon, one of the roughest spots in Wild Horse Valley.

"I hate to disappoint you, Henry," remarked Judge, after they had ridden some distance over the back-breaking trail, "but I have a feeling that you think I am enjoying this trip."

"No, I am not disappointed in the least," assured Henry. "In fact, it has been an education to me. Never before did I realize what a complete mastery you have over profanity. During that last quarter mile of narrow trail you swore continually, and never repeated the same cussword. That, my dear Judge, is art. It should have its place in the Hall of Fame, along with wife-beating, child-slapping and dog-kicking."

"Thank you, sir," nodded Judge gravely. "I never suffer silently. I have discovered, by the way, that my stirrups are too devilish long."

"Well," replied Henry, "I hope you remove your curse from this entire country and place it upon your stirrups. However, when the horse trots you invariably lose one or both stirrups. Why don't you get a side-saddle, Judge? They look like perfect comfort."

"And wear a skirt, I suppose," flared Judge.

"Well, of course, the skirt would be optional, Judge."

"Yes, I suppose!" snapped the suffering Judge. "If you have found your entire quota of fault with me, sir, will you please explain just why the devil we are in the depths of Jawbone Canyon?"

Henry nodded somberly. "One reason, my dear Judge," he

explained, "is because when we are deep down in this semi-cool retreat we cannot hear the jeers of the world; and the only other reason is that I am still optimistic over finding some trace of the whereabouts of Sandy Crane and Dusty Cole."

"I believe the first reason is paramount in your mind, Henry."

"There is a grain of truth in that, Judge."

"As a matter of fact," sighed Judge, "we are merely stalling for time. Neither of us have a single idea."

"As a matter of fact," retorted Henry, "you are wrong; I have several ideas. One very good one, which I polished several hours after retiring last night. My goodness, it was so bright! But—" Henry sighed deeply—"I discovered that several of the wheels were missing—and I don't know where to find them. Shall we proceed?"

"You seem to be directing this follow-the-leader foolishness," retorted Judge. "Proceed."

Some distance farther up the canyon Henry discovered an old trail that led out of the main canyon, up through brush and broken rock and into a narrow side canyon. There the trail ended. Henry was obliged to find a way over the broken rock to the heavily-brushed rim.

They clawed their way up, leading their horses. Henry said nothing, but Judge was voluble in denouncing him as a path-finder. When they at last reached the top they mounted again and threaded their way through the mesquite. The rim was so heavily brushed that they could not see into the canyon.

Judge was cursing the thorns of the mesquite when abruptly Henry drew up. From somewhere had come the nicker of a horse. There was nothing unusual about the nicker of a horse in the range country, and Judge mentioned the fact sarcastically to Henry.

"In the canyon, I believe," remarked Henry, ignoring the sarcasm.

"There is no law against horses going into a canyon," reminded

Judge sourly. "I believe you demonstrated that a few minutes ago, sir."

Henry dismounted and handed his reins to Judge. Then he worked his way painfully through the mesquite toward the rim of the small canyon. When be came back his shirt was in ribbons and his hands bleeding, but he was flushed with triumph.

"The blue-roan and the gray horse are in the canyon," he told Judge. "There is less than an acre of open ground, and brush fences have been made at both ends. I could also see a trickle of water."

"By jove!" exclaimed Judge. "I believe we have made a valuable discovery, Henry. When I heard the nicker of that horse—"

"You reminded me of the law concerning such things," finished Henry. "You have the greatest hindsight I have ever known, Judge."

Judge was not mollified. "But what are we going to do?" he queried.

Henry did not answer. He mounted and led the way to the highest point along Jawbone Canyon. There they dismounted in the shade of some scrub oak to study the situation.

"An ideal place to conceal the horses," he remarked. "There are no trails near it, and the brush on both sides is so thick and tall that even from here there is no indication of the canyon."

"All of which," said Judge, "would indicate that Dusty and Sandy are holed-up not far from here. Perhaps in Jawbone Canyon, Henry."

"Not likely. They are both too smart to be caught in a hole."

"They might he hiding in the canyon with the horses."

Henry polished his nose thoughtfully. "That is possible."

"They must have food, Henry."

"I have thought of that. Still, they have friends, who might give them food."

"And shelter, too," sighed Judge.

"Exactly. I suppose we may as well sit here during the heat of the day and keep an eye on things. The shade is adequate and the breeze is not too blistering. We will loosen our saddles and take life easy, Judge."

"Anything is better than that devilish saddle," answered Judge. He eased himself up against the nearest scrub oak.

CHAPTER XII

"MARIHUANA QUE FUMAR"

UNTIL NEARLY SUNDOWN they dozed in the shade. Then, nothing having happened, Henry aroused his deputy. As they tightened their saddles and prepared to ride back to Tonto City, Judge groaned wearily over his sore muscles.

"We will circle Jawbone Canyon," decided Henry, "cross that low pass in the hills and reach the road at the Spotted Horse mine."

"Every muscle in my body protests against the ride," declared Judge sadly.

"Muscle!" scoffed Henry. "You haven't had a muscle since you were thirty years of age. You mean that your skin aches."

"Well, it is not my fat—at least."

Henry grunted. He led the way over the unfamiliar range. It was the first time that either of them had ridden on that side of the canyon. After a while they found an old cattle trail which made the going easier. Riding at last into a small clearing, they found an old shack, composed of weathered boards, box parts and tin of every description.

Seated in the shade near the doorway was an old Mexican, ragged and dirty. As they rode up close to him, he looked at them critically through his small, blood-shot eyes. Henry glanced at Judge.

"Do you know this colorado-maduro gentleman, Judge?" he asked.

"I do not believe I have ever had the pleasure," replied Judge.

97

He turned to the old Mexican and said:

"Have you some water, my friend?"

"No entiendo," muttered the Mexican.

"Agua dulce?" questioned Judge.

"Si, poco," whined the Mexican.

He got slowly to his feet, tugged at his ill-fitting trousers, and turned toward the closed door of his shack. Then, suddenly, he whirled. He held a gun in his hand.

Judge was out of his saddle, and Henry was just starting to dismount, as the Mexican, his skinny shoulders against the wall of his shack, started throwing lead.

So unexpected was the shooting that both Henry and Judge were too amazed even to move. The little Mexican, his skinny right hand jerking high with each shot, was throwing lead from the big Colt .45 almost into their faces.

Henry slumped against his saddle, clawing his gun loose. As the Mexican sent his last shot over his head, Henry fired once. The heavy bullet blasted the Mexican back against the rough wall. The gun fell from his hand and he slid to the ground.

For several moments there was silence. Then Judge said:

"Huh—Henry, I believe we have killed a man."

"My goodness!" gasped Henry. He slid weakly from his horse and went over to the Mexican. It was true. The man was dead.

"He—he went crazy, Henry," said Judge. "You are all right?"

"About as good as I ever am, Judge. My goodness!"

Henry reached down and picked up the Mexican's gun. He looked it over carefully and turned to Judge.

"My gun," he said quietly. "The one Dusty Cole took that day in the courtroom."

"Are you sure of that?"

Henry showed him the brand *JHC* scratched on the butt.

"But where on earth did this Mexican get that gun?" queried Judge.

Henry shook his head. "Queer," he remarked. "Mighty queer.

Perhaps we'd better search the shack, Judge. I can hardly understand why he went crazy and tried to kill us. I just wonder—"

He broke off. He had been examining the ground in front of the door, where there were a number of cigarette butts. He looked at the dead Mexican's shirt-pocket, from which the yellow strings of a cigarette tobacco package were dangling. Removing the nearly empty sack, he placed it in his own pocket.

"What is your reason for doing that?" queried Judge.

"I am fairly certain that our departed friend was a smoker of marihuana," replied Henry, "but I want to be sure. I shall have Doctor Bogart analyze this stuff. The gentleman was entirely too sudden for a normal person—and shot too badly. Six shots at six paces—and not a hit. I believe we should examine the interior of this shack, Judge."

Henry reached for the crude fastening of the door. At that moment a bullet ripped out a foot-long splinter of wood just above the latch, missing his hand by six inches. From back on the brushy slope came the rattling report of a rifle.

Henry jerked back, looked wildly around. Judge ran toward his horse.

Pwee-e-e-e-e! Another bullet struck a few inches from Henry's feet and went singing into space.

Flup-p-p-p-p-p! One narrowly missed Judge's head. He dived back for the protection of the shack, with Henry in close pursuit.

THEY MADE it almost together. Safe for the moment, they leaned against the wall and looked at each other.

"This is—er—extraordinary, sir," declared Judge.

Then, instinctively, they ducked. Another report echoed back from the hills, preceded by the whining song of a ricocheted bullet.

"Do you suppose they are trying to shoot *through* this shack at us?" queried Judge.

"I am not a mind-reader, sir," replied Henry stiffly. "However, that bullet did not strike the shack."

He went cautiously to the corner and peered around toward the front of the shack. He turned quickly back, walked past his deputy and peered around the other corner. Finally he came back.

"I do not believe you will develop any more saddle sores between here and Tonto City, Judge," he said quietly. "Our horses have pulled out and are now going home."

Judge stared in amazement at Henry. "You forgot to tie them!"

"I only rode *one* of them, Judge."

"Yes, I suppose that is true. Horseless, helpless and—and—"

"Harassed," finished Henry. "If it were not for your blood-pressure, I would advise that we start running."

"Do not hesitate on my behalf, sir," replied Judge. "When I get as frightened as I am now, high blood-pressure is merely a figure of speech. But I do not relish a bullet in the back."

"In the kidneys, as it were," mused Henry. "No, the thought is not pleasant. I believe our wisest move would be to stretch out here, each of us facing a corner, in case of attack, and wait for darkness, which is not far away. Then we may quietly steal for home."

"I prefer the word 'slink,' Henry."

"Very well. We will strike out the word 'steal' and insert the better word 'slink.' Any more corrections, Judge?"

"You might 'lie down' instead of 'stretch.'"

"As you please," replied Henry soberly, "but I am going to stretch. It keeps me lower to the ground."

EARLY THAT morning, shortly after Henry and Judge had left Tonto City, Laura Morris and Molly Hope came to town. They went straight to Judge Myers' house and awakened him. Laura handed him a note.

"A little old Mexican brought it at daylight," she said.

Judge Myers rubbed his sleepy eyes before looking at the penciled words on some cheap paper. They read:

Dear Laura:

The bearer promised to deliver this to you. Sandy and me are on our way to Mexico. I reckon I went crazy when I met your father that night. But they'll never take me alive. Give my boots to one of the boys. I want you to know that I'm sorry for what I done but it can't be helped now. I hope you can forgive me.

Dusty

Judge Myers lifted his head and looked at Laura.

"I guess the law was right," she said miserably.

"It sometimes is right, my dear," nodded the Judge. "I was all wrong—I believed him innocent. I am glad he is leaving for Mexico; glad that he confessed the truth to you. I would not say anything about this note."

"We wanted you to see it," said Laura.

"Thank you very much, Laura. But are you sure this is Dusty's writing?"

"Very sure, Judge. Dusty wrote in my autograph album. Molly and I compared it with this note."

"I see. Do you mind if I keep this note and show it to Henry Conroy? Henry is very discreet, you know."

"Keep it as long as you please"

"Strange that he would write a confession," mused the Judge. "I hardly understood the boy. By the way, what sort of a Mexican delivered the note? Can you describe him?"

"Well, he was very old, not very big, but very dirty. He— he had eyes like a monkey—small and round, the whites very reddish. He couldn't speak English—or wouldn't."

"Did he ride a horse or a mule?"

"Why, I don't know. I didn't see him leave the ranch. He was barefooted."

"You had never seen him before, Laura?"

"No, I don't remember of ever seeing him before."

"Very likely a newcomer from across the Border. If the sheriff can pick him up, we may get a line on just where the boys went."

"You won't make it public—about the—" Laura hesitated.

"Regarding the confession? No, there is no need for that, Laura," assured the Judge.

Laura and Molly went back to the ranch, trying to console each other. Judge Myers went to Henry's office, only to find that Henry and Judge Van Treece were out in the hills. He found John Campbell, the prosecutor, at his office, and told him that he had definite evidence that Dusty and Sandy were in Mexico. Campbell quizzed him about the evidence, but got no results.

"Well, I'm glad," said the lawyer. "No, I don't mean that I didn't want to hail them into court. But after all, in my own heart I doubted that Dusty was guilty. Guilty of robbery—yes. But if they're going to stay across the Border, and out of Wild Horse Valley, I'm sure that everybody will be satisfied."

"It is quite a relief," agreed the old judge.

AFTER DARK, and with no moonlight to betray them, Henry and Judge left the shack and started for town. While there was no moonlight to betray them, there was also no moonlight to guide them; and they were a weary, bedraggled pair of blood-hounds of the law when at last they stumbled in at the Spotted Horse mine.

They told their story to Mack Taylor and Tuck Nash. The mining pardners gave them whisky, strong coffee, and then cooked a big meal.

"I know where that old shack is located," said Taylor, "but I didn't know it was occupied. That old Mexican must have moved in there recently."

"Must be a crazy hermit," remarked Nash. "It's a wonder he didn't kill both of yuh."

"That ain't as interestin' as them rifle-shooters," said Taylor. "Who in the devil would try to dry-gulch yuh at the cabin?"

"It might be Dusty and Sandy," suggested Judge.

Taylor laughed at the suggestion.

"Judge, why on earth would Dusty and Sandy do that? You

didn't have 'em cornered. Heck, I don't believe they'd hurt anybody, unless they was cornered."

"You might give a better theory, Mack," said Judge. "It is the only one I could originate."

"I wish I could, Judge. But it seems unreasonable. You say all this shootin' started when you went to open the door of the shack?"

"That is true," nodded Henry. "These beans are exceptionally good, Mack."

"Glad yuh like 'em, Henry. After supper I'll hitch up the team and take you fellows home in the wagon. The road is rough, but it beats walkin'. How about a little more whisky?"

"Thank you, but I believe I shall only take coffee. I find that a pint is about all my system requires—at one sitting, of course. Judge and I have been tapering off lately."

"Yes," agreed Judge soberly. "Last Wednesday we almost stopped abruptly. Merely a quart apiece. It was a shock to our system."

"I should think it would be," said Mack Taylor. "Only a quart! Why that's not enough to keep a baby alive!"

AFTER SUPPER they jolted the five miles to Tonto City. Judge and Henry climbed out at the office, found Oscar alone there.

"W'ere in de ha'al have you been?" he wanted to know. "Yust a vile ago both hurses come home. Ay am scare like ha'al."

Henry knew there was no use of explaining things to Oscar; so they merely said that the horses had pulled loose and come home. When Oscar told Henry that Judge Myers was looking for him, Henry limped over to the judge's home. The judge explained about the note and handed it to Henry to read.

"My goodness!" exclaimed Henry. "Well, of all things!"

"With them in Mexico, we may breathe easier, Henry."

"Did Laura Morris describe that Mexican, Judge?"

"Yes, she did," replied the judge, and gave the description.

"Well, well!" exclaimed Henry. "I shot and killed him this evening."

"You... did... what?"

"He attempted to kill me—with the gun Dusty Cole jerked out of my holster in the courtroom. So I shot him—dead."

Judge Myers shook his head violently for a long moment.

"I am afraid that something is wrong with my hearing, Henry. Will you repeat what you just told me?"

Henry told him the whole story, omitting the horses in the canyon, while Judge Myers sat and listened in amazement.

"With our horses gone we were obliged to leave the dead man where he fell," concluded Henry.

"This makes a worse puzzle than ever," declared the judge.

"Hm-m-m," mused Henry, as he polished his nose. "I wonder."

CHAPTER XIII

RIDING DOUBLE

IT WAS AN assorted cavalcade that left Tonto City next day. Judge was too stiff and sore to mount his horse; so Henry took Frijole, Oscar, Thunder, Lightning, John Campbell, the prosecutor, and Doctor Bogart, the coroner. They took an extra horse on which to bring out the dead Mexican. Mack Taylor joined them at the Spotted Horse mine. Henry had told no one about the horses in the small canyon.

Mack Taylor knew the exact location of the old shack; so they had no trouble in finding the still-warm ashes of what had been that shack. It had burned to the ground, and all that was left were the twisted sheets of tin and a pile of ashes.

Of the corpse there were no remains at all. The old shack had been built over what seemed to have been a natural depression in the ground, or an ancient prospect hole, now nearly filled with the burned debris. They poked through all the ashes, but were unable to locate anything that might have been the Mexican.

"Rather strange, Henry," mused John Campbell, as they stood and contemplated the ash-heap which had been the shack.

"Why, yes, it does seem strange," admitted Henry soberly. "I am sure there was no fire around here when we left last night. The body was not close enough to have been consumed, even had it not been removed."

"I'm sure there wasn't any sign of fire in this direction when I drove back from town last night," said Mack Taylor. "I'm sure I could have seen the light of it from the road."

"It would burn very quickly," remarked Henry. "It is fortunate it did not spread to the dry brush and cause a conflagration."

"What about yore two Mexicans, Henry?" queried Taylor. "Have they ever seen this one you shot last night?"

"They say not, Mack."

"We never see heem," declared Lightning. "He mus' be stranger from mine."

"Well," smiled Doctor Bogart, "as long as it is impossible to perform an autopsy on a burned shack, suppose we go home."

The rest were in agreement. They all mounted and the cavalcade, having achieved absolutely nothing, started back.

SHORTLY AFTER they arrived back in Tonto City, Nick Borden, recently made manager of the Yellow Warrior mine, came to see Henry at his office. Nick was well known in Tonto City, having owned and operated the Smoke Tree mine for about a year.

"Well, Henry, the plot seems to get thicker," he said.

"Perhaps it is the smoke of the burned shack, Nick," said Henry.

"Well, I never thought of that. I was talking with Judge, and he gave me a description of that old Mexican. I've seen him."

"You have? Where?"

"Up at the Yellow Warrior. Several times I saw him, hanging around, possibly looking for a meal. A dirty-looking old character."

"Hm-m-m," mused Henry. "That is interesting, Nick. Hanging around the cook-shacks?"

"Well, I don't believe I ever saw him down there. I found him hanging around the office. He couldn't talk English, and I only know a few words of Mexican; so I told Jim Bradford, the assayer, to have the boys run him away from there. Jim talks the language pretty well; so he had a talk with the old boy, and he went away. Jim had worked for a mining outfit in Sonora for several years."

"Was that the last time you saw this Mexican, Nick?"

"Yes, he never came back again, as far as I know."

"Was that before the gold was stolen from the stage?"

Nick Borden squinted thoughtfully for several moments.

"Come to think of it—I believe it was that same day. I could ask Jim Bradford about it; he would remember."

"It is of no importance, Nick. That stage robbery is a puzzle to me. You and Bradford were the only ones who knew about the shipment. Dusty and Sandy must have known that shipments are never made by stage. They should have known that there is never enough money on that stage to make it worth robbing—and still they robbed it."

"Coincidence, I suppose."

"I wonder. When did you and Bradford decide to send that gold?"

"The morning of the day it was shipped."

"I see. Were you intending to ship that gold soon, whether on the stage or otherwise?"

"That's right, Henry; I wanted it out of the safe at the mine."

"That safe is not very strong, Nick."

"It sure isn't. I've asked for a better one, but that takes time."

"You have guards at the mine office?"

"A night watchman. Bradford sleeps in the office, which is securely locked. Oh, the gold in the safe is well guarded. Shipping is our greatest risk."

"You should have more guards, Nick."

Nick Borden laughed. "It would take more than Dusty and Sandy to crack our safe, Henry. Don't worry about that."

LATER IN the day, Judge limped in and took his accustomed seat.

"I hope you are through combing the hills, Henry," he said painfully. "The only place I am not blistered is on top of my shoulders. I suppose you have done a lot of thinking about what happened to the old Mexican and his shack."

"Well," admitted Henry dryly, "I have had it on my mind. The shack never set itself on fire, and the dead Mexican did not walk away. Further than that, I admit being nonplussed. By the way, I gave that sack of tobacco to Doctor Bogart, and his test showed that it was well impregnated with marihuana."

"After all, it is not unusual to discover that an old Mexican liked his marihuana, Henry. It grows wild, I believe."

"So do its users, I believe, Judge. Nick Borden tells me that he had seen that old Mexican around the Yellow Warrior several times."

"That Mexican," replied Judge, "was old enough to have been around the world several times. I suppose he was up there trying to get a free meal. Or does his presence at the Yellow Warrior mean something to you?"

"I do not know, Judge. At times I feel that I am on the verge of a great discovery. I am like the man who thought he had invented a non-refillable bottle, only to find that it was so constructed that he could not fill it for the first time. Sometimes I feel that in the role of a detective, I am badly miscast."

"I feel the trace of a giggle," admitted Judge. "Still it may be the after effects of some baking soda I took a while ago."

"You may giggle, if you feel the urge," said Henry soberly. "As for me, I feel the need of liquid inspiration. Wouldst?"

"Wouldst," agreed Judge quickly, getting to his feet. "By the way, I saw Thunder and Lightning a while ago, heading for the Bar M—going, I believe, to break bread with Juan Mendoza."

"I hope they have better luck than they had the last time. Those two seem to be harbingers of disaster."

Side by side, keeping perfect step, sheriff and deputy a moment later crossed the street to the Tonto Saloon. There they filled their glasses, bowed low, and drank a silent toast to each other.

"That's my idea of two gentlemen takin' a drink together," remarked the bartender. "You fellers are re-fined. A lot of these snake-hunters around here make fun of yuh—but not me. I says,

'They may be a funny pair of old coots, but they can be gentlemen when they feel like it.'"

Henry and Judge bowed to the bartender, and then to each other. Drinking was a ritual with them—even to the last drink....

THE USUAL evening crowd gathered in Tonto. Henry squinted closely at his watch.

"What is the time, my friend?" queried Judge.

Speaking very clearly and spacing his words carefully, Henry replied:

"It... is... exactly... a quarter... of... shix."

"The days mus' be short, shir," remarked Judge. "It ish dark."

"The clock," said the night bartender, "says it is nine-thirty."

"That is all right," said Henry a trifle soberly. "I hold no malice toward a clock—none what'ver."

The interruption and exclamation was caused by none other than Lightning Mendoza. He galloped into the saloon, hatless, his eyes wide, spouting Mexican in a shrill voice.

He saw Henry, rushed up and grasped him by the lapels of his coat.

"Dios mio!" he shrilled. "My brodder ees keeled! I tell you, he ees keeled! You know my brodder—sure! Sure, you know my brodder. Well, for Hiven's sake, he ees keeled!"

"You—you really startle me!" gasped Henry. "What killed him?"

"Thees two men on a horse! They keel heem—sure. You know my brodder? Hees keeled—*muerto!*"

"These two men on a horse," parroted Henry. "Which two?"

"Madre de Dios, w'at ees the deeference? Thonder ees died."

"Well, well!" exclaimed Henry.

"Thees two men on a horse keel heem with a seex-shooter."

"Where did this happen?" queried Henry.

"On the road to—w'at the devil ees the deeference? My brodder ees dead. I see hem fall off the horse. Thees men keel heem, and then they go like hell. W'y don't you catch heem?"

"Your brother? Too late—he has already fallen. I believe—my goodness!"

Hatless, panting, his hair standing on end, Thunder Mendoza was stumbling into the saloon. He stared at the crowd, brushed a lock of hair out of his eyes and gasped at Lightning:

"W'y the devil you don't wait for me? I yell your head off, and all you do is wheep the horse and leave me to run t'ree mile all by yourself."

"Dios mio!" gasped Lightning. "My leetle brodder! You are alive? *Dios,* I could kees you!"

"Leave those kees on your face; I don't want heem."

"Well, Thunder, perhaps you can tell us what happened?" suggested Henry. "Your *leetle brodder* seems rather excited."

Thunder scratched his tousled hair for a moment.

"You know w'ere thees road from the Yellow Warrior come to the other road? Good. We are there. Thees two men on one horse ride like hell. They see us. One man tak' shot at me. My dang horse jomp and I forgot to jomp weeth heem. That ees all. W'en I'm get dirt out of your eye, thees men are gone and thees brodder from me ees go like hell."

"I see. You had to walk to town, eh?"

"Walk? You theenk I'm walk? You theenk I'm walk t'ree mile in t'ree minute? Huh?"

"Fair walking speed," remarked Judge.

"This is all rather queer," declared Henry, as sober as he ever was. "Why would two men on one horse shoot at these boys? It is not consistent. You two haven't done anything, have you?"

"Sure," nodded Thunder. "We go see our cousin."

"Yes, of course. That may be the reason they shot at you. But—"

He broke off. A rider was drawing up in the front of the saloon, sending a shower of gravel across the porch. "Who's this?" someone near the doorway asked.

A moment later Nick Borden came striding in. The crowd went silent at sight of the tall mine boss.

"There's hell to pay at the Yellow Warrior," he announced at once. "Two men emptied the safe and murdered Jim Bradford a little while ago."

"Two men on one horse?" asked Henry.

"That watchman killed one horse," replied Borden.

Henry turned to the crowd. "One of you notify Doctor Bogart and ask him to go at once to the mine. I shall be with you as soon as I can saddle a horse, Nick."

CHAPTER XIV

THE BARRED DOOR

THE OFFICE BUILDING at the Yellow Warrior was a pine and tar-paper building about twenty-five feet long and fifteen feet deep. At the east end, attached to the office building, was a ten-by-twelve quarters for the watchman, with a door entering the office.

Borden had closed the office and had it guarded, while he went for the sheriff and coroner. Nothing had been touched. Tied to a chair, almost in the center of the office, was the body of Jim Bradford, the assayer, his back toward the front door.

Bradford had been gagged and blindfolded. Directly in front of him was the safe, the door wide open. Only some worthless papers had been left therein.

"They got about five hundred ounces of gold," said Borden.

The dead horse lay about fifty feet from the office, and they examined him by lantern light. It was the gray horse, its neck broken by a rifle bullet.

"I'll get the watchman and let him tell the story," said Nick Borden. "I guess he can walk up here."

Mike Bruno, the watchman, his head bandaged, one arm in a sling, came back with Borden. He was pale and weak, but told a clear story.

"I was in the office talkin' with Mr. Bradford, who was workin' on some figures. Then I went into my quarters, got some tobacco, and went out my front door. It was dark, and I didn't see anyone, but somethin' hit me an awful blow on the right shoulder. It knocked me down and made me terrible sick. I felt like every bone in my body was smashed. Then I heard a voice sayin', 'Sock him another one to make it safe.'

"Well, I guess they did, 'cause I don't remember what happened. Then I woke up, one big mass of aches. I realized it was a robbery. My six-shooter was gone—they'd took it. But I gritted my teeth and crawled into my room, where I keep a rifle. I could hear them in the office by this time.

"I managed to get outside again. I was goin' into the office, but I realized I wasn't in any shape to put up a good fight; so I limped out a little ways, just as they opened the door. Well, I cut loose at 'em, but the kick of that gun hurt me so bad that I almost fainted. I guess my shoulder was hurt bad.

"I knew they shot at me, but I don't know how many times. I was down on my knees, I know that much. Then they went runnin' to the horses, and I managed to fire another shot, and I killed the gray horse. But they both got on one horse and pulled out."

"You did well for an injured man, Bruno," said Henry. "Most men would have been willing to take it much easier."

"I'm paid to guard the place," said Bruno.

Borden sent the watchman back with two men to help him to his bed. Then he turned to Henry.

"I imagine the Yellow Warrior will offer a stiff reward for the murderer of Bradford," he said. "They tied him up, probably forced him to give them the combination of the safe, and then shot him dead. You've got to get those men, Henry."

"Yes, I must do that, Nick. Can you furnish a vehicle to take the body back to town? So they got five hundred ounces of gold."

"About nine thousand dollars' worth, Henry."

"They are doing very well for inexperienced robbers," remarked Henry. "Nine thousand dollars for a dead horse. You heard the shooting, Nick?"

"I sure did. Mike's old forty-five-seventy roars like a cannon. But it was all over when we got here from my cabin."

WHEN ARRANGEMENTS had been made to take the body back to Tonto City, Henry himself rode back. He found Judge at the hotel, and they went up to bed. Henry told the watchman's story to Judge.

"I am at a loss what to advise," sighed Judge. "Dusty and Sandy have certainly started a reign of terror in Wild Horse Valley; and I am afraid it will not stop until both of them are dead or behind the bars. I suppose that the Yellow Warrior will add to the reward."

"Nick Borden said they might."

"Dusty and Sandy are dangerous men, Henry. When they murder a helpless captive—they are capable of any deviltry. I do not believe that savages would do a thing like that. Both men must be mad."

"I wouldn't be surprised," agreed Henry. "I feel that I am getting a bit mad myself."

"I talked with John Campbell this evening," said Judge. "He says that the commissioners are already discussing a possible man to fill your position. It seems that they want a man of dynamic personality."

"Eh?" Henry looked up from pulling off a tight boot. "Oh, yes. Well, they might appoint Oscar Johnson."

"I said 'dynamic'—not 'dynamite', Henry."

"My mistake, Judge; they sound so much alike."

NICK BORDEN rode in from the mine next day to announce that the Yellow Warrior was offering two thousand dollars for information which would lead to the arrest and conviction of the men who murdered Jim Bradford.

Borden talked the matter over with John Campbell, the prosecutor, and Edwin Corley, one of the county commissioners. The county was offering two thousand for Dusty Cole and a thousand for Sandy Crane. Mack Taylor and Henry Harrison Conroy joined them in front of the court-house, and discussed the rewards.

"That makes five thousand for Sandy and Dusty together," said Mack Taylor.

"When and if it is proved that Dusty and Sandy killed Bradford and robbed the mine," corrected Henry.

"Not much chance to miss on that," smiled Taylor. "The gray horse shows who they were, I'd say."

"I am inclined to give them the benefit of the doubt," replied Henry. "Anyone might ride a gray horse."

"That gray horse is not conclusive evidence, I'm afraid," agreed the lawyer. "However, it seems to be the same horse that one of them rode out of town the day Dusty escaped."

"Will those rewards read 'Dead or Alive'?" queried Taylor.

"They will not!" snapped Henry.

John Campbell laughed at Henry's vehement reply.

"Well, I agree with the sheriff there," he said. "Unless we can absolutely prove that Sandy Crane had a hand in killing Bradford, I don't believe we would be justified in pronouncing a death sentence upon him, if and when he is cornered. And since they must be together, that would have go for Dusty too."

"I don't know about yore theory," said Taylor. "Seems to me time's past to show mercy for either of them."

"That's a matter of opinion, of course," said Campbell. The group broke up then. Campbell went to his office with Nick Borden. Henry wandered up to Judge Myers' office, went in and sat down.

"Henry," said the judge soberly, "I'm afraid that Wild Horse Valley would hang both of us, if they knew what we had done. Is there any possible chance that it was not Dusty and Sandy—last night?"

"Their gray horse was killed, Judge."

"That's what I heard. I went out to the Bar M to visit with Molly. She has recovered from the shock of Sam's death to a point where she can smile again. Women are queer, Henry. Laura still believes in Dusty Cole.

"Mack Taylor came out while I was there, and I had a talk with him. He wants to marry Molly as soon as he can—but I'm not so sure of Molly. I told her she should wait a while, at least; and she said I need not worry about that part of it. Laura said that if you did not capture Dusty Cole pretty soon, she would go out and capture him herself."

"Good!" laughed Henry. "I will swear her in as a special deputy and give her a star. I wonder what she will think, when she hears that Dusty lied to her."

"Lied to her, Henry?"

"His note said he was heading for Mexico."

"That's right—it did. He must have changed his mind."

"Perhaps they felt the need of more money," sighed Henry.

Henry went on back to his own office. A little later Doctor Bogart came in, bringing the battered bullet which he had taken from the body of Jim Bradford.

"Unmistakable proof," said Judge, "that Bradford was killed by a bullet."

"I can swear to the evidence, Judge," smiled the doctor.

Henry's smile was enigmatic. He pocketed the battered lump of lead, yawned widely and walked out, heading directly for one of the two assay offices in Tonto City.

LAURA MORRIS, Molly Hope and Jim McDonald sat on their horses in the shade of some scrub-oak on the top of a hill and looked off across the rolling expanse of Wild Horse Valley. The two girls, grown restless at the ranch, had wanted to ride into the hills; so Jim McDonald had gone with them. They had heard what happened at the Yellow Warrior mine.

"If we could only find Dusty," spoke up Laura. "Just to think he's out there, hiding like a hunted animal…"

"Well," drawled McDonald, "he may be hidin', but as far as I can see, he ain't hunted. They're talkin' about askin' Henry Conroy to resign, and appointin' another man in his place."

"Who would they appoint?" queried Molly Hope.

"I dunno. Somebody was sayin' that they kinda favored Mack Taylor. But you can hear lotsa things. Henry's all right. He's funny, and he don't never seem to be doin' anything, but I like him. He ain't a man you'd select for an Arizona sheriff, but he's done well enough. He's shore made folks laugh."

Just then Molly pointed to a dark spot in the hills, far off to their right, and asked Jim McDonald what it was.

"That's the old Lost Injun mine," answered the Bar M foreman. "I dunno where it got its name. They done a lot of work over there, years ago, but never hit anything worth while. After it was abandoned and the location ran out, an old hermit prospector named Alex Moss located it. He had an idea that somebody was stealin' his high-grade ore, which there wasn't any, so he made a heavy oak door and locked up his main tunnel. I'll betcha it weighs two hundred pounds with all the iron he bolted onto it, but danged if the old coot didn't swing that door all by himself.

"That was quite a lot of years ago. Old Alex died, and nobody ever relocated the mine again. There's several old buildin's left. That yaller dump you can see from here shore cost plenty money to put there. If yuh want to we can go past there on our way back to the ranch. It ain't out of the way."

"Let's do that," said Molly.

Laura nodded. "We might as well. I've heard Dad speak of that mine, but I've never been there."

"Yore dad knew Old Alex," said McDonald. "If I ain't mistaken, he helped the sheriff carry the old man's body over to Tonto City."

McDonald led the way along the side of the hill and down to an old trail which led over to the mine. Arriving at the old hermit's tumbled-down cabin, they left their horses and climbed up the trail to the old tunnel. McDonald explained about an old shaft on the hill which had been intersected by the main tunnel, and told of the many big stopes which had been worked out.

It was quite a climb up to the old portal, but when they arrived they found the huge oak door still in place on its massive iron hinges. There was no lock left, but the huge, hand-made hasp was held in place by an old horseshoe. They went up to the door to examine it. Jim McDonald removed the old horseshoe, pulled back the rusty hasp and started to swing the door open.

It was Jim McDonald's last conscious act. At that moment a heavy bullet smashed into his body, driving him sideways away from the door. He sprawled in a heap on the broken rock.

The thud of that bullet was as audible as though someone had swung a heavy hammer against McDonald's back. It was echoed by the rattling report of a rifle shot from somewhere near. Laura screamed and backed against the partially opened door.

Another bullet thudded into the heavy oak.

Molly Hope started to run, but tripped and went sprawling. At that moment a third bullet splattered against one of the heavy iron hinges of the door. Laura Morris thought that Molly had been hit. She reached out quickly and grasped Molly around the shoulders. Exerting every ounce of her strength, she dragged her to the narrow opening of the door. By bracing her body against it she managed to open it far enough to drag Molly inside the tunnel. As she managed to drag the door shut behind her, another bullet splintered the edge, only a few inches above her head.

Frightened and out of breath she knelt in the darkness beside Molly. "You're not hit, Molly?" panted Laura.

"No, I—I fell down. Who is it? Laura, they killed Jim McDonald! Who can it be? They—they were trying to kill us."

"I don't know," Laura answered. "We can't get away now. Maybe when they see who we are—listen!"

They could hear footsteps on the rubble outside—footsteps, which came boldly up to the door. The two girls held their breath, expecting someone to open that door. But it did not open. Instead, they heard the rasp of metal, a slight bump against the door, followed by a harsh laugh of derision.

Straining their ears, they heard the man mumbling over the body of Jim McDonald, but could not hear what he said. Then they heard him grunt, as he lifted the inert body and began dragging it away.

When the sound died, Laura stumbled over to the door, put her shoulder against it and shoved with all her strength. It was no use—the door was fastened from the outside.

CHAPTER XV

A RESIGNATION

WHEN HENRY SAW all the commissioners at the inquest over the body of Jim Bradford, he knew exactly what was going to happen. Edwin Corley looked sourly at him, and the others merely nodded coldly. As soon as the inquest was over Henry went straight to his office, and in a few minutes Edwin Corley came in. He started to speak, but paused when Henry handed him a sheet of paper.

Corley scanned it closely, looked curiously at Henry, and folded it carefully.

"You are a mind-reader, Mr. Conroy," he said.

"Thank you, sir," replied Henry gravely. "Except for the uncaught criminals, I believe that everything is in good order. Now if you do not mind, I shall move my personal effects immediately."

"Oh, that's all right," assured Corley. "No hurry. I shall—"

Corley broke off as Mack Taylor came in.

"I was talkin' with a couple of the commissioners at the Tonto Saloon, Corley," said Taylor. "They told me that I was goin' to be appointed sheriff."

Corley showed embarrassment, but nodded quickly. "That's right," he said.

"Sorry," drawled Taylor. "Thank yuh a lot, Corley, but I haven't any use for the job; I'm runnin' a mine."

"Why, I—I thought you said—the other day—" hesitated Corley.

"I was jokin'," laughed Taylor. "I never had any idea of acceptin' that job. Why the devil don't yuh leave Conroy on the job? He's a better man than you can get."

"We demand results," replied Corley firmly. "Conroy has not been able to give us any. We decided you would be the right man for this job, Taylor. Of course, there are men who would jump at the chance to be sheriff of this county."

"Nerves, more than anything else," said Henry.

Judge at that moment came striding in, his lean face grim and determined.

"More hell to pay, Henry," he said. "Chuck Miller just rode in from the Morris ranch, bringing queer news. Yesterday Laura Morris and Molly Hope rode away from the ranch with Jim McDonald. They didn't come home all night. This morning they discovered Jim McDonald's body, tied to his saddle, on a loose horse at the corral gate. Jim had been shot through the back."

"Good Lord!" gasped Corley. "McDonald dead—those women—"

He turned to face Henry.

"Get out and do something!" he snapped. "As sheriff of this county, you've got to stop these things."

"My star is in the upper right-hand drawer of the desk," said Henry quietly.

"Wait a minute!" snapped Mack Taylor. "You say that McDonald is dead and that Laura and Molly are missin', Judge?"

"Those are the facts as related by Chuck Miller."

"But that ain't reasonable, Judge. Who would harm a woman... Where's Chuck Miller?"

"He's over at the Tonto. What is this about your star, Henry?"

"My star," replied Henry quietly, "has set."

"You—you resigned?"

"Yes, Judge. The Shame of Arizona is history. We will take all our personal effects and go out to the ranch."

"But, confound it, we haven't any sheriff!" wailed Corley. "Just at a time like this—!"

They were interrupted by the hurried entrance of Judge Myers. He was pale and breathless. He had been told of his daughter's disappearance.

"I heard about it, Judge," said Henry. "I know how you feel. But I am no longer the sheriff. Mr. Corley has my resignation."

"We've got to have a sheriff," said Corley. "We've got to."

"Of course," said Henry, "there are many men who would jump at the chance to be sheriff of this county."

"Who?" queried Judge Myers.

"I am waiting for Mr. Corley to answer that question," replied Henry.

Corley looked nervously around. Already Mack Taylor was on his way across the street to seek more information from Chuck Miller.

"I—I can't just mention one at this moment," Corley said.

"Until you can make an appointment," said the judge, "I am of the opinion that you yourself must act as sheriff, Mr. Corley. And under the circumstances, I would advise that you act swiftly in getting more information concerning Laura Morris and my daughter. Do not forget that they did not come home—and their escort was murdered."

"Well—I"—Corley rubbed his chin nervously. "Well, I don't know what to do, Judge. Don't even know where to start. I never had any idea of—wait a minute! Conroy, I never asked for your resignation. You—you just gave it to me. You're still the sheriff. I won't have that resignation, I tell you. Look at this, will you!"

Corley took the resignation from his pocket and tore it into bits. Then he whirled and went swiftly from the office.

"Well?" said Judge Myers.

Judge Van Treece shoved his hands deep in his pockets and rocked on the balls of his feet as he looked quizzically at Henry, Henry who was slowly polishing his red nose.

"It seems to me," said the latter quietly, "that the Shame of Arizona is going into an extra edition."

EVERY ABLE-BODIED man in Tonto City, seemingly, wanted to join a searching posse; so it was a large group of riders that Henry and Judge led out to the Bar M. Even Thunder and Lightning came along in time to join. Seeing them, Henry asked where Frijole Bill was.

"He's no shape from riding, thees Frijole Beel," Lightning answered.

"Been making some more of his devil's brew, eh?" queried Judge.

"Thees making don't hurt heem. He ees saying to me, 'Thees ees great lee-ker. T'ree dreenk, and hees either make or break you.' *Por Dios,* I'm theenk hees break."

"Sure," agreed Thunder. "I'm see Frijole weeth twenty feet, two-by-four, and I'm ask heem what ees he building. He ees saying, 'W'at the hell you mean building? Thees ees boggy-wheep.'"

Arrived at the Bar M, the riders crowded into the ranchyard. The body of Jim McDonald had been laid out in the bunk-house, and there Doctor Bogart made his examination. McDonald had been shot with a soft-nose bullet, and the doctor said his death had been instantaneous.

Henry examined the saddle and rope, but nothing could be learned from them. The rope was one which belonged to McDonald. And while they were crowded in and around the bunk-house Juan Mendoza, the cook, brought word that both Laura's and Molly's horses had come back, still saddled and bridled. There was no blood on the saddles.

Chuck Miller and Dan Keefer, the two cowboys present now, had left the ranch before McDonald had ridden away with Laura and Molly; so they had no idea where he had intended taking them. Juan Mendoza hadn't much more to offer.

"I know notheeng," he declared. "They say they be back for sopper las' night, but nobody ees coming."

"Sure," declared Lightning, "he don't know notheeng. I am the smart one from hees familee—and I don't know notheeng myself, personally."

"There is nothing unusual in that statement," said Henry.

He turned to the crowd of riders. "If any of you gentlemen have any suggestions, I would like to hear them," he said. "Someone murdered McDonald and tied his body on his saddle. There could be nothing in the theory that those two girls are lost. Laura Morris knows this country too well for that. Their saddle horses came home. Under the circumstances I believe it is evident that the girls are held captive. Why, where and by whom, I have no idea.

"If any of you know someone who hated Jim McDonald badly enough to murder him, I would like to know it."

"Mebbe they didn't exactly hate him," suggested a cowboy.

"Jist wanted to see him jump, I suppose," remarked another.

"Mebbe he found out somethin'," said the first cowboy. "It jist might be that they ran into some range brandin'. Things like that have happened, yuh know."

"Thank you for the suggestion," said Henry. "Gentlemen, I can see no use of us riding all over the hills. It will require more than a show of force to solve this problem. Wild Horse Valley is a big slice of the state, and there are a thousand places where the two ladies might be held captive."

The crowd agreed with Henry. Mack Taylor came to Henry and took him aside. Taylor's face was gray and drawn.

"I don't reckon I've got to tell yuh how I feel toward Molly Hope," he said. "Anyway, that's my business. But we've got to do somethin', Henry. Yuh can't let a thing like this drag out."

"What would you suggest, Mack?" asked Henry.

"I don't know. Heck, there's nothin' to work on."

"Exactly. Try and calm down. It may require cool heads to solve this problem."

BACK IN Tonto City, Henry found the town seething with

excitement over the missing girls and the murder of McDonald. Henry returned to sit in his office, squint-eyed in thought, while Judge Van Treece paced the street, hunched, red-eyed, his bony hands locked behind him. Oscar Johnson sprawled on his cot in the office, a harmonica hidden in his huge paws, as he droned *Sweet Adeline,* the only tune he could play.

"Ay have yust been vondering," said Oscar, after a long period of so-called music.

Henry glanced at him curiously. "Wondering, eh? Wondering about what, Oscar?"

"Oh, yust vondering."

"That is remarkable," sighed Henry.

"Yah, su-ure. Ay vars yust vondering where dose girls are."

"Well, it is wonderful to think that you have got around to it at last. Have you arrived at any conclusion?"

"Ay don't know vat that means."

"Have you made up your mind as to where they are?"

"Oh, yust missing, Ay guess."

"My goodness! Oscar, have there ever been any detectives in your family?"

"Va'al, Ay don't like to talk about it."

"There is nothing wrong about it."

"Va'al, Ay guess not, but my fadder he don't like it."

Henry squinted one eye at Oscar, trying to puzzle out what the big Swede meant.

"You see," confided Oscar, "it vars in Nort' Dakota. De officers arrested my brodder Yulius. Ay vars younger den Yulius."

"Why did they arrest him, Oscar?" queried Henry.

"Dey said he vars defective."

Henry closed both eyes this time and rested his head in his hands. His old swivel chair made sounds like a lost turkey in the woods trying to locate the flock.

"Ay vill put some axle-gris on the yunction of dat chair," offered Oscar, and got heavily to his feet. "Ay don't know vere

Yulius is now—he never wrote to me. Ay guess it vars because he never learned how to write."

Oscar went out to get the axle-grease, closing the corridor door behind him. Henry lifted his head and wiped away his tears.

Mack Taylor came in, just then, smiled at Henry.

"Well, I just heard that yore resignation was refused, Henry."

"Torn to bits and scattered to the four winds," replied Henry soberly. "Mr. Corley seems to have lost his nerve. By the way, how long have you known Jim Bradford?"

"Jim Bradford?" Mack Taylor looked closely at Henry. "Why, I don't know how long. I knew him slightly—down in Sonora several years ago."

"A pretty square fellow, wasn't he?"

"None better," declared Taylor stoutly.

"That robbery has me puzzled," replied Henry. "It was an inside job, as they say."

"What do yuh mean, Henry?" asked Taylor curiously. "It couldn't have been an inside job—not when they murdered Bradford."

"They didn't murder him; he was accidentally shot by the watchman."

"Accidentally shot by the watchman?"

"He shot at the two men as they came out. Bradford was tied to a chair, directly in line with the doorway, and the bullet killed him. I had the bullet weighed at Hansen's Assay Office, and it is a forty-five-seventy."

"I'll be danged! But that doesn't indicate an inside job."

"That is true, Taylor. But Bradford was badly tied. His gag was ineffective. Why, he could have spat it out. I fully believe that Bradford was in on the robbery. More than that, I believe Bradford passed the word, when that first gold shipment was made from the Yellow Warrior. He passed the word to that old Mexican I shot at the cabin in Jawbone Canyon, and the Mexican carried the message to the men who robbed the stage."

Mack Taylor looked out into the street, his eyes narrowing in concentration.

"Maybe yo're right, Henry," he said. "It sounds reasonable. Go to it, workin' along that line. And if yuh need help, call me."

"Thank you, Mack. You are the only one I've told about this; and I may need you, before this is settled."

"It's sure nice of yuh to tell me, Henry. Have yuh figured out anythin' that might help us find Molly and Laura?"

"Not yet. I'll let you know if anything turns up."

"All right. I reckon I'll go back to the mine."

A moment later, Henry leaned in the doorway of his office and watched Mack Taylor ride out of town. He looked the other way to find Judge Myers walking down to the office. The judge was nervous and worried. Before either had said much, however, John Campbell came in to talk about the missing girls.

"Every man in Wild Horse Valley is at your disposal, Henry," he said.

"Except the two men who could really help me, John."

"Who are they?"

"That is what I have been trying to figure out ever since that stage robbery."

"Corley told me that they wouldn't accept your resignation."

"I refuse to be flattered, John," smiled Henry.

"Good sheriffs are scarce."

"They must have been—to elect me," said Henry soberly.

"The commissioners still have faith in you," declared the lawyer.

"Don't lie, John," said Henry. "Corley did not want the responsibility of handling the job, and no one else wanted it—not even me. I have no illusions over my own ability. As a comedian I could get past on my funny nose and my ability to mis-juggle things. I am all out of practice as a juggler—and I have found out that a red nose is not of any advantage in suppressing crime. However, while I may be baffled—I am not stumped."

CHAPTER XVI

THE EMPTY CABIN

JUDGE VAN TREECE, saddling his horse in the dim lantern light of the little stable, tugged and yanked on a latigo. In the next stall, Henry grunted as he lifted a heavy stock saddle to the back of his chunky bay.

"Crazy damned idea—riding at night!" grunted Judge. "Go ahead and blow up like a balloon, you jug-headed monstrosity!"

"I resent that, Judge," said Henry. "I am not a jug-head."

"I was speaking to my horse, sir," retorted Judge. "Let me tell you something! You are going to get a kick in the belly if you don't look out."

"Still speaking to the horse, sir?" queried Henry.

"Certainly. No matter how I feel toward you—I am still speaking to the horse. Riding out at night! Two old wolves—prowling, I suppose."

"I like that word 'prowling', Judge. As though either of us could prowl. We might stumble and creak—but never prowl. Our prowling days were over years ago."

Henry backed his horse out of the stall and looked at the saddle in the lantern-light.

"A trifle far back," he remarked. "But it makes for easier riding. Ready, Judge?"

"I shortened my stirrups a little, Henry. It might make for easier riding."

"Very likely give you a permanent bend in the knees. Blow out the lantern as you come past."

Henry led his horse to the door, swung it open and stepped outside. And as he did so, flame seemed to blaze right in his face. His eardrums were all but shattered from an explosion.

Henry went backwards and down, falling against the knees of his frightened horse. The horse reared back into Judge, knocking him aside. Luckily both horses whirled back into the stalls then.

Judge, gasping and choking, fell on his knees beside Henry.

"My God, Henry!" choked Judge. "Speak, Henry! Whoa horses! Whoa, you fools! Henry! Can't you say something, Henry?"

"Haitch is for hockleberry," whispered Henry.

"Henry, are you shot?"

Henry groaned and sat up in the dark, puffing heavily.

"Shot? No, I do not believe I am, Judge. I caught my heels on that threshold and sat down very, very hard. Was that a shot?"

"It certainly was a shot. Are you sure you are not hurt?"

"I feel no pain, except where I sat down. Yes, I—I do believe I have a few powder burns on my face. Nothing disfiguring—just a slight stinging sensation."

He drew a deep breath and got slowly to his feet.

"I suppose we had better go, before someone comes seeking the sound of that shot, Judge. There is no use letting the town know that someone tried to kill me."

THEY LED the horses out and rode away from the rear of the jail. They could hear voices out on the street, evidently townsmen seeking the cause of the shot.

"Who on earth would want to murder you?" queried Judge, as they circled around to reach the main road.

Henry chuckled quietly. "I do not know, Judge. Perhaps it is someone who doesn't care who they kill, just so they get a fat one."

"I see no cause for levity in the situation, sir."

"Perhaps not—they did not shoot at you, Judge."

"Would it be amiss if I asked where we are going, sir?"

"I hope," replied Henry, evading the question, "that you did not forget to bring your gun this time."

"No, I have the cumbersome thing. But do you anticipate shooting?"

"We just had some, Judge; and there may be more to come."

Judge fell silent then. But after a mile of silence he remarked:

"Those damnable goose-pimples are annoying me again."

"If you care to go back, I'll go alone, Judge."

"No, I—I couldn't do that, Henry. Something—something might happen to you. But I have a feeling that again two fools are rushing in where angels fear to tread."

"I wish you would not speak of angels, Judge."

"Fear not, Henry, Angels are all young spirits."

"My spirit is young enough, sir... We turn here."

"You are going to the Spotted Horse mine?"

"I believe the road ends there, Judge."

"In my opinion," stated Judge, "you are leading me on another of your wild-goose chases. It is as dark as the inside of a black cat on a moonless night—and there will be no moon tonight."

"It will be an ideal night for the old wolves to prowl, Judge."

"That doesn't lower my goose-pimples to any extent, sir."

"It really is dark," admitted Henry. "If it were not for your complaints and the uncertain footsteps of that jaundiced brute you are riding, I could believe myself alone out here."

"Your sarcasm assures me that I have company, sir," retorted Judge.

They plodded slowly on through the darkness.

They were only a short distance from the Spotted Horse mine, when both men jerked up on their reins. From somewhere ahead they had heard a dull *plop*, which sounded very much like a shot. For several moments they remained silent, listening.

"It sounded very much—well, it could have been a shot," said Judge. "I do not understand why there should be shooting out here."

"I am very much in the dark," chuckled Henry. "Suppose we proceed, Judge."

"With due caution, I hope, sir. An officer of the law might not be exactly welcome, you know."

"They rarely are, Judge; and I am naturally cautious."

There was a light in the cabin at the Spotted Horse, but not a sound to break the stillness. They drew up a short distance away, dismounted and dropped their reins to the ground. As quietly as possible they approached the cabin. In the dim light from a window they could see a saddled horse. The door was closed.

"Goose-pimples," muttered Judge, as Henry led the way to a window.

MOVING IN close, they peered inside the cabin at a queer sight. Tuck Nash was standing toward the middle of the room, braced against the rough table. His face was the color of putty in the yellow lamplight. One side of his light-colored shirt was soggy with blood.

As they watched him he turned from the table and walked drunkenly toward the door, passing from their line of vision. They heard him fumbling with the latch and heard the door creak open. They crouched below the window and waited. Judging from the sounds, Tuck Nash was trying to mount the horse in front of the cabin.

At last he rode past them, not more than ten feet away. He was going slowly, but he disappeared quickly in the darkness. Henry and Judge hurried to their horses and followed him. They had no way of knowing what speed Tuck Nash was traveling, nor whether he had stayed on the road to Tonto City. But Henry felt sure that Nash was too badly injured to ride fast.

About a mile from Tonto City they found Tuck Nash. In the darkness they would have ridden past him, but Henry's horse snorted wildly, swerved against Judge's mount and nearly unseated both riders. They spurred back, dismounted and lighted matches.

Tuck Nash was dead, sprawled on his face in the center of the road. They drew him away from possible wheels or hoofs, and stood there in the darkness, wondering what to do.

Finally Henry said: "Judge, you go to town and get some of the boys to come back with you—right away. I am going back to the Spotted Horse."

"But—but what is it all about, Henry?"

"I am not sure—yet. Bring the boys to the Spotted Horse."

"You—you'll be careful, Henry?"

"I have no idea of establishing a precedent this evening, my dear Judge. Please hurry."

Henry lost no time in getting back to the cabin at the Spotted Horse. The door was still open. He left his horse and went in fairly close, hunched down behind some bushes. If Mack Taylor had shot Tuck Nash, Henry wondered if Taylor would return. And why had Taylor killed Nash? Back in Henry's mind was a hazy reason for the shooting, but it seemed far-fetched. Still, it might be the solution.

Henry must have crouched there fully fifteen minutes before he heard the sound of a horse walking on the hard ground. Then he saw the horse and the man pass between him and the dim light from the window. The man was on foot, leading the animal.

They stopped at the doorway and the man looked into the cabin, but Henry was unable to distinguish who it was. After a few moments the man led the horse to the little stable, only a short distance away.

Henry could hear sounds from the stable, and wondered why the man was spending so much time out there. On his hands and knees, Henry crawled forward in the darkness, until he was fairly close to the stable. Judging from the sounds the man was saddling another horse. Finally he walked back to the cabin, closing the door behind him.

Henry got to his feet and stepped over to the stable. There he discovered that the man had packed a horse. Plainly he planned on making a trip. Henry quickly untied the animal and gently led it away into the brush. There he tied it securely.

There had been no sound from the cabin. Henry hurried back, intending to look through the window, only to discover that in his absence it had been covered. Backing away from the cabin he crouched in the brush, waiting for the man inside to make his next move.

Henry had barely hunched down when the man came out, leaving the door open. He went straight to the spot where he had left his horse. Henry heard his grunt of surprise when he discovered the pack animal was missing. He could hear the man walking around in the darkness for possibly five minutes.

Then he came back to the stable, mounted his horse and rode slowly past the cabin toward the road. At the road he spurred into a swift gallop, going toward Tonto City.

Henry got stiffly to his feet and walked over to the cabin. He was sure that man who had ridden away was Mack Taylor, and that Taylor believed Tuck Nash had stolen the pack-horse. Now he was on his way to overtake Nash.

Henry walked into the cabin and looked around. The air reeked of kerosene, and a closer examination showed that the two bunks at the rear, as well as the chairs and floor, had been saturated with the stuff. On the table were a dozen sticks of dynamite, tied together and fused with about six inches of fuse. Henry rubbed his nose and pondered. What was the dynamite for, and why had the house been soaked with kerosene?

Before he had reached any decision, a slight noise at the door caused him to turn quickly.

Full in the doorway stood Mack Taylor, his heavy six-shooter covering Henry. Taylor's face was white and drawn, but his eyes glittered dangerously in the lamplight.

"Reach down, unbuckle yore belt—and let it drop," he ordered.

CHAPTER XVII

THE FIGHT IN THE CELLAR

SLOWLY HENRY OBEYED. The heavy belt and gun thudded on the floor. Taylor motioned him to move aside while he secured the gun.

"The smart sheriff of Tonto Town, eh?" snarled Taylor. "Thought I pulled out, eh? Damn little brains you've got, Conroy. I found that pack-horse, but I left him there while I out-smarted you. You've got a lot to learn yet—but yuh won't never learn it, 'cause this is the end of yore trail. Sorry, but Wild Horse Valley will have to appoint another sheriff—and it won't be me."

"Going to Mexico?" queried Henry.

"Exactly. What did yuh do with Tuck Nash?"

"Tuck Nash, I believe, has gone to Tonto City."

"Yo're a liar, Conroy. Nash is dead."

"I doubt that, Taylor. Dead men rarely mount a horse and ride away."

There was a flicker of fear in Taylor's eyes.

"He was dead, I tell yuh, Conroy."

Henry shrugged his shoulders. "I am afraid that this is one time you failed to get your man, Taylor. You broke with him, after he murdered Jim McDonald, I believe."

"What the devil do you know about that?" snarled Taylor.

"Common sense. I may be wrong, but I do not believe you would harm Molly Hope. It had to be Tuck Nash. Why did you and Nash murder Peter Morris—merely to steal that fifteen thousand dollars he was to invest in your mine?"

"Well, I'll be damned!" gasped Taylor.

"Without a single doubt, sir."

"You know a lot, don't yuh?" sneered Taylor. "Well, it won't never do you any good. Pete Morris was too danged greedy. He promised us fifteen thousand for a third interest, and then tried to hold us up for a half. Tuck had one of Sam Hope's knives that night."

"I guessed that," said Henry. "You wanted to throw the blame on Sam Hope, so you could get his widow. You never realized that circumstances might place the blame on Dusty Cole. Where have you kept those two cowboys, Taylor?"

"Kept them?"

"Certainly. You wore their clothes—you and Nash. You kept those two boys, waiting for the rewards to mount up and read 'dead or alive'. You wanted to collect extra money."

Taylor laughed harshly. "You know a lot, Conroy. All right. For yore own information, those two boys were in that cellar under the old Mexican's shack—until we took 'em out and burned the shack. Then we put 'em in the Lost Injun tunnel. Nash was up there and saw Jim McDonald and the two women goin' into the tunnel; so the danged fool killed McDonald and locked the two girls in the tunnel. Too much whisky and marihuana, I reckon."

"I suspected that," nodded Henry. "He gave Sam Hope marihuana, too. That is why Sam rode into that hitch-rack that night. I suppose you shot Sam that night."

"Nash shot him. Had to do it, 'cause Sam knew too much. He came to tell you that he knew where Dusty and Sandy were. But how did you figure out that me and Nash had any hand in this deal?"

"Raw gold isn't so easy to dispose of, Taylor," replied Henry. "It could be handled by a mine outfit. Someone had to tell you about that Yellow Warrior shipment. Only Borden and Bradford knew; so I concentrated on Bradford. That old Mexican was the key."

"Well, Conroy, you've got more brains than I figured. Smell the kerosene? I soaked five gallons into this place. This cabin will burn very nice. You noticed the dynamite bomb? Enough dynamite to blow this place to hell. Now go ahead and figure out what's goin' to happen to you."

HENRY WAS straining his ears, praying every moment that Judge and the posse might arrive. He wanted to stall for time.

"Where are the girls, Taylor?" he asked. "They haven't done anything against you. Neither have Dusty and Sandy. With all of us gone, they will starve to death. At least be man enough to let someone know where they are."

"Do you think I'm a fool?" snarled Taylor. "They know nearly as much as you do. With them alive, Mexico wouldn't be big enough to hide me. I've got it all figured out. Before I touch a match to this shack, I'll put the old Mexican's remains in here. There'll be enough bones left to show that I died, too."

"You mean—" Henry stared wide-eyed.

Taylor laughed and pointed back toward the two oil-soaked bunks.

"There's a trap-door back there, Conroy. It ain't a big cellar, but it's big enough. They're down there—now. Nash brought 'em in tonight. He wanted Molly Hope—the danged hop-head. We cut down on each other, and I got him first. I don't care what you done with the body; the bones will check out all right—if there's any left."

"You would murder all those innocent people, Taylor?"

"My life is worth more than anything else to me, Conroy. Back up."

"You are going to force me into that cellar?"

"That's right. And when yo're down in there, I'll toss in the dynamite, fasten the trapdoor, touch off the kerosene, and have light enough to start south with the gold. Neat, eh?"

Henry tried to force a laugh, but merely choked.

"You will never get away, Taylor," he said hoarsely. "They are surrounding the place now."

Taylor laughed, came forward to jab the muzzle of his gun into Henry's belt-line.

"They're settin' around Tonto City, yuh mean. You told me yourself that I was the only one you'd told about yore suspicions."

Henry shook his head, his mouth too dry for conversation. He wanted to tell Taylor something, anything to delay him. Taylor was laughing harshly, punching him backward. Henry nearly collapsed against one of the bunks and his nostrils filled with the scent of kerosene. Taylor flung the trap-door open, grasped Henry by the sleeve and whirled him around.

It was Taylor's intention to slash Henry over the head with the barrel of his revolver. Instead, his heel slipped on some oil and he missed. His hand, clenched around the butt of the heavy gun, barely brushed Henry's sleeve.

Henry, making a clumsy attempt to avoid the blow, sagged into Taylor, his outflung arms slipping down around the murderer's legs. Rasping out a curse, he slashed again with his gun, but Henry's weight had thrown him off balance. Taylor was pitching sideways over the edge of the trap, twisting, cursing, but unable to help himself.

He crashed down on the trap, clawing at it with both hands, losing his gun in a desperate attempt to free himself from those gripping arms. He got hold of the trap-door and clung to it—but just then Henry toppled off the edge into the cellar, dragging him with him. Taylor clung to the door until it shut against his fingers; then he let loose and they crashed down into the darkness together.

JUDGE VAN TREECE'S entrance into the Tonto Saloon was dramatic. He strode in, flung up his hand for silence, and roared:

"Tuck Nash was shot and killed tonight! His body is about a mile from here on the road to the Spotted Horse. The sheriff has gone back to the mine, and he is asking for every rider in town to come out there—quick!"

The response was gratifying. Moments later at least a dozen riders spurred out of town, and they included Judge, Oscar, Thunder and Lightning, Frijole Bill and John Campbell. The latter had borrowed the horse of a cowboy who was too drunk to ride. Well armed and ready for anything, the dozen riders thundered along the road toward the Spotted Horse.

Campbell tried to ride and ask questions of Judge at the same time, but with little success.

Several horses shied at the sight or scent of Tuck Nash's body beside the road, but swept on.

There was no caution used by this posse in approaching the lighted cabin. They swept up in a body, dismounted swiftly and crowded into the narrow doorway. There they halted, listening, wondering.

"Kerosene!" exclaimed the lawyer. "Where is everybody?"

They moved in further.

"Dynamite bomb on the table!" Judge said.

"Ay hear somet'ing," said Oscar.

From under the floor came a rasping, bumping sound. The posse looked at each other in wonder.

"Yudas Priest! Look!" choked Oscar.

The trap-door was raising up slowly. At last it crashed over against the legs of a bunk. The head and shoulders of a man came into view, the face covered with blood and dirt. It was Mack Taylor, choking, spluttering, trying to get loose from something.

The crowd surged forward in amazement.

"Good Lord!" gasped the lawyer. "Why—why, that's Henry Conroy!"

Mack Taylor was making ineffectual attempts to dislodge Henry. The sheriff had his head buried in Taylor's midriff, both arms locked around his waist and was hanging on for dear life. As the crowd watched in stunned amazement Mack Taylor swayed and fell back down into the cellar, with Henry on top of him.

There was an eloquent *thud*.

"My goodness!" exclaimed Henry in an exhausted whisper. "Do we have to go through that all over again?"

Henry's words seem to bring the posse to their senses. Quickly they dragged Henry and Taylor back out of the cellar. Taylor was too weak to resist, but Henry seemed to have his senses.

"Handcuff Taylor!" he gasped.

"Yeeminee-e-e!" shrilled Oscar from the cellar. "Ha'are are de vimmin! Yah, by yiminee! An ha'are is Dosty and Sandy!"

THERE WERE plenty of willing hands to take them out. Except for bruises and fright, Molly and Laura were all right. Dusty and Sandy, whiskered, dirty, half-starved, were able to talk. Henry's right eye was swollen shut, his nose twice its original size, and he seemed one mass of scratches and bruises.

The ropes were quickly removed from the captives.

"I thought we were goners," panted Dusty. "What month is this?"

"Never mind the month," said Sandy huskily. "We've been in holes for a year. My gosh, what a life we've led! Has anybody got some ham and eggs in their pocket? Where's Nash? Let me get my hands on that feller—jist once."

"Nash is dead," informed Judge. "Taylor shot him tonight."

"Henry," said Campbell gently, "do you feel like talking?"

Henry smiled, in spite of his battered features.

"Talk? My dear Mr. Campbell, I could sing. But perhaps Mr. Taylor would prefer telling his own story; it would not hang him any higher. Will you please lift my right hand up? Higher, please. I thank you very much."

"Is your shoulder hurt, Henry?" queried Judge anxiously.

"Oh, not at all. I merely wished to be acclaimed the winner."

And Henry Harrison Conroy toppled over in a dead faint.

"Thonder!" yelped Lightning. "Let alone! Leesten, my leetle brodder, you monkey weeth those dynamite bum you get our head blowed off jus' below my waist. Have leetle senses! Let alone."

Dusty limped over and knelt beside Laura. She smiled at him through her tears, but neither of them spoke. Henry opened his eyes and looked around. That is, he opened one eye. Frijole handed him a pint bottle.

"Is that the stuff that makes buggy-whips out of two-by-fours?" whispered Henry.

"Yeah, and that's jist what you need right now."

John Campbell had been questioning the exhausted Taylor, and now he came over to Henry.

"Henry," he said, "I want to apologize for anything I might have thought about you as a sheriff. You have cleared up all the mystery, saved a lot of valuable lives and even recovered every ounce of the stolen gold. No officer could have done better."

"Henry does not want praise," said Judge loftily.

"Like the devil, he don't!" exclaimed Henry. "He loves it!"

"I presume that squelches me," sighed Judge. "Or perhaps you are delirious, sir?"

"There might be something to that theory, too, Judge," chuckled Henry.

Judge grinned.

"Va'al," stated Oscar, "Ay can say, it turned out yust like Ay knew it would. All along Ay have suspected—somebody."

FIFTEEN MINUTES later the cavalcade was on its way to Tonto City, stringing along the dark road. Thunder and Lightning rode together, far in the rear.

"W'at ees a mysteree?" Thunder asked. "W'at ees, pleeze?"

"I'm never hear from one," replied Lightning.

"I'm hear Jodge saying one ees gone."

"I'm won'ner w'ere he ees gone. Leesten, my leetle brodder, I'm do *mucho* leestening and *mucho* looking tonight, but there are many theengs I cannot get through your damn head. Dosty Cole ees going be hong for keeling Peter Morris. Sure. That ees setttle. Then w'y is Peter Morris' daughter keesing Dosty Cole tonight?"

"Sure," agreed Thunder. "She kees heem t'ree time."

He nodded sagely.

"Sure. You are seeing w'at 'appen. You see Henry and Meester Taylor fight een the cellar. You see these dynamite bum on the table and thees oil pour over everytheeng. You are looking. W'at you theenk from all these things happening? You leesten, too, and you hear theengs from leestening. W'at you theenk?"

"Hm-m-m," muttered Thunder. "Hm-m-m."

"Por Dios! I am askeeng you question and you make noise like rosty heenge. My leetle brodder, you are ver' domb. W'y you not spik? Can't you say sometheeng?"

"Haitch ees for hockleberry," replied Thunder.

"Gracias," said Lightning. "I fill that you agree weeth me."

And they drifted on down the road in the dust of the cavalcade.

HENRY HITS THE WARPATH

Even though all the varmints of Wild Horse Valley are ag'in' him, the white-haired, fumble-fingered custodian of Tonto's law is determined that his record for incompetence, square-shooting, and fiasco shall not be besmirched

CHAPTER I

"HENRY," SAID "JUDGE" Van Treece soberly, "Oscar Johnson is up to something. That vitrified Viking has been drinking liquor all the afternoon with a drummer, and he is full of both whisky and nonsense."

Henry Harrison Conroy, Sheriff of Tonto City, gravely considered his deputy, who stood beside the desk, one bony hand resting on a dog-eared copy of the brand register.

Sheriff Henry Harrison Conroy, formerly a brilliant luminary of tanktown vaudeville, made three separate and distinct efforts to lift his boots to the table-top, grunted in disgust and subsided. He rubbed his huge, red nose and fixed his small, squinty blue eyes on Judge, and remarked:

"I find that my hinges do not function properly—and I sigh for the days of my youth, when I was so supple that I could easily put an ankle behind my neck. Oh—er—yes, of course—you mentioned Oscar."

Judge Van Treece, tall and gaunt, with the features of a melancholy hawk, looked wearily upon Henry. Judge Van Treece, once a renowned criminal lawyer, had drunk himself right out of the profession, and was well on the way to total submersion when Henry Conroy came to Tonto City.

Henry had inherited the JHC spread in Wild Horse Valley, and had come to claim his inheritance, blessed with a complete lack of knowledge of the cow country. With his derby, spats and gold-headed cane, he had found himself elected sheriff of Wild

Horse Valley on a write-in ballot. This was very funny. Realizing that it had all been done as a joke, Henry appointed Judge as his deputy, and made Oscar Johnson jailer. If Arizona wanted a laugh—he would play to the gallery for all he was worth.

Oscar Johnson was a huge Swede, uneducated, belligerent, and always in trouble. Where none existed, Oscar created it. His courtship of Josephine Swenson, maid at the Tonto Hotel, was, in matters of matched size and strength, a battle of Titans.

"Yes, I mentioned Oscar," Judge replied ponderously. "There is something in the wind. Oscar and that clothing salesman went to supper together, and a while ago I saw them enter the hotel together. They were both listing heavily to starboard. And I need not remind you that when Oscar gets to a point where he lists, he is dangerous. At such a time he is, chemically speaking, ninety percent alcohol."

"How blissful for Oscar!" Henry exclaimed quietly.

"Blissful! A man in Scorpion Bend declared publicly that there isn't three sober breaths drawn in the sheriff's office in a month. No wonder they call us 'The Shame of Arizona'."

"That, sir," declared Henry, "is base calumny. The man does not know whereof he speaks. Last Wednesday you were sober. Please do not interrupt me, Judge. Tuesday night you dropped

*Sheriff Henry's cavalcade was magnificent—and
only Henry knew that danger flags were flying*

OSCAR

and broke that jug in which we had a gallon of Frijole Bill's
prune whisky. You were so depressed that you forgot to drink
anything on Wednesday."

"Well," remarked Judge quietly, "a man must fast—at times."

"True, Judge—true. Now that we have a railroad of our own,
linking us with the outside world, we must—well, meet civili-
zation half-way."

"I still prefer the stagecoach, Henry. I protested openly, asking
that Tonto City be afforded passenger service—not a damnable
caboose at the rear of a cattle or ore train. Damnable grades and
creaking curves—and one train a day. An antiquated engine,
spewing cinders, and—what on earth?"

THE OFFICE-DOOR flew open and in staggered Oscar Johnson, clad in a misfit dress-suit, which had split at elbow, knee
and down the middle of the back. The pants, which extended
to a point about six inches above his shoe-tops, exposed yellow
shoes with white spats.

Oscar's shirt was a happy combination of red and lavender,
topped by a tall, bat-wing collar, unfastened at one end. While,
hanging down the back of his neck was a bright blue four-in-

hand tie. In one hand he carried a silk top-hat, which looked as though it had been caught in a stampede. Oscar's nose was swollen and scarlet; one eye had assumed a deep purple hue, and was tightly closed.

He kicked the door shut behind him and limped over to a vacant chair.

"What on earth happened to you?" gasped Henry.

"Me?" queried Oscar in a weak voice. "Ay am de wictim of romance."

Henry closed his eyes tightly and made gurgling sounds in his throat.

"Romance?" queried Judge weakly. "Where on earth did you get those clothes, Oscar?"

"Ay *vars* svell looking, Ay'll tell you," whispered Oscar, mournfully.

"My goodness!" breathed Henry. "Wh-where's the romance?"

"Yosephine," sighed Oscar. "She yall like ha'al—Yosephine did."

"I knew it!" exclaimed Judge. "The moment I saw you, I—"

"Hold it, Judge," choked Henry. "Let Oscar tell it."

Oscar shifted his position, groaned twice and said:

"Ay vars going to elope, and Ay—"

"With Josephine?" interrupted Judge.

"Yah, su-ure. She vanted romance. She vanted me to put a ladder up to her vindow—and steal her avay."

"Who from?" queried Judge weakly.

"Ay never dit find out, Yudge. Das ha'ar drummer he tell me he vill fix me up in vedding clothes, and ve got drunk togedder and—yeeminy, Ay am von mass of hurts. Das hat is too small; so ve tied it on vit a string.

"Ay got de ladder oop to Yosephine's vindow and made de climb oll right. De vindow is open and Yosephine has yust closed her valise, ven Ay look in de vindow and Ay says, 'Hallo, Baby.'"

"Keep going, Oscar," whispered Henry. "Don't stop now."

"Va'l, she yust took von look at me, yalled bloddy morder, and hit me sqvare in de face vit her valise. Va'l"—Oscar tried to smile, as he fingered the ruined top-hat—"de ladder vent over backvard—and Ay vars on it."

Henry buried his face in his arms, while Judge covered his mouth with a blue bandanna. Finally he managed speech: "And so you did not get married."

"You can see for yourself, Yudge. Ay am not in shape for matrimony."

"Let us all be calm," whispered Henry. "At a time like this it is good to try and repeat poetry. It—it takes the mind off things at hand. For instance, any simple nursery rhyme, such as—Oscar, take that hat off your head!"

"Vedding clothes—huh!" snorted Oscar.

"Were you going to take a bridal tour?" asked Judge.

"Ay vars not! Ay love her, Yudge. Ay vouldn't strike her vit anyt'ing. Take a bridle to her! Huh! Ay am a yentleman."

"Now, listen!" wheezed Henry. "This must cease—at once, sir! By gad, if no one else will protect my blood-pressure, I shall do it myself. Oscar, you take those—er—clothes back to their owner. At once, sir!"

"Ay am de owner, Hanry," replied Oscar. "Ay bought 'em."

"You—you bought 'em?" gasped Judge.

"Yah—su-ure, Ay bought 'em. He told me dey vars like iron. Huh! Ven Ay hit de ground dey bost like a vatermelon. Yudas, Ay am a mess."

"The best thing you can do is to find Josephine and apologize," said Henry.

"Me—apologize to Yosephine? Who de ha'al do you t'ink threw dat valise—me?"

"I suppose you are right."

"Of course, Ay am right. Ay vars dere—Ay ought to know."

"Oscar, have you seen Thunder and Lightning this evening?"

queried Judge, by way of a diversion. Thunder and Lightning were two Mexicans employed by Henry at his JHC ranch.

"Yah, Ay seen 'em," nodded Oscar. "Each von had bottle tequila. Dey ride dobble on that Yeronimo mule."

"Henry, I told you they'd spend that money for tequila," declared Judge. "Overalls, indeed! Socks and drawers! You gave them each a dollar and a half—and they spent it for tequila. You are a trusting soul. Why on earth you keep them I can't figure out. They won't work."

" 'They toil not, neither do they spin'," quoted Henry, "but where on earth might a man find two people who can do more gymnastics with the King's English than those two blessed Mexicans."

"From an economic standpoint—"began Judge, but stopped.

FROM OUTSIDE came the staccato thudding of hoofs, the *r-r-r-r-rip!* of gravel, as a rider skidded his animal to a stop in front of the office. The three men were staring at the door, as boot-soles slithered across the wooden sidewalk.

A man flung the door open; stopped on the threshold, panting.

"Is the sheriff—" he blurted, when from somewhere behind him came the report of a shot. The man in the doorway was falling forward, dead before he reached the floor....

From the street, thudding hoofs mingled with a crash, a yelp of alarm or pain. Oscar Johnson, in spite of his bruises, leaped over the dead man, dodged a rearing gray shape, which was Geronimo, the mule, and went galloping after a man who was running up the badly-lighted street.

Oscar could really run, and in front of the Tonto Hotel he made a diving tackle, bringing down his man, who was carrying a shotgun in both hands. As they crashed down in a cloud of dust, the shotgun roared, and part of a front hotel window left its moorings, adding to the general excitement on the main street.

People came running from every direction. Henry and Judge

were examining the dead man, as loiterers crowded in, wondering, questioning.

"It's Johnny Brent," Judge told them. "Someone shot him from behind, as he stood in the doorway."

"One of the JP outfit," growled a voice outside. "Patterson said he'd get square."

"Oscar Johnson's got the killer!" yelled a voice. "Caught him in front of the hotel; and he still had the shotgun."

Oscar shoved his way through the crowd, and the prisoner was Lightning Mendoza, frightened almost white. His nose was skinned, where Oscar had skidded with him on the gravel. Oscar didn't know whom he had captured until he saw him in the lamplight. He shook the little Mexican violently.

"Easy, Oscar," Henry warned. "What happened, Lightning?"

But Lightning couldn't talk. Eyes wide, jaw sagging, he looked from face to face, trying to realize what had happened. Someone shoved Thunder forward roughly, and the two brothers bumped into each other.

"Who push?" Thunder demanded indignantly.

"I did!" snapped a hard-faced cowboy. "Don'tcha like it?" He strode forward.

"Sure," nodded Thunder, unhappily. "I don' mind from leetle push."

"Now wait a minute, you folks," said Henry calmly. "*I* shall handle this. Lightning, did you shoot Johnny Brent?"

"Johnny Brent ees shot?" blurted Thunder.

"With the shotgun that Lightnin' had," said a cowboy.

"*Madre de Dios!*" howled Lightning, suddenly discovering that he had a voice. "I'm keel not'ing. Me and our brodder ees riding these mule, and for eenstance a horse ees trying for getting on the mule and all t'ree from us get knocked down. W'at ees going on, that ees all I hope—and pray."

"Well, that clears that up," said Henry calmly. "Now, Lightning, can you tell us why you had the shotgun?"

"W'at shotgun?" Lightning queried, looking at his empty hands.

"The shotgun you had when Oscar caught you, Lightning," explained Henry kindly. "You remember that, do you not?"

Lightning shook his head.

"Ay t'ink he shoot ha'al out of de hotel vindow," offered Oscar.

"You look as though you'd been in a fight yourself," said one of the cowboys.

"Yust keep your face out of my business," replied Oscar with the hauteur of a Caesar.

DOCTOR BOGART, the county coroner, bustled in with his little black bag and fussed adroitly over the dead man.

Henry turned to Thunder Mendoza. "Thunder, perhaps you can tell us what happened. Now take it easy."

"Sure," agreed Thunder eagerly. "I know everytheeng. W'at you want for knowing?"

"What were you and Lightning doing out there and what happened?"

"Me and my brodder go home on Heronimo, theese damn mule. That ees sometheeng—I hope. All from a sodden we are hearing gon go *boom!* Then a horse ees trying for get on the mule, too. That ees all."

"I see," nodded Henry. "You heard someone fire a shotgun, and then a rider collided with your mule. But where did Lightning get that shotgun?"

Thunder turned to Lightning and said:

"W'at you do weeth that shotgun?"

Lightning blinked foolishly, looked at his empty hands and wiped them on his hips.

"I am escared that my leetle brodder ees gone loco," he told Henry.

"If I may interject the cold light of reason into this disjointed interview," said Judge, "I might say that following the collision, Lightning, acting in sort of a daze, secured the shotgun, when the original owner dropped it; being dazed from the day of his birth, and not materially helped by the aforementioned collision, he likely ran and ran, until overtaken; and in the scuffle which ensued, the shotgun was accidentally discharged."

"That ees exactly from w'at happen!" Thunder exclaimed.

"What was that?" queried Henry curiously.

"Listen!" exclaimed a cowboy. "I saw them two drunken Mexicans get on their mule about a minute before the shot was fired. They rode the mule bareback, and it's a cinch they didn't have no shotgun."

"Thank you, sir." Henry nodded gravely. "You did not happen to see the man who fired the shot, did you?"

"No, I didn't, Sheriff."

Henry turned to Oscar and ordered him to release Lightning. Campbell, the prosecutor, had arrived. They shooed the crowd outside, leaving only the coroner, prosecutor, sheriff and deputy with the body. Henry told what they knew about it. Johnny Brent had been riddled with buckshot, killed instantly. John Campbell looked gravely at Henry.

Johnny Brent owned a small spread south of Tonto City, and Johnny Brent had just lost a suit in which he had claimed that the JP spread, a large outfit owned by Jim Patterson, had been stealing his calves. The JP outfit beat Brent in court, and Patterson had told Johnny Brent that he would get even with him for bringing the suit. So much they all knew.

"I believe I know what you are thinking, John," said Henry.

"It was a cold-blooded killing, Henry," said the lawyer. "Buckshot in the back—from behind. From your testimony, it would seem that Brent needed your services—and in a hurry."

Henry nodded sadly and picked up the shotgun. It was old, cheaply made, ten-gauge, with short double-barrels. He opened the gun and took out the shells. They were old-fashioned, brass shells, had been reloaded many times, as evidenced by their thin edges. Except for the imprint of some hardware store, there were no identifying marks on the gun.

"Don't look like it had been shot for a century," said the lawyer. "Probably dug up special for this occasion."

Henry looked thoughtfully at the lawyer. "I was wondering about Old Shep Hart," he said.

Shep Hart lived with Johnny Brent. He was a grizzled old rawhider from Wyoming, who had gained his nickname from working in a sheep country.

"Why wonder about him?" queried Judge.

"Johnny Brent rode fast and far, judging from the lather and sweat on his horse," replied Henry. "He might have ridden for help, Judge."

Judge Van Treece scratched his thinning thatch thoughtfully. "You would think of something like that," he said wearily.

"I *could* ride alone," said Henry.

"Yes," nodded Judge, "you could. But if Johnny Brent rode for help, what could you do alone?"

"Well, I might ride back here to get you," smiled Henry. He turned to the doctor and said, "Doctor, you don't need us. So we will go and see how things are at Brent's *rancho*. Judge, call Oscar and have him help you saddle the horses. And—wait a minute—show Oscar which end of my horse the head is on. I do not want the saddle on backward again."

"I shall saddle him myself. Henry."

"Then have Oscar show *you* which is the head-end."

CHAPTER II

FIFTEEN MINUTES LATER, Judge climbed into his saddle. At the same time, Henry Harrison Conroy struggled stoutly to assume a sitting position in his own. The greatest trouble in Oscar's life was to find a horse strong enough to carry Henry around.

"Ay t'ink ve should hang de Mexican and settle everyt'ing," declared Oscar. "He had de shotgon, and he run avay."

"Your word against his—and we saw *you* with the shotgun, Oscar," replied Henry.

"Yah, su-ure," Oscar agreed.

"As a rebuttal," remarked Judge, "he should have remarked that he was with us when the murder was committed, Henry. Oscar, you are not bright."

"By Yudas, das vars right!" exclaimed Oscar.

"Send him your bill, Judge," Henry chuckled. "That amounts to legal advice. Shall we shake up these equines before they go to sleep under us?"

"Shake up yours and perhaps mine might get excited. Or else fall apart."

It was nearly midnight when the three rode up to Johnny Brent's little ranch house. There was not a light in the place, but this was not surprising. They dismounted at the sagging porch, called loudly for Shep Hart, and pounded on the door.

There was no answer. Cattle bawled quietly around the creaking old windmill, and a rooster crowed sleepily from inside the stable. They pounded some more, but nothing happened. Henry tried the door and found it unlocked. They stepped inside and Henry lighted a match.

"Good glory!" Judge exclaimed. "Quick, Henry—light that lamp!"

With shaking fingers they lit the lamp and surveyed the room.

Sprawled on the floor, his shoulders against a bunk, was old Shep Hart, dead for hours. Lying across his legs was a 30-30 carbine, and the floor was littered with empty 30-30 cases. There were many .45 cases, too. Henry levered the rifle, but found it empty. Shep's Colt .45 had been cast aside—empty.

The windows had been shot out, and there were a score of bullet holes in the flimsy door. The three officers looked uneasily at each other.

"Your hunch was right, Henry," Judge whispered.

"I saw something that perhaps you overlooked," said Henry. "Johnny Brent's gun and belt were empty."

"Yudas Priest!" exclaimed Oscar. "Dey have a var here."

"Evidently," nodded Henry gravely. "I wish I knew who'd won it."

He made a tentative examination of Shep Hart. "Shot to shreds," he told Judge. "It looks as though they cross-fired him. I wonder how Johnny ever got away from here."

"That is something we may never know, Henry. Well, we can do no good here; so we may as well go back and notify the coroner. I've seen raw and hideous murder before—but nothing so raw and hideous as this. We've got to get them, Henry. We've got to hang them."

"What chance have they to escape?" Henry queried soberly.

"Their chances of escape are about ninety to ten, I would say."

"You are very modest, Judge. You give us ten points. Ten percent. Nine-to-one against us. I wish I had a drink."

"I wish I had a quart," sighed Judge. "By the way, this was to have been Oscar's wedding night—and look what happened!"

"Yah, su-ure," sighed Oscar. "She t'rew a valise at me. Ay am t'rough vit vimmin for life. Ay hope Ay can find de clothes-drommer. Ay don't t'ink he fit me. Ay look like a busted skveese-organ."

"Yes, I think we better go home," said Henry.

NEWS OF the battle at the Brent Ranch spread quickly, and next morning the valley was well represented in the posse that went there with the coroner. Judge noticed that there was not a man from the JP spread, and mentioned it to Henry.

John Campbell, the prosecutor, saw it too, and rode in beside Henry to talk about it.

"They are the only ones ever had trouble with Johnny Brent," he remarked.

Henry nodded. "That same old finger of suspicion, John," he said. "I often think of it when I get angry. A foolish threat, made in the heat of anger, always swings that accusing finger. Oh, I will admit that Jim Patterson was mad. His pride was hurt. The case was dismissed from lack of evidence—so Patterson was not exonerated."

"And he *is* hot-headed, Henry."

"Very true, John. I see we have two representatives from the Circle M with us."

"Oh, the two in that near buckboard. That's Peter Hatton, the new owner. The driver is Len Stryker, his foreman. Hatton has only been here a few days. He looks like a man who had eaten well but unwisely, Henry."

"Liquor, John. Being what I am, I hesitate to criticize; but liquor alone gave him that paunch and those jowls. I understand he paid a pretty penny for those twelve thousand acres."

"I believe he did. He's going into the cow business on a big scale, I understand. The railroad people are building a siding and loading corrals on the Circle M for Hatton's exclusive use."

"I heard they were. I don't believe that Hatton employed any local punchers. At least, I haven't heard that he did."

"No, I believe not. He brought in four, including Len Stryker. I don't know where they came from."

At the Brent Ranch Henry was introduced to Peter Hatton, after the coroner had made his investigation and the body had been removed to a wagon.

"It must have been a hell of a fight," Hatton remarked. "The poor devil sure got salivated. Must have been caught in a crossfire between them two windows. I hear this pardner was buck-shotted in yore office doorway last night, Sheriff."

"Yes." Henry nodded. "He was. Fine boy, too."

"Had trouble with the JP outfit, I heard."

Henry looked narrowly at Peter Hatton. "Matter of public record," he said quietly.

"Oh, I mean the threats that passed between Patterson and Brent."

"Men often speak threateningly, under stress of anger." Henry smiled his most lamblike smile.

And Hatton smiled at Henry. "You shore juggle words, Sheriff. You ain't a native of Arizony, are yuh?"

"Only by adoption, sir. Our mission here is finished so we may as well go back to Tonto City. It has been a pleasure to meet you, sir."

"Yeah—well, that's fine," Peter Hatton said. "See yuh later."

As they walked to their horses, Campbell said: "Henry, I don't believe you like Peter Hatton."

Henry smiled slowly and shook his head. "Queer people," he said.

"You mean that Hatton is queer?"

"No—Henry Harrison Conroy. For over thirty years I featured my big, red nose, John. It was plastered on bill-boards from New York to San Francisco. And today I formed a dislike for Peter Hatton, because he never took his eyes off my proboscis, while talking with me—and I know he was laughing at it—internally."

"It seems to me," interjected Judge, "that murder gives it an added sheen. Or it might be the sun."

"I feel," remarked Henry stiffly, "that under the circumstances we should avoid personalities, Judge. What did you deduce from an examination of that room? I saw you sniffing like a blood-hound—or was that merely a recurrence of your hay fever?"

"I am not in the habit of sniffing—like a bloodhound, or otherwise, sir. And I would have you know that I lay no claim to any hay fever. It would seem that at least one member of the sheriff's office should show some inclination toward investigating this mystery. It would look better, I think. All you did was polish your nose and make banal remarks."

They managed to climb on their horses. Henry, with his ten-gallon hat tilted over one-eye, squinted at the lanky Judge. "And your solution is what?"

"I believe that Johnny Brent and Shep Hart were together in the house when trouble started. Brent's horse was tied at the front porch, and in some way he managed to ride away for help. Some of the attackers followed him and shot him in our office doorway."

"Marvelous," Henry whispered. "All we have to do is to find who the attacking parties were. Have you any idea why the attack was made, Judge?"

"You might inquire at the JP, Henry."

"That is also elementary, Judge. With my mind all set on a mystery—you shame the noonday sun by parading the obvious."

"There must be some reason for the attack, Henry. The JP threatened Johnny Brent. The JP are the only ones who have a motive."

"You overlook one thing, Judge."

"What is that, sir?"

"The fact that anything can happen in Arizona."

"In this case I must disagree."

"Oh, that is perfectly all right, Judge. Glad to have you. If you ever agreed with me, except on the age of whisky, I would be afraid that my opinion was not worth expressing."

THEY CAME back to Tonto City, where the body was placed with Johnny Brent's. Jim Patterson, owner of the JP outfit, and two of his riders, Tod Ellers and Eddie Lee, were in town; and they all had been drinking heavily. They followed Henry and Judge to the office.

Patterson was tall and dark, high-cheeked as any Indian, hard-faced, his eyes bloodshot. He was past forty, lean and hard as an ironwood pool, his gun swinging in a short holster against the leg of his worn chaps.

"We been listenin' around, Conroy," he told Henry harshly, "and some of these fools are hintin' that me and my boys had a hand in them killin's. 'Cause I told Brent that I'd pay him back for that suit against me, they figure I killed 'em both. All right—suits me. Next move's yours."

Henry rubbed his nose, swallowed painfully, a weak smile on his lips. "It—it was a—er—nice evening for it, Mr. Patterson," he said.

"You—you admit it, Patterson?" gasped Judge.

"Who sold you any chips in this game, you moultin' sand-hill crane?" Patterson demanded angrily.

"Thank you, Mr. Patterson!" blurted Henry. "I have tried and tried to think up an apt description for Judge. That is a jewel, I assure you. Moulting sand-hill crane. Good—in fact, very good."

"What are you talkin' about?"

"A—a beautiful description," explained Henry. "I would like to shake your hand, sir. If you do not mind—"

"Get yore hand away from me! Yo're both crazy. C'mon, boys."

Jim Patterson and his two men stalked outside and headed for the hitch-rack, without a backward glance toward the office doorway, where Judge and Henry stood together.

"Both crazy," murmured Judge. "Damme, I believe he's right."

"To think otherwise would only be to prove his point, my dear Judge. But he came here with malice aforethought and with two gunmen—and we sent him away, talking to himself. Genius is always crazy. And sometimes vice versa."

"Oh—are you a genius?" queried Judge.

"Rather—a squirming genius, Judge. The man was looking for trouble—and you—you moulting sand-hill crane—asked him to admit a murder. Tck, tck, tck, tck! Your stupidity revolts me."

"I do not believe in beating around the bush."

"That is no excuse for parading through it with a brass band. Judge, I love life. I find it good. So I believe I shall go out to the JHC for the night—away from the roar and rattle of Tonto City, the petty annoyances of murder mysteries and the smell of dank jails. I crave solitude and peace."

"And a liberal portion of Frijole Bill's prune whisky," Judge added.

"Wouldst retire to solitude with me, sir?" queried Henry soberly.

"Wouldst. The solitude doesn't appeal to me; but there is something in Frijole Bill's prune whisky that actually warms the cockles of my heart."

"Warms! Man, the cockles of your old heart were incinerated after your first drink of that stuff. Mine were, I know. After that, cauterization set in. An autopsy on either of us would have to be done by a chimney-sweep. Let us go at once, Judge; Jim Patterson might wonder what I meant—and come hack for an explanation."

CHAPTER III

THE INQUEST OVER the two bodies brought out no new information; so the six-man jury brought in the usual verdict— killed by parties unknown. Jim Patterson attended the inquest, sitting there grim-faced, alert, hostilely on the defensive. The crowd watched Patterson as much as they did the coroner and witnesses. But there was no hint in the questions nor testimony that might link the killings to the JP outfit.

Oscar Johnson was jubilant again. He and Josephine had once more reached an understanding, and Oscar was in the office, caressing weird discords out of an ancient accordion, when Henry and Judge came from the inquest.

"When Ay am happy Ay like to play de skveeze-organ," he told Henry.

"Happy?" queried Henry, hanging his sombrero on a nail.

"Yah, su-ure. Ay explained everyt'ing to Yosephine."

"That is mighty interesting, Oscar. But it would seem that the explanation should have come from Josephine."

"It vars from Yosephine. She t'ought Ay vars a ghost."

"Oh, my goodness! A ghost of whom?"

"De ghost of a man Yosephine saw long time ago. He vars very smort and he vore a tall hat. She say Ay look yust like him."

"Who was the man?" queried Henry.

"Villiam Yennings Bryan."

"Well," choked Henry, "there is a—er—certain resemblance. You both have two arms and two legs."

"Yah, su-ure. But ve are not going to elope next time. Ay put my fute down on it. Ay say to her, 'Yosephine, next time dere vill be no monkey business, you bet you. You vill marry me in cold blood. You vanted romance, and all Ay got vars a ruined suit, a lot of bomps, and a busted ladder. Next time Ay vill run de shindig myself.'"

"Good for you!" Henry applauded, wiping his eyes. "I salute you, Oscar."

"T'ank you, Hanry. Now, how far on de odder side of Scorpion Bend is Niagara Falls?"

"Well, I—how far? Oh, possibly twenty-five hundred miles."

"Yumpin' Yudas! Every time Ay open my mouth, Ay get a fute in it!"

"SANDY" CRANE rode up to where a small crew of men were building a loading corral on the Circle M spread, and dismounted from his nervous horse. The sight of building activity, the rattle of hammers, did not soothe the fretful disposition of that half-broke sorrel. Sandy gave the animal a little extra footage on the tie-rope and rolled a cigarette.

Sandy was young, tall and gaunt, with sad brown eyes and a wide mouth. His nickname had been shortened from Sandhill. When Laura Morris married Dusty Cole and sold the Circle M to Peter Hatton, she purchased the Bar N, with the intention of raising fancy stock. Because Sandy and Dusty were closer than the famed Damon and Pythias, it was natural that Sandy should stay with the Bar N. Sandy heard that the railroad company had built a siding on the Circle M; so he rode over, neighborly-like, to take a look at it.

Sandy was upset over the killing of Johnny Brent and Shep Hart. Sandy liked them both—and he didn't exactly cotton to Jim Patterson. Sandy always rode with a Winchester on his saddle because he had little faith in certain brands of humanity.

With his sombrero tilted low over his eyes he surveyed the construction. The foreman climbed down and came over near him.

"Like to see somebody?"

Sandy looked him over soberly, nodded shortly. "Yea-a-ah."

"Who?"

"George Washin'ton," replied Sandy.

"George Washington? You—you mean the original George Washington?"

"Yea-a-ah."

"He's been dead for years and years, feller."

"Uh-huh. But that don't stop me from wantin' to see him, does it?"

"Oh, I see." The foreman turned, wiped his brow with his sleeve and spat dryly. "You ain't with the Circle M, are you?" he asked.

"Yuh hadn't ort to say 'ain't'. You should say am not. No, yo're right—I ain't with no Circle M; I'm with the Bar N. How's all yore folks—and what was yuh before yuh started carpenterin'?"

"What's that got to do with it?" demanded the foreman.

"That loadin'-chute," explained Sandy. "It's wide enough for a cow to turn around in. The the'ry of a loadin'-chute—"

Sandy paused and turned his head. From a mile or so away came the whistle of a locomotive. Instinctively Sandy drew the restless broncho closer, taking a firm grip on the tie-rope.

"Don't reckon my steed ever met a train," he said, grinning widely. "You better move, pardner, 'cause this might be a merry-go-round in a minute."

The carpenter foreman moved quickly back to work, as an ore train came rumbling down through a cut, cars swaying from side to side. The road-bed was new and badly in need of ballast. Sandy's terrorized horse was dragging him in a circle, as the train rattled and clanked to a stop, with the caboose opposite the new corral. A grimy brakeman, with a valise in each hand, climbed down, while behind him came a girl, wearing a gray suit. He helped her down, waved a signal to the fireman, and the train rumbled away.

THE GIRL looked all around, ignored the carpenters, who had ceased work to look at her, and came out toward Sandy, who had his horse under control again. Sandy got one close look at her, drew a deep breath and fumbled for his hat. She was the most beautiful woman he had ever seen.

"How do you do?" she said smiling.

"Well—howdy, ma-am," replied Sandy, eloquently. "I—I wasn't expectin' a lady."

"Mr. Hatton received my wire, didn't he?"

"Why, I—I dunno if he did or not, ma'am. Yuh see, I ain't—am not—"

"You are from the Circle M, are you not?"

"No, ma'am, I ain't—I are not from the Circle M. Yuh see, I wish I was."

The girl laughed and looked around. "How far is it to the Circle M ranch house, Mr.—?"

"Crane, ma'am. Sandy Crane. The ranch house? Why, it's 'bout five miles, as the crow flies. Around the road it's mebbe seven."

"Since I can't fly," she said, "it would mean a long walk. I can't understand why Mr. Hatton did not meet me."

"You—you ain't Pete Hatton's wife, are yuh?"

"You are quite a hand at guessing, Mr. Crane." She smiled. "How about me being his daughter?"

"Gee, that'd shore be great."

Sandy noticed a cloud of dust across the mesquite-covered mesa, and pointed it out to the girl.

"Looks like somebody comin' from the Circle M," he said. "Yeah, that's what she is. A buckboard, with the team on the run. Mebbe yore train was ahead of time."

"After riding in that caboose all the way from Scorpion Bend, I doubt that it is ever ahead of time."

"I've rode it," grinned Sandy. "Yuh have to spur the seat and hang onto leather. Well, here's yore buggy, Miss Hatton."

Peter Hatton whirled the buckboard team in a circle and came to a stop near them. Sandy got the valises, while the girl went over to the buckboard. Peter Hatton looked keenly at the tall cowboy, as he stacked the valises in the back. Then he swung the team around and drove away in a flurry of dust, without so much as a thank-you to Sandy Crane.

Sandy stood there, looking after them, a puzzled expression in his eyes. One of the carpenters laughed shortly and Sandy whirled around, but the men were all busy. None of them looked in his direction. Sandy had never met Hatton; just knew him by sight. He climbed into his saddle, spurred across the track and headed south.

"That's jist another hombre I don't like," he told his horse. "He might at least have kissed her, I'll bet I would. Purty as a june-bug's ear. Cowboy, you've got somethin' worth dreamin' about."

SANDY STOPPED at Tonto City, intending to tell Henry about the arrival of Peter Hatton's beautiful daughter, but Henry and Judge were out at the JP ranch. Henry impressed on Jim Patterson that the visit was in no way official as they sat on the big front porch of the rambling old ranch house.

"I'm not sayin' anythin'," Patterson declared. "There ain't a damn bit of evidence against me; so why should I talk about it?"

"Everybody liked Johnny Brent," Judge offered.

"I didn't!" Patterson snapped.

"At least, you are frank, sir," Henry remarked. "What puzzles me is that only Brent and Hart were killed. From the number of shots they fired, I am rather surprised that there were so few fatalities."

"Wild shootin', I reckon," Patterson growled.

"Bugs" Taylor, the cocky little horse-wrangler of the JP, sauntered up to the porch, grinned at Henry and Judge and sat down on the steps.

He rolled a cigarette carefully, reached in his pocket and drew out something that glittered. Henry craned his neck. The shiny object was a brass shotgun-shell. In fact, it was two shotgun shells, a ten-gauge and a twelve-gauge, which Bugs had fitted together, making a match-safe.

"Kinda cute, eh?" he chuckled, holding it up for all to see. "Lotta old twelve-gauge shells around here, but I had a hard time findin' a ten. It shore makes a watertight matchbox."

Henry glanced sharply at Jim Patterson, whose face was tense, his narrow-lidded eyes fastened on the back of Bugs' neck. Brass ten-gauge shotgun-shells—like the ones in the shotgun that murdered Johnny Brent. Bugs put it back in his pocket and leaned back, puffing on his cigarette.

"Possibly you are right, Patterson," remarked Henry.

"About what?" queried Patterson quietly.

"Wild shooting."

"Oh, there is no doubt of it," said Judge quickly. "I am afraid it is going to be an unsolved mystery, gentlemen. Henry, I suggest that we ride back home before that sun gets too hot."

"I—I believe it would be a wise move," Henry agreed.

A mile down the road, Henry chuckled thoughtfully. Judge looked at him curiously and said:

"I should be pleased to learn of anything funny that may have occurred to you." His mouth was filled with lemons.

"Your suggestion that we ride home before the sun gets too hot. The hottest part of our day is around noon. It is now four o'clock, and at least ten degrees cooler than at noon."

"I was feeling the heat very much, Henry."

"Increased no doubt by the sight of that brass shell, Judge."

"And the expression on Jim Patterson's face. He could have gladly wrung Bugs Taylor's neck. I—I rather expected you to take the shells away from Bugs—as vital evidence."

"As a matter of fact, you thought nothing of the kind. You were *afraid* I might. I'll wager that by this time Bugs Taylor is shy one matchbox, and that eager eyes are searching out every brass shell on the JP."

"And we had the evidence in our grasp, Henry."

"Quite right, sir. The only obstacle would have been Jim Patterson's forty-five. Judge, I am not a hero. Marching bands and flying colors fail to bring a lump into my throat. I might, if properly drafted, die for my country. But, damme, sir, I absolutely refuse to die for my county. That doesn't cover enough territory."

"I know, Henry. But it only strengthens my belief that you are—well, a bit timid."

"If you want the truth, and are willing to admit your share of the episode, I would say that we were both scared stiff, Judge."

"Yes, I believe you have expressed it quite correctly, Henry. But the fact still remains that more and more the evidence points to the JP outfit as the killers of those two men."

Henry nodded thoughtfully. "I believe you are right, Judge; the country does need rain. A brush-fire at this time of year might ruin all of Wild Horse Valley. Yes, you are entirely right, sir."

"I surrender," sighed Judge. "If I carried a sword, I would pass it to you—hilt first, sir."

"If you carried a sword," declared Henry, "we would not be riding together, Judge—because you wouldn't know the hilt from the point."

CHAPTER IV

HE TOLD THE stage-driver that his name was Albert Novelle, and he tried to induce the driver to drink from a bottle with him. But the road from Scorpion Bend to Tonto City required sober, steady nerves; and Albert Novelle drank alone. Albert was young, dressed to the point of dudishness, and as the stage-driver expressed it, "Didn't know a chuckwalla from a chuckhole."

Albert arrived in Tonto City during the siesta period, and went to the Picador Bar, a cantina frequented mostly by the Latin element. This was odd. Most strangers would have found the Tonto Saloon more convenient to the coach-station, whereas the Picador was hardly visible at fifty yards.

"Frijole" Bill Cullison, together with Thunder and Lightning Mendoza, had come in from the JHC ranch that afternoon, driving a pair of half-broken horses to the ranch buckboard. Frijole did the driving, Not because he was any good, but because Thunder and Lightning were the worst drivers in Arizona. Thunder and Lightning were in the Picador Bar, gulping tequila, when Albert Novelle sauntered in.

"Buenas tardes, señor," Lightning greeted affably. Albert's eyes took in the cool interior of the place.

"Good afternoon, gentlemen," he replied a trifle shakily. Albert had taken over a pint of liquor during his stage-ride; and now he was inclined to be affable and patronizing.

"What is the best drink the place affords?" he asked, leaning against the bar and eyeing the bottles on the back-bar closely.

"The best for dreenkeeng ees tequila," declared Lightning. "You do not onnerstand dreenkeeng tequila?"

"You swallow it, do you not?"

"For sure. Firs' you take leetle beet salt on the hand—so. Leek heem off the hand, then take the leeker een your face— so. *Mucho bueno.*"

Albert grinned and reached for the salt dish. "Fill 'em up," he told the bartender.

Tequila does not taste as potent as it really is. Neither does it manifest its powers at once. It lurks rather deceitfully in one's interior. After imbibing five or six drinks of tequila, Albert merely grew a little more patronizing.

"Where," he asked, "is the Circle M ranch?"

"Firs'," explained Lightning, "you do not go south, because those ees the wrong way for going."

"East ees jus' as good for wrong going," added Thunder.

"It seems," hiccoughed Albert, "that we have north and west left."

"Take your peek," Lightning shrugged. "One ees wrong."

"Before we draw the grand prize in this guessing contest, suppose we have another drink?" suggested Albert. "Fill 'em up, bartender."

THAT ONE drink became several. Albert was a lavish host, and the two Mexicans were entirely willing to be thus entertained. Suppertime came and passed. Frijole Bill, deep in a draw-poker game at the Tonto, forgot the passage of time. By nine Novelle and the two Mexicans were magnificently, and certainly complacently, under the influence.

Albert had long since confided that he was a college graduate; that he couldn't remember the name of the college; that he had had lots of money all his life; but just now he was fighting for existence. Someone had doublecrossed him. He was supposed to be wealthy—and wasn't. Albert cried a little, especially when Thunder and Lightning sang a song about a cockroach.

After several hours Albert remembered that he had asked the way to the Circle M. But by that time neither Thunder nor Lightning could tell him which way it was.

"I can go to heem," declared Lightning, "but I'm not knowing one way from a hole in the ground."

"I'll give fi' dollars t' anybody who'll take me there," declared Albert.

Lightning grew thoughtful. Five dollars. That was a lot of money. Five dollars to be taken to the Circle M—and it was such a short way. Not over six and a half miles. Crooked road, yes; but what was the difference? Lightning nudged Thunder, who was clinging with both hands to the bar.

"Leesten, lettle brodder, from me," he said. "Togedder we weel take theese *caballero* to the Circle M een the bockboard."

"Sure," agreed Thunder, "and then Frijole Beel weel keel hell out from bot' of you. I am escared—unless I do the driving."

"*Mmmm,*" mused Lightning. *"Por Dios,* we weel bot' do the driving. You tak' one line, I tak' the other. How you fill 'bout those?"

"Sure. You get those fi' dollar firs'."

The advance payment was easily secured, and the three of them managed to get outside, with only one bad jam in the doorway; and Lightning led the way past the Tonto to the hitch-rack. Thunder and Albert got into the buckboard, while Lightning untied the team.

"Whoa!" yelled Thunder, and surged back on the lines.

The half-broke team whoaed to such an extent that they backed one complete circle in the street, during which time Lightning managed to crawl over the rear end. The equipage went out of town, the team galloping wildly, while Lightning, his legs dangling, yelled:

"Alto! Alto! Alto!"

There was no brake on the buckboard, and Thunder's surge on the lines merely loosened the tugs.

"You're goin' li'l fas', are you not?" queried Albert, clinging with both hands. He had long since lost his hat.

"Alto!" yelled Lightning weakly. "Thonder! You are not een the right direction. *Madre de Dios*, we weel all be keeled from dying, you fool—that ees all I hope!"

The flying buckboard rocketed from chuckhole to chuckhole, while Albert clung to Thunder, and Lightning clung to the back of the seat, yelling to Thunder please to stop and consider. It was not through any expert driving that the equipage stayed on the road. In fact, it was too dark for a driver to see all the curves.

A mile of fairly level going gave Lightning an opportunity to figure out some way to get control of those lines. With Thunder humped over, the best he could do was claw at his shirt, only to be bounced madly when they struck more chuckholes.

But now Thunder sagged back, and Lightning threw both arms around his neck in a stranglehold.

"Geeve up those line!" he yelled in Thunder's ear. "Or I squizz!"

At that moment the team left the road and started cross-country, crashing through mesquite and cactus; the buckboard bounced like a tin can tied to the tail of a frightened dog. Down the steep slope, of a swale they went, the skidding vehicle cutting brush like a scythe.

Lightning caught a momentary flash of men around a lighted lantern, before the careening buckboard threw them head over heels into the brush.

MIDNIGHT CAME, and with it went the last of Frijole Bill's wages. "I reckon I'll be goin'," he declared. "In fact, I know blamed well I'll be goin', 'cause I'm tired of tryin' to make a pair of deuces beat two pairs. I guess I'm a born optimist. *Buenas noches.*"

But Frijole had no way of going home, except on foot. The buckboard and team were gone. Frijole went to the Picardor, where the bartender explained that Thunder and Lightning had taken a very rich man to the Circle M.

"He geeve them five dollar," explained the bartender. "Have dreenk?"

Frijole accepted a drink. "You like to go to funerals?" he asked.

"Somebody ees dying?" the bartender asked anxiously.

"Uh-huh. Couple Mexicans. *Hasta luego, amigo.*"

Frijole Bill borrowed a horse and rode out to the Circle M. There were no lights at the ranch house, and neither was there any sign of Thunder, Lightning or the buckboard; so Frijole Bill came back, went into the hotel and awoke Henry and Judge.

"If they worked for me," declared Judge sleepily, "I would kick them all the way to Mexico."

"And I'd help yuh, Judge," Frijole complained.

"You have no idea how tired you would be," yawned Henry.

"But what's to be done?" wailed Frijole. "By this time they've likely wrecked the whole darned thing."

"Then it is too late to do anything," soothed Henry.

"And perhaps killed themselves," added Judge. "Who was this very rich man, Frijole?"

"I dunno. He paid 'em five dollars to take him to the Circle M—and they never got there. The Lord knows where they are. That team wasn't even half-broke. If I ever get my hands on— who's that?"

Someone was coming down the hall toward their open door, heading for the light, it seemed. A moment later Thunder and Lightning halted in the doorway. Bloody and dirty, their clothes in ribbons, they stood there, looking like the victims of a careless hurricane.

Henry rubbed his nose and squinted at the two apparitions. "Talk. One at a time," he said gently. "No use pooling conversation. Lightning, suppose you tell what happened to you."

"One man ees keeled," whispered Lightning.

"The rich man?" asked Judge.

"Was he reech man?" asked Lightning.

"How in the devil do I know?" Judge blurted out. "There were only three of you—and neither of *you* is dead."

"Pretty queeck, I theenk," groaned Thunder.

"That's right," said Frijole. "Pretty quick—y'betcha."

"Come in and shut that door, before you wake the hotel," commanded Henry. "All right, now, who got killed, Lightning?"

"I don't know heem," replied Lightning, "He ees stranger from me."

"Begin at the beginning," ordered Judge. "You are unintelligible."

"There ees no begeening, Judge," stated Lightning. "The man ees geeve us five dollar for taking heem to the Circle M."

"Well, where in the devil did you take him?" asked Frijole.

Lightning shrugged his shoulders. "I theenk not," he replied.

"Very likely not," agreed Judge. "Where is that man?"

"*Quien sabe?* The damn bockboard upset in the brush. I find Thunder on hees head in mesquite. We never find those bockboard. Then we find the man who ees dead. The lantern ees gone, but I have match and—"

"What lantern?" queried Henry.

"I don't know—ees gone."

"All right. You used a match to look at the dead rnan."

"*Por Dios,* how you know those?"

"You just said you did. Was it the man you started to take to the Circle M?"

"No, theese ees deefferent dead man."

"Different dead man?" queried Henry. "Were you making a collection? How many, in all?"

Lightning looked at Thunder. "How many you see, my leetle brodder?"

"Seex or seven," declared Thunder. "All dead."

"I think he's crazy!" snorted Frijole.

"Where did all this happen?" asked Henry. "Can you take us to the spot?"

The two Mexicans looked at each other. Thunder said, "I don't theenk it was."

"Well, we seem headlocked. Frijole, get a room for those two, and one for yourself. In the morning we may be able to puzzle out where they went and what happened."

"I hope," said Lightning.

"You *hope?*" snorted Frijole. "What do yuh hope?"

"I hope I leeve that long."

CHAPTER V

EARLY NEXT MORNING Sandy Crane, coming to town from the Bar N, found Albert Novelle wandering dazedly along the road. Albert was no longer handsome and dapper. His suit was ruined, his hat gone, and his face scratched, gouged and bumped. One eye was swollen almost shut.

Sandy drew rein and eyed the wreckage critically. Albert seemed totally indifferent to his careful scrutiny. Albert gave the impression of no longer caring.

"Yo're a mess, feller," Sandy told him. "How old are yuh?"

"I'm twenty-two," replied Albert in a dreary monotone, and sounded as if he could give Methuselah cards and spades.

"How on earth didja manage to git in such a shape in such a short len'th of time?" queried Sandy soberly. "My, my, you must have started poppin' brush early in life. Gotta name?"

"I am Albert Novelle."

Sighing, Sandy drew his left foot from the stirrup. "Hook a toe in there and pile up behind me, Albert, and I'll take yuh to Tonto City."

"I have never been on a horse," said Albert. "I do not believe I could climb up there. I've had a terrible night."

"Insomnia?" queried Sandy. "Mebbe yuh drank too much coffee."

"Coffee!" Albert's laughter was bitter. "Have you ever drank tequila? You place a little salt—"

"I know," interrupted Sandy. "Where'd you drink it? Never

mind; it don't make any difference. Git on behind me and we'll go bye-bye."

"I—I wonder if I could? Really, I am shattered from walking."

"Yeah? Well, git on."

Between the efforts of two of them, Albert managed to straddle the horse behind the saddle, and they went on toward Tonto City.

"I am looking for the Circle M," Albert explained.

"Yea-a-ah? The hell yuh are! Huh! Say, do you know Peter Hatton's daughter?"

"I—I don't even know Peter Hatton. I wish to find Jane Laird."

"Jane Laird? Never heard of her. Do yuh have to wish?"

"I do not believe I understand."

"Neither do I, Albert. But what are you doin' out here in the hills this mornin'—lookin' like yuh do?"

"Last night," explained Albert, "I hired two Mexicans to take me to the Circle M. At least, I dimly remember such an arrangement. But it seems that the team ran away and—"

"Thunder and Lightnin'?"

"Why, yes, that is their names."

"Oh-oh! There goes another JHC buckboard. So you hired them two, eh?"

"Was I wrong in doing that?" queried Albert. "I—I meant no wrong."

"Jes' foolish," said Sandy. "Here comes a reception committee."

A cavalcade composed of Henry, Judge, Oscar, Frijole Bill, Thunder and Lightning came around a curve in the road. Sandy drew off the road and waited for them.

"*Por Dios*, there he ees!" yelled Lightning, pointing at Albert. He screamed his delight at the reunion.

"Oh, hello," said Albert, wincing.

"I picked him up back here a ways," explained Sandy. "Says he wants to get out to the Circle M."

"Same theeng like las' night, eh?" grinned Lightning.

"Keep your nose out of this, Lightning," Judge ordered. "You've had too much to say."

Albert introduced himself to the white-haired sheriff.

"Mr. Novelle," said Henry, "have you any idea where you—er—busted up last night?"

"I haven't the least idea," replied Albert. "I know we did, though."

"I see. Yes, the evidence points to that fact. Did you see a dead man?"

"Dead man? Was there a dead man?"

"I hope not. Did you see a lantern?"

"A lantern? Well, I saw a bright light, but it was more like—well, like a pyrotechnic display."

"It's shore an education—jist a-ridin' with him," said Sandy.

"As a matter of fact, you do not know what happened," said Judge.

"I'm afraid you are right," sighed Albert. "I had no idea that tequila was so powerful."

"You may as well take him to town, Sandy," said Henry. "His grips are at the hotel. The stage-driver did not know what else to do with them."

"I'll try and git him there, Henry. Somebody ort to take him out to the Circle M, before he starts bouncin' off into the brush again."

"Oh, I'm docile now," Albert assured him, smiling wearily.

THE SHERIFF'S cavalcade found the spot where the careening buckboard left the road, and it was an easy matter to follow the tire-furrows into the deep swale, where the occupants had left the vehicle. They found the buckboard, upside down in the brush, little the worse for its wild voyage through the mesquite. Pieces of harness indicated that the horses went right ahead.

Here they found what seemed to be a half-dug grave, but there was no corpse. On top of the pile of dirt was the circular indentation of a lantern-bottom. Henry pointed it out to the others as evidence that Lightning had been right—for once in his life.

Frijole, Lightning and Thunder went on, hunting for the horses, while Judge, Henry and Oscar rode back to Tonto City. Albert had taken a room at the hotel, where he cleaned up, changed clothes and bought Sandy a drink.

"Tell me somethin' about this here Jane Laird," Sandy suggested.

"I really know nothing about her," replied Albert. "Queer, isn't it?"

"Lotsa women I don't know—and it never struck me as bein' queer."

"But I was supposed to marry this one—when I became of age."

"And you don't even know her?"

"I haven't seen her since we were ten years old."

"I'll be a stepchild to a sidewinder!"

"We were betrothed at ten."

"Are yuh sure she's at the Circle M?"

"Reasonably sure, yes."

"Uh-huh. Albert, did I tell yuh about Peter Hatton's daughter?"

"I believe you mentioned her. What about her?"

"I ain't been able to sleep since I seen her—and everythin' tastes alike to me. You want to go to the Circle M, don'tcha? Well, so do I. If I took yuh out there—I might see this yere angel that flew into my life—off an ore train. Let's wait until the cool of the evenin'. No use ridin' in the heat."

"You are manna from Heaven," said Albert.

"I'm Crane from New Mexico," corrected Sandy. "Well, here's to both of your back teeth—may they stand the shock."

PETER HATTON answered a knock on the ranch house door that evening, and scowled with surprised annoyance at sight of his visitor, Samuel Eckles, attorney-at-law from a small Wyoming town. He closed the door and listened to the departure of the horse and buggy that Eckles had hired to bring him from Tonto City. Eckles tossed his hat to the table and sat down in a rocker. Eckles was small, emaciated, with a hooked nose, very little hair, and a wise expression.

"Of all the cursed, dusty, rough trips I ever had!" he snorted.

Hatton glanced toward the stairway and came closer to Eckles. "Why did you come here?" he asked roughly.

"Has Albert Novelle been here yet?" asked the lawyer.

"Novelle? No. What about him, Sam?"

"He came to see me. Some fool told him that Jane Laird was on her way down here. He demands an accounting of his father's estate—and he's no fool, Pete. Where's Jane?"

"Upstairs. Keep yore voice lower. I've been tryin' to get her to go home. I told her to go and talk to you, 'cause I didn't have anythin' to do with it. Claims she has been robbed."

"So does Albert Novelle," sighed the lawyer. "Blame it, they won't listen to reason."

"Make 'em listen. It was yore scheme."

"Albert Novelle insinuates that his father was murdered. He wants to talk with Jane. He—he told me that I was a crook, and that he'll send me to the penitentiary."

"Well, that's true, Sammy," grinned Hatton. "I'm in the clear. I've got a deed to everything—and you've got to depend on my word to give you a square deal. If anybody goes to the penitentiary—it won't be me."

"You'd doublecross me, Pete?"

"I'd doublecross anybody, Sammy. This is my chance for a stake, and I'm goin' to keep it. If Novelle comes to me, I'll refer him to you."

"You can't do this to me, Pete Hatton," breathed Eckles. "I own half this ranch. I own half of everything."

"Try and get it," replied Hatton, sitting down across a small table from the white-faced lawyer. "You didn't dare show any of the papers. Crooked, but cautious, that's you, Sammy. I'm not sayin' that you killed Jim Laird, 'cause I can't prove it. But I had enough on yuh to drive yuh into a corner and make yuh play the game my way. Now, I've got all the chips on my side of the table; so what's the answer?"

"Pete, you wouldn't do that to me," whined Eckles. "Why, I came all the way down here to warn you against Novelle. I can handle him, but"—Eckles leaned across the table, his jaw tensed—"but before I do that, you've got to play the game my way. One word of what you are going to do—and you're through. They'd hang you, my swell-headed friend. There's law in Wild Horse Valley—but it wouldn't help you one bit."

"I see," nodded Hatton coldly. "You threaten to tell, eh? Yes, I'm afraid you might, Sammy. It is something I've wondered about."

"Novelle might tell, too," said Eckles. "Jane might tell."

"That's right," agreed Hatton coldly. "They *might*—but you *would*."

Sam Eckles got slowly to his feet, facing Hatton. "You understand me perfectly, Hatton," he said quietly. "You will play square with me—or I'll ruin your game in Wild Horse Valley."

"Is that yore last word, Sammy?" queried Hatton.

"That is my last word," replied Eekles firmly. His eyes were quick. They saw his danger—but there wasn't time enough to do anything but gasp....

THE RANCH house shuddered from the concussion of Hatton's forty-five, shot from under the table-top. Eckles' body, jackknifed from the shock of the bullet, fell forward, half under the table.

Hatton was on his feet. A door banged upstairs. Hatton jerked forward and blew out the lamp. From the darkness at the head of the stairs came a woman's voice: "What's happened?"

Peter Hatton laughed shortly. "My gun fell off the bed and hit on the hammer. Nobody hurt, my dear. Sorry if I woke yuh up."

"I thought I heard voices a while ago."

"That was Len. He came to ask me somethin'."

Hatton listened for the closing of the upstairs door before he moved. Without lighting the lamp, he dragged Eckles' body out on the porch, then carried it down beside the stable, where he left it. Then he went to the bunk-house. All the crew were at Tonto City. By the light of a lamp he examined himself carefully, but there was no blood on his clothes.

Someone in Tonto City must know that Eckles had come to the ranch, but in case of an investigation he could say that his men had taken Eckles back to Scorpion Bend. Just what to do with the body was a problem; he decided to wait until the boys came home. Mopping his head, he went back to the bunk-house.

Peter Hatton did not know that Sandy Crane and Novelle were sitting on the corral fence out there in the darkness. They had arrived just ahead of Sammy Eckles in the livery-rig, and Albert had seen Eckles in the light from the doorway.

Sandy had secured a horse for Albert—a staid old plug. After Eckles entered the house, they tied their steeds to the corral fence to wait a while before announcing their arrival. They had heard the shot, and later had seen Novelle carry his victim down to the stable.

"Do you really suppose he killed him?" Albert whispered.

"Yeah, I reckon," replied Sandy. "But you didn't like him, anyway."

"I know—but murder—Sandy."

"Yeah. Do yuh know, I never shot a man that I didn't have it on my conscience for hours afterward. That's why I never was a success as a killer—I've got a conscience."

"Don't you think we should notify the police, Sandy?"

"The which? Police? Oh, yeah. But there's no hurry. While I'm out here, I'd shore like to see Miss Hatton. And you want to see Jane Laird."

"I—I do not believe I—well, don't you realize that murder has been done? We should do something—at once, too."

"*Sh-h-h-h!* Not so loud. He might take a shot at us."

"That is true. Let us go back to town, Sandy."

"Uh-huh. Well, let's go down and take a look at the corpse."

"No, no, no!"

"All right, I'll do the lookin', Albert. C'mon. I know right where he left it."

They climbed down and made their way carefully to the stable. The body was no longer there. They circled the stable, but there was no sign of it.

"Didja ever hear of such dang fools?" marveled Sandy.

"Who—us?" Albert queried.

"Sure. There ain't no corpse. Yuh see what yore mind can do to yuh? Blamin' an innocent man. Yore lawyer is prob'ly in bed in the house."

Albert sighed. "I still do not want to go to that house tonight."

"Write yore own ticket," said Sandy. "C'mon."

As they reached their horses they heard Hatton leave the bunk-house and go back to the ranch house. After he closed they door and lighted a lamp in the main room, they rode away from the ranch.

On the way to town they met the four cowboys from the Circle M, but drew aside to let them pass. Hatton was waiting for his boys, and drew Len Stryker aside to tell him what happened.

"We'll handle it all right," said Len. "There won't be any slips on this'n. Where'd yuh say yuh put him?"

"I'll show yuh, Len. All the others need to know is that a man died."

Peter Hatton took Len down beside the stable, but the corpse had not returned. Hatton cursed viciously. "The skunk played possum! Len, we've got to stop him. Get the boys together— we're goin' to Tonto City and see that he don't talk. C'mon."

IT WAS about an hour before daylight when someone knocked on the door of the sheriff's office, waking Oscar Johnson. Oscar listened sleepily to the visitor, whom he left in the office, while he went to arouse Henry. Both Henry and Judge being heavy sleepers, Oscar had nearly to tear down the door of their room at the hotel.

"Ay yust vish to say," Oscar stated, "that a man is at de office, and he vishes to speak vit de shoriff."

"My goodness—at this hour," yawned Henry. "What is his business?"

"Ay didn't ask him," replied Oscar, "but Ay t'ink he has been testing out de inside of a threshing machine. He looks veak, and he is hoomped up, like he has belly-ache. He say somet'ing about bullet in de belt-bockle."

Henry reached hastily for his boots.

"Did he give his name, Oscar?"

"De man is not in shape to give anyt'ing, Henry. He looks like all de vind had been knocked out of him, and he can't get it back."

"Interesting, Judge," observed Henry. "An epidemic…"

They dressed hurriedly, clattered down the stairs, and headed for the office. But it was empty.

"Are you sure you did not dream it, Oscar?" Henry inquired.

Oscar scratched his head foolishly. "Ay don't t'ink so, Hanry."

"He said he would wait for you?" Judge demanded.

"Yah, su-ure. Ay never saw de man before. By yimminy, Ay vonder if it vars a dream. De son-of-a-gon, he look yust as natural. Ay—vell, by golly, he ain't here."

"Bullet in the belt-buckle!" snorted Judge.

"Wait a minute!" Henry exclaimed. Half under the corner of his desk was an envelope, addressed to *Samuel Eckles, Attorney-at-law, Bender, Wyoming*. Inside was a letter.

"Eckles—Eckles—Eckles?" queried Henry.

"Yust like a hen," remarked Oscar.

"Someone must have dropped this recently," said Henry. "I know no one named Samuel Eckles. Listen to this, Judge."

Dear Sir:

Your letter of the 12th was a painful surprise, but not exactly convincing. For that reason I am making a trip to your town.

I can't believe that my father died broke and that there is nothing left of the estate. In fact, it looks fishy to me. You say that before he died he turned all his assets over to Jim Laird. Why? There must be a reason. My father was a conservative business man.

For years the Laird and Novelle interests have been the largest of their kind in that state. You also say that Jim Laird died shortly after my father's demise, and that it was discovered that the estate of Jim Laird had dwindled to a paltry few dollars.

Well, I demand an accounting. I want to know just why my father did not leave a cent. You say that Jane Laird's share of her father's estate did not exceed a few thousand dollars. I intend to contact Jane Laird, and between us I expect we will ferret out the truth. Expect me in about ten days.

Very truly yours,
Albert Novelle.

"Nothing very enlightening about that letter," Judge said, frostily.

"Yust might have been dropped by de man who vars here," suggested Oscar.

"You may be right, Oscar," nodded Henry. "The letter was sent from Chicago on the seventeenth of this month. The contents means nothing to us. I haven't any idea who Samuel Eckles may be, of course."

"I suggest that we go to bed, Henry." Judge yawned.

"Meeting adjourned." Henry nodded. "If he shows up again, Oscar—sit on his head and yell."

SANDY CRANE took Albert Novelle to the Bar N for the night, Next morning they rode out to the Circle M again. Albert was sure that Jane Laird came to the Circle M—and he had recognized Sam Eckles. Albert had talked with Eckles in Wyoming, but the lawyer had not mentioned that he was coming to Tonto City.

"Somethin' fishy," Sandy declared. "We heard the shot fired, Albert. And we both saw a man carryin' somethin' down to the stable. 'Course it was too dark to see what he had, but—well, jussasame—"

Hatton met them on the front porch and Albert introduced himself.

"How do you do?" Hatton nodded coldly. "What is yore business?"

"I came to see Jane Laird."

Hatton's brows lifted slightly. "Yo're a little late, Mr. Novelle. Miss Laird is on her way to Scorpion Bend. One of my men took her and Mr. Eckles, a lawyer, in a buckboard. They didn't want to ride an ore-train caboose."

"Yuh can't blame 'em for that." Sandy grinned. "I've tried it. How's yore daughter standin' the heat, Mr. Hatton?"

"My daughter? I haven't any daughter."

"Huh?" grunted Sandy. "Why—uh—you remember meetin' her over at the sidin', don'tcha?"

"Oh, yeah," smiled Hatton. "That was Miss Laird."

"Well, I'll be a stepchild to a sidewinder!" snorted Sandy. "She said she was—well, what do yuh know about that?"

"Did Miss Laird say where she was going?" asked Albert.

"I believe she was going to New York," replied Hatton. "Mr. Eckles was goin' with her as far as Chicago."

"We," said Sandy, "are not interested in Eckles."

"Perhaps I am," remarked Albert. "I want to get my hands on that crooked little shyster—when there are no police around."

"He is Miss Laird's lawyer, I hear," said Hatton. "Dunno much about him myself."

"You are very fortunate, Mr. Hatton," said Albert. "Good morning, sir."

They rode back to Tonto City, where Sandy introduced Albert

to Henry and Judge. It was evident to them that Albert was the writer of the letter they had found in the office, but neither of them mentioned it.

"Do you," queried Henry, "know a lawyer by the name of Eckles?"

"I certainly do," replied Albert firmly. "I went out to the Circle M this morning and they told us that Eckles was on his way back to Scorpion Bend."

Sandy grinned slowly, his eyes squinted in deep thought.

"Just what is in the back of your mind, Sandy?" queried Henry.

SO SANDY CRANE told them what happened at the Circle M last night, but first he told about meeting the girl at the train—the girl who intimated that she was Peter Hatton's daughter. Henry said to Albert:

"Just why did Jane Laird come here to see Peter Hatton?"

"I haven't any idea, Mr. Conroy. A man in Bender, Wyoming, told me that she had gone to Tonto City. He said it was her ranch—but I guess he was mistaken; it belongs to Peter Hatton."

"And why did you come here—merely to be with Miss Laird?"

Albert Novelle told his story to Henry and Judge. Judge paced the floor, his brow furrowed in thought.

"The firm name was Laird and Novelle?" he asked.

"That is right, Mr. Van Treece."

"By dad, I remember it now! Lair and Novelle. Sheep!"

"The biggest sheep outfit in the state," added Albert.

"Just where does Peter Hatton come in?" queried Henry. "Why did Jane Laird come to see Peter Hatton?"

"Jane Laird might be able to answer that question," said Albert.

"She's shore beautiful," sighed Sandy, "but she lied to me."

"And," continued Henry, "you boys thought that Peter Hatton shot Eckles and dumped his body beside the stable."

"I reckon we imagined too much," grinned Sandy.

"Evidently," mused Henry. "Well, I wish you luck, Mr. Novelle."

After they left the office, Henry and Judge looked thoughtfully at each other.

"We know," said Henry, "that Eckles hired a livery rig in which to ride to the Circle M. The driver came back alone. Sandy and his companion imagine that Eckles was shot and killed at the Circle M. At an ungodly hour this morning, Oscar tells us of a small man who looked as though he had been through a threshing-machine, and who needs the services of a sheriff. But the man is gone, leaving a letter on the floor. Now we hear that someone from the Circle M has taken him to Scorpion Bend, along with a beautiful, but untruthful lady, who is on her way to New York. It doesn't make sense, Judge. If the man was in the condition as described by Oscar, how on earth did he get back to the Circle M—and why would he go back there?"

"We," reminded Judge, "can only concern ourselves with cases where the law has been violated, Henry. As far as I can see, nothing wrong has been done. We cannot constitute ourselves as guardian angels for this elusive Mr. Eckles; and it is no crime for a beautiful woman to lie to a cowpuncher. They all do it, I believe."

"You have taken a weight off my mind, Judge," said Henry solemnly. "I would buy a drink."

"I feel that it is about time we got back to normal, Henry."

CHAPTER VI

IT WAS ABOUT noon next day when Henry and Judge rode up to what had been Johnny Brent's ranch house. Somehow it had managed to burn itself to a huge heap of cold ashes. Henry had suggested a search of the ranch house to see if they might find any clue as to the cause of the battle.

They dismounted and walked around the ruins. Every timber and shingle of the place had been consumed. The stable and sheds had not been injured, nor had the fire spread to any of the surrounding brush.

"Mighty funny," remarked Judge. "Mighty funny, Henry." He looked like a man who has just found a snake in his bedroll.

"Not funny, Judge—queer. Note the heap of ashes in what was the center of the room. That would indicate that all the furniture had been stacked in the center. I believe I shall do a little wading in the ashes. It is possible that—well, we seem to have visitors, Judge."

Jim Patterson, owner of the JP, and two of his men were riding in behind them, looking curiously at the charred ruins. Patterson nodded coldly as he rode up.

"Place burned down, eh?"

"That is evident," Judge replied coldly. Henry tucked his pants inside his boots, secured a heavy stick, and walked into the ashes. As he poked around in the large pile of ashes, Patterson said to Judge:

"What's he lookin' for?"

Judge shrugged his shoulders. "I wouldn't have any idea, Patterson."

"Fire must have been set," remarked a cowboy. "Nobody livin' here, was they?"

"Not as far as we know," replied Judge.

Henry was very busy now, shoving ashes aside. He turned and called to Judge: "See if there is an old broom in the stable, Judge."

Judge found a worn-out broom in a shed and gave it to Henry, who proceeded to do considerable sweeping. Finally he came back, a grim expression on his usually placid features.

"A man burned in that fire," he said. "The body is mostly consumed, but enough is left to show that it was once a man."

"Someone burned to death?" queried Patterson.

Henry held out his open hand, on which were two small, dark objects.

"Those were in the ashes below the remains, Patterson," he replied. "They are melted bullets—melted out of the body, I believe. That would indicate that the man was dead before the house was fired. Whoever used this as a funeral pyre, piled all the furniture in the center of the house, placed the body on top, and tried to make a complete job of destroying the body. However, the human body requires a lot of heat before it turns to ashes."

Patterson and his two cowboys looked grimly at the two officers. Patterson said, "They'll prob'ly blame me for that, too."

"Are any of your men missing?" queried Judge.

"They are not. Why ask about my men, Judge?"

"Oh, merely curiosity, Jim." Judge looked elaborately disinterested.

"The question is well put, at that," said Henry. "Unless I am mistaken, the dead man who burned in that fire was either killed or wounded in the battle here. They did not dare notify a doctor or the officers—and they had to dispose of the body."

"That sounds reasonable, Conroy," nodded Patterson. "Find out who is missin'. I'll do all I can to help yuh."

"Thank you," said Henry. "I believe our next move is to summon the coroner, before removing the remains. An autopsy might give us a clue as to who the man was. Dentistry is traceable, I believe, and there might be other clues."

Jim Patterson nodded. "I wish yuh luck, Sheriff. If yuh need any help, call at the JP."

THEY RODE on, and in a few minutes Henry and Judge mounted and started back to Tonto City. But they did not go far. Henry led the way off the road, where they concealed their horses, and crawled to a spot where they could overlook the burned building. They could not see Patterson and his cowboys.

"Do you expect them to come back, Henry?" queried Judge.

"If he is guilty—yes, Judge."

But Patterson and his cowboys did not come back; so, after an hour, the two officers went on to Tonto City, where Henry told the prosecutor about what they had found. The coroner had gone to Scorpion Bend and would not be back until late; so they were obliged to postpone further investigation until next day.

Oscar Johnson overheard the conversation, and Oscar told it in the Tonto Saloon. Several men asked Henry about it, but he set his lips and tried to look wiser than he felt. There was wickedness in the Valley; it made Henry very angry, and a little sick. Henry was a crusader born.

Next morning, along with the coroner, they went to Johnny Brent's ranch, but their trip was useless. The huge pile of ashes had been flattened, and the remains were missing.

"Too much information," sighed Henry. "Who was in the saloon when you shot off your mouth, Oscar?"

"Everybody," replied the big Swede. "Ay didn't count 'em."

Judge drew Henry aside. "Perhaps Patterson knew we were watching yesterday, Henry. When we left—well, it isn't a bad theory."

"Just as good as any other, I suppose," smiled Henry. "However, it does prove that a body was burned in that fire."

"Prove? The body was there, Henry."

"Did you see it, sir?"

"No, I—well, I took your word for it. Didn't you find a body?"

"If I had, do you suppose I'd have been foolish enough to leave it for anyone to take away or destroy? I merely *believed* that a body had been burned; the body which was to be buried when those two Mexicans and young Novelle broke up the burial."

"But you found the bullets!"

"Remember, Judge, that house was *full* of bullets, after that war. A sifting of those ashes might disclose half a hundred hunks of melted lead."

Judge nodded solemnly. "But the fact still remains, Henry—that we are no nearer the solution than we were the day it happened."

"Oh, yes, we are—several days nearer. Remember the old saying, 'Murder will out,' Judge? I believe it is true. But I may say, sir, that there is more behind this than the fact that a young man accused a big cowman of rustling calves, and the big cowman threatened him. Damme, sir, I believe I am on the point of a big discovery."

"Perhaps it is the heat," Judge said, with sympathy. "I have known cases where it induced a belief in something like a non-refillable bottle, or perpetual motion. Suppose we ride across country to the JHC. I'm sure that Frijole Bill will be glad to dig up some of his two-day-old prune whisky."

"Yes, I think that would do very nicely, Judge. You are very thoughtful."

After two hours of hard riding they reached the JHC ranch house, where they found Frijole Bill Cullison, half asleep on the shady porch. Frijole Bill was sixty, a skinny, half-pint in size, with a small, lean face and long mustaches. He shut one eye, so as to get the proper focus, and grinned widely.

"Just a word of warning, Frijole," said Judge soberly. "Do not tell us any lies about Bill Shakespeare. If you have anything to drink—"

"Lie about Old Bill?" queried Frijole. "My goodness, Judge! Why, I—sh-h-h-h-h! Go easy and I'll show yuh somethin'. No noise, remember."

Frijole stepped off the porch and moved quietly to the corner, where he motioned to them to go easy. Cautiously they eased their way to the rear of the house. On the back porch, beside the steps, sat a huge, gaunt, gray old rooster, with only an occasional feather decorating his skeletal frame, and one long, ragged feather in his tail. He was fast asleep.

Frijole craned his neck and looked all around. "Bill!" he called quietly. "Bill, whereat's that bobcat?"

"Now, listen, Frijole—" began Judge.

"I left 'em asleep together not more'n ten minutes ago," declared the old cook. "Sweetest sight yuh ever seen. Yuh see, every time Bill Shakespeare got full of prune mash he'd track that wild-cat down and whip hell out of him. Well, sir, I dumped some mash this mornin', and Ol' Bill filled up. I wasn't payin' no attention, until I hears a awful rumpus goin' on out here; so I runs out. Ol' Bill's got too much aboard, and he's done tied into the biggest rattler that ever crawled out of Mummy Canyon.

"Well, sir, I'm shore scared that Bill's done chose too much. This yere whiz-adder is ten, fifteen feet long and as big around as my leg, right at the forks; so I does myself a hop, skip and a jump into the house to git me a gun. But before I get outside agin, I hears a lot of spitting and splutterin'. Yuh don't have to believe me, but there's that big, ol' bobcat a-helpin' Bill Shakespeare tie that rattler in knots. Fact. Returnin' good for evil. I'm shore plumb amazed; so I gets myself another drink, and then I finds them two, Bill and the bobcat, sleepin' side by side on the back porch, jist like a couple little kids. What didja say, Judge?"

"I just cleared my throat," said Judge weakly. "Is there anything left in the jug?"

"Shore. I bottled this mornin'. I never seen anythin' age as quick. Why, yuh can't even git the cork into the jug, before it starts sproutin' gray whiskers. Set down and I'll git a jug."

Frijole hurried away. Henry sat down and mopped his brow. Bill Shakespeare opened one eye, gazed balefully at Henry, but went to sleep again.

"Look!" whispered Judge.

Around the corner of the house came a black-and-white kitten, dragging the remains of an eighteen-inch gopher snake. Henry and Judge looked at each other, and Henry shook his head sadly.

"Our very best lies have a basis of fact," he said.

THE NEXT afternoon Henry sauntered down to the Tonto depot, a rough, unpainted structure, recently completed. It was little used by passengers, because they preferred the stage to a rough-riding caboose at the end of a slow-moving cattle or ore train. Len Stryker, from the Circle M spread, came out and mounted his horse. He nodded curtly to Henry and rode away.

Henry entered the little building and leaned through the ticket window, watching the operator tap out a message.

"I noticed Mr. Stryker leaving," he remarked casually.

The agent nodded and filled his pipe. "The Circle M must be shipping cattle here," he said. "Do you know a man named Eckles, Sheriff?"

Henry pricked up his ears. "What about Mr. Eckles?"

"He must be connected with the Circle M. Stryker brought a telegram, signed by Eckles, ordering a man named Anderson to load and ship immediately. The wire went to Bender, Wyoming."

"Oh," said Henry quietly. "Signed by Mr. Eckles."

"Samuel Eckles," said the agent. "Perhaps he is a buyer."

"Yes—perhaps," agreed Henry. "Getting warm. This new lumber draws the heat."

"And," added the agent, "there isn't enough to do here to forget the heat."

Henry went back to the office and told Judge about the telegram.

"But Eckles has gone to Chicago," said Judge.

"It seems to me," remarked Henry, "that somewhere among the kindling lurks an Ethiopian. Mr. Eckles and a Miss Laird are taken to Scorpion Bend, from which city they proceed eastward. Today Mr. Eckles sends in a signed telegram from the Circle M."

"Possibly he came back, Henry. You're still trying to build a mountain from a molehill. Doggone it, why not go to the Circle M and find out? Saw Sandy Crane and Albert Novelle a while ago. Useless pair of young men. Oscar is with them, adding tone to their uselessness. By the way, Oscar said he was going to ask for a leave of absence, in order to marry Josephine. Personally, I hope they go so far that they cannot come back again."

"I believe I have an idea, Judge!" exclaimed Henry.

"Regarding Oscar?"

"Oscar, my dear Judge, does not require ideas; all he needs is an opportunity. Continue your siesta, while I take a little walk."

Henry went back to the depot, where he spent about fifteen minutes, after which he came back to the office and informed Judge that the sheriff's office was about to indulge in a horse-back ride.

"You are a confounded old fool," complained Judge. "No normal human would ride at this time of day. But that is like you, Henry. No consideration for anyone. I may fry in my own grease, as far as you are concerned."

"I shall be with you, my antiquated weasel, riding between you and the sun, offering as much shade as my meager body may afford."

"The sun," reminded Judge, "will be on our backs."

They rode in at the Circle M. Len Stryker was there, and told them that Hatton was somewhere back in the hills.

"We were coming out this way, anyway," explained Henry blandly, "and the depot agent asked us to deliver two telegrams that came today."

Stryker reached for the telegrams when Henry took them from his pocket, but Henry drew them back.

"You see," he explained to Stryker "these telegrams are special,

and may only be delivered to the proper parties. One for"—
Henry read the names carefully—"one for Jane Laird and the
other for Samuel Eckles."

"Well, I'll tell yuh," said Stryker, "they ain't here now—but I
can see that they get 'em."

"Sorry," said Henry, "but I cannot leave them. I will give
them back to the agent, and he can hold them until the proper
parties call."

"Well, yeah, that's all right, I reckon," said Stryker. "Yuh don't
know who they're from, do yuh?"

"They are sealed," replied Henry, examining the envelope flap.
"No way to determine where they are from, of course."

On the way back, Henry remarked:

"I still feel that everything is not right, Judge. Stryker was
nonplussed for a moment, offered no information regarding
the whereabouts of the two people, and was unduly curious as
to the origin of the two telegrams."

"Such a stupid time of day to deliver telegrams," complained
Judge. "I thought you had an idea. Idea, indeed! I might have
known. The whole sheriff's force, riding in the worst heat of the
day—to act as messenger boys. At times, sir, I really feel that your
brain is weakening. Ideas! Pah! Ride all the way to the Circle
M—delivering telegrams."

"And not be able to deliver them, Judge," added Henry. "All
this long ride—and not even that satisfaction. Continue, sir,
with your castigation, and I will add any small detail you may
have overlooked."

They found Oscar at the office, well-filled with spirits
frumenti, and grinning widely.

"Ay am putting on a party next Thursday night, and Ay vish
to inwite you both," he informed them.

"What sort of a party, Oscar?" queried Henry.

"Va'al, Ay am going to ved mit Yosephine—Ay hope. Ve are
goin' to ved in Scorpion Bend. Ay am inwiting both of you, Free-
holey, Thonder and Lightning, Sandy Crane and dis new faller,

Olbert. Olbert say he vill pay for de sopper, and Free-holey vill furninsh de prune yuice."

"And you," added Judge dryly, "will furnish the bride."

"Ay hope," sighed Oscar. "Ay have had my ops and downs."

"Love is like that, Oscar," said Henry. "Speaking for Judge and myself, we will be greatly honored to attend your marriage. You are very kind."

"Yah, su-ure," grinned Oscar. "Ay am great faller, you bat you."

"Are you going to Niagara Falls?"

"Ay don't know yet, Yudge. Ve talk it over, and Yosephine says if Ay ain't got money enough for both of us to go, she will make de trip and send me a postal-cord. Anyvay, it is only vater going over a tall rock."

"At any rate, Josephine has a sense of humor," remarked Henry. "What minister will perform the ceremony?"

"Ay have been getting prices," said Oscar. "De best deal ve can get is from a Yustice of de Peace. He vants two dollars."

"Close with him at once," advised Judge. "I will pay the justice. What will you do, Henry? If Albert Novelle will pay the supper bill, and I pay the minister, while Frijole furnishes the prune juice—what is left for you to buy?"

"Very likely—a new belt," replied Henry. And added, "For myself."

CHAPTER VII

JOHN CAMPBELL WALKED heavily into the sheriff's office and sat down. Henry tried to put his feet on the desk-top, failed dismally and squinted inquiringly at the prosecutor, while Judge cleared his throat raspingly. They both knew that the commissioners had been in session, and had called John Campbell into their conference.

"I presume that you have read the latest paper from Scorpion Bend," said Campbell. "The leading editorial is—"

"We have," interrupted Judge. "The heading is, I believe, 'Wild Horse Valley—A Murderer's Paradise.' Correct me if I am wrong, sir."

"You are perfectly right, Judge," the lawyer sighed. "I have just finished a long discussion with the commissioners."

"Of course, they resent the slur," said Henry.

Campbell's brows lifted slightly. "I regret to say—they quite agree with the editor, Henry."

"As far as that is concerned—so do I," added Judge grimly.

"Suppose we made it unanimous?" queried Henry. "I hate to be outdone."

"They say that nothing has been done to solve the murders of Johnny Brent, Shep Hart and the unidentified man, cremated in the Brent ranch house fire. Three apparent murders and one of those not even identified."

"In fact," remarked Henry, "my office is getting so damned lax, sir, that we cannot so much as name our dead. I believe that

198

is the common viewpoint. What we need is a crystal ball. But we do know two of the victims, John. I hope the commissioners credit us with that."

"Had I been sheriff," said Judge firmly, "I would have Jim Patterson behind the bars—at least for an official questioning. Did the commissioners suggest such a thing, John?"

"The commissioners haven't any ideas, Judge; they leave that to the law-enforcement officers. They do resent publication—or I might say, reasons for publication of such an editorial."

Henry shook his head sadly. "I am not a man who asks for much. All my life I have gone along my path, perfectly willing that the other man get the breaks, asking little for myself. But if there is anything in luck, or divine favors, all I ask is that some day I find the editor of that paper, with his head caught in a barbwire fence, a section of two-by-four lying handy, and Henry Harrison Conroy arriving on the scene in the same frame of mind as he is at the present moment."

"He said," quoted Judge solemnly, "that the voters of Wild Horse Valley had elected a red nose, only to discover later that even the olfactory nerves had been atrophied from continuous jug-sniffing."

"Judge," reproved Henry, "we have all read it."

"I am sorry, sir. But, damme, the man has a sense of humor. When he says—"

"Judge," interrupted Henry, "you have too much sense of another man's humor, and not enough of your own. You will please excuse him, John."

"Certainly," nodded the lawyer gravely. "But what is to be done, Henry?"

"Rome," replied Henry, "was not built in a day."

"But they say that Nero fiddled, while Rome burned," reminded Judge.

"I am not a fiddler, sir!" snapped Henry. "I lay no claim to—"

Oscar Johnson came in; and Henry stopped to look inquiringly at him.

"Ay vars yust talking vit de depot agent," Oscar stated, "and he said to tell you that he had borglars last night."

"Burglars? My goodness! Pickpockets in Tonto City, next. What did they get, Oscar?"

"He says he can't find anyt'ing missing."

"Some tramp prowler, I suppose," sighed the lawyer.

Henry chuckled quietly. "I feel that Tonto has grown up, John."

"I wish *you* would grow up," said Judge soberly.

"That gives me a real idea," smiled Henry.

"Growing up, sir?"

"No—burglars, Judge."

The prosecutor yawned and got to his feet. "I wish you luck, Henry," he said. "Something should turn up."

"If only our toes," added Henry thoughtfully.

FEW PEOPLE in Tonto City knew that Josephine and Oscar were going to Scorpion Bend to get married, but they did wonder and grin at the cavalcade which went up Main Street. In front were Henry and Judge in the JHC buckboard, drawn by two half-broken steeds, while behind them rode Sandy Crane, Albert Novelle, Frijole Bill, with Thunder and Lightning bringing up the rear, riding a pair of mules.

Judge, clad in rusty black, drove, while beside him, straight and round and dignified, sat Henry Harrison Conroy, clad in a black cutaway, pearl-gray trousers, spats, patent-leather shoes, a black derby hat carefully balanced on his head, his hands clutching a gold-headed cane.

Josephine, who had never ridden on a train, chose to gain her first experience at rail travel by accompanying her groom-elect to Scorpion Bend in the caboose of an ore train, which *might* arrive at its destination at eight o'clock that evening.

"All we need is a gaslight flare, a colored banjo-player and a few bottles of colored water," declared Judge grimly, as they drove out of Tonto City.

"My hair is too short," said Henry. "But, at that, I have always felt that I would have been a success with a medicine show, Judge."

"The three commissioners and the prosecutor were in front of the courthouse, watching our parade."

"Was that where the applause originated?"

"There was no applause, sir," growled Judge. "What you heard was the frightened milling of horses at the Tonto hitch-rack."

"Anyway," sighed Henry, "I doffed my hat, Possibly that is the first time that the Great Conroy ever acknowledged the fright of a broncho."

"I am afraid, sir, that Tonto City looks upon us as a couple of inefficient old fools."

"I appreciate that—all except the 'old,' Judge," replied Henry. "I am not growing old. An occasional twinge of rheumatism, perhaps; but that even attacks the young. My mind is as clear as it was at thirty."

"Fortunately, I did not know you at thirty," said Judge soberly, "so I am unable to draw my own conclusions. But I do know this much—Tonto City would be very pleased if we did not come back."

"I am afraid you exaggerate, sir."

"I would hate to repeat what they are saying about your regime as sheriff of Tonto."

"Then it must be rather bad," sighed Henry. "Outwardly, perhaps, I am not deadly efficient—but inwardly, sir, I am—well, I must grope for a word, if you do not mind. While I am searching my vocabulary, please try and keep the left-hand wheels of this equipage on the grade. I do not care to go to glory, with something unsaid."

"I suppose we will swelter all the way to Scorpion Bend, and then have to wait hours for that ore train to arrive," complained Judge. "I don't see why Oscar did not put his foot down and insist that Josephine make the trip in a buggy."

"I am afraid that Oscar has put his foot down for the last time,

Judge," remarked Henry. "From now on, Josephine's foot will be the one that is put down. His marriage may not be a prison bar, but it is little more than a parole. I feel genuinely sorry for the boy—and I don't care if the train doesn't reach Scorpion Bend in time for the ceremony."

"There is no time element involved, Henry; the justice of the peace lives there."

LATE IN the afternoon, hot, dry and dusty, they reached Scorpion Bend. Henry's splendor was somewhat wilted and grimy.

"Henry, yuh look like a lily that had been drug," said Sandy Crane.

"Just a withered old bouquet," sighed Henry.

"Stand in some water, and mebbe you'll revive," suggested Sandy.

"I never expected to come to that, Sandy. I do believe that a drink or two might at least put a shine on my dusty nose."

Henry gave Thunder and Lightning some money for tequila, while the rest of them repaired to a thirst-emporium.

"Ees Henry getting married?" queried Thunder, as he and Lightning hurried to a saloon.

"Leesten, my lettle brodder," said the very wise Lightning, "you come all the way for a wedding, and I don't know yet who is marrying?"

"Por Dios, I'm theenk we come see fight."

"Fight? Who spiks of fighting?"

"Somebodee ees saying that this weel be fight from night to morning."

"Sure. But when people are married the fight ees legal. Stop talking, and get the face feexed for tequila."

At eight o'clock they all met at the depot to await the coming of Josephine and Oscar. The garrulous depot agent growled:

"It'll get here, when it arrives. That ore train hasn't any schedule."

Thirty minutes later the headlight came in view, the engine

laboring under the drag of the heavy train. Another train pulled in and stopped some distance east of the depot, where a switch would allow them to turn onto the track leading to Wild Horse Valley and Tonto City.

The heavy ore-train rumbled and clanked into the station, drawing the dusty caboose even with the platform. Josephine and Oscar dismounted, tired and dusty, to be greeted warmly by the small crowd.

"Next time Ay will walk," declared Josephine wearily. "Ay never vars so rattled in my life. Yerkety-yerk, boompity-boomp! Sving your pondner! Vedding trip!"

That other train was clanking over the switch, its headlight centering on the platform. Henry turned and watched it, as it came in behind the depot. Lights from the platform illuminated the slow-moving cars. Henry yelled:

"Sheep! Sheep, heading for Tonto City, Judge! Look!"

The crowd whirled around. The cars were not fifty feet away, and the crowded sheep were visible through the slatted sides of the cars.

"Stop it!" yelled Judge. "In the name of the law—"

"Yudas Priest!" howled Oscar. "Voolies!"

Forgetting Josephine, forgetting his marriage, Oscar went galloping across the high platform, straight for the slowly passing cars, while Henry, his derby in one hand, his cane in the other, headed for the caboose, with Judge running a close second.

With a flying leap, displaying uncanny agility for his bulk, Henry landed on the back platform, while Judge managed to grasp the handles, his coat tails flying, and swung aboard. The conductor met Henry at the doorway, but Henry knocked him aside and stumbled into the car.

Peter Hatton and Len Stryker were there, in the dimly-lighted caboose, facing him in the aisle.

"Stop this train!" panted Henry, shaking his cane. "You—you cannot take sheep into Wild Horse Valley!"

"Can't I?" rasped Peter Hatton. "Stop me, Conroy."

A gun flashed in the car-lights, as Hatton covered Henry and Judge, neither of whom had a gun. Len Stryker reached over, took Henry's cane away from him and flung it through the doorway. The train had gained speed now, as it struck the down-grades. Henry drew back from the menace of the gun.

"Set down—you two!" ordered Hatton.

"Wh-what's this all about?" quavered the conductor.

"Keep yore nose out of this," ordered Hatton. "Yo're paid to run the train; this is private business."

"But you cannot do this, Hatton," protested Henry.

"No? Well, I'm doin' it, Conroy. I know my rights. Once I get sheep into Wild Horse Valley—nothin' can stop me. I know how much range belongs to the cattlemen. You two set there and enjoy the ride. As soon as we've unloaded at the Circle M sidin', you can go home."

"My goodness!" gasped Henry. "I see it all now, Judge."

"See what?" asked Judge huskily.

"The reasons for those murders. It proves my ideas. Don't you see it? Laird and Novelle—sheep. They bought the Circle M. Shep Hart was an ex-sheepman from Wyoming."

"What's that got to do with it?" asked Hatton grim-faced, tensed.

"You couldn't let him tell us who you are, Hatton."

Len Stryker swore bitterly, "And you said he was a fool, Pete."

"He is," replied Hatton, his voice brittle. And added: "For tippin' his hand that way. Not a brain in his head. But the sheep go onto the Wild Horse range, Len—nothin' can stop that— not now."

BUT HATTON reckoned without the vitrified Viking. Oscar had caught the ladder of a sheep-car and climbed to the top of the train, where he started on a dog-trot toward the engine. Oscar was unarmed, clad in his Sunday best. As he ran he threw away his coat and hat, leaping from car to car; the train gathered speed.

At the last car he leaped down to the tender, sprawling over the coal, and came upright in the engine cab, a huge, coal-streaked figure, howling at the top of his voice:

"Stop de train! Stop de train!"

Possibly the fireman thought Oscar was a crazed tramp, because he swung a brawny fist at Oscar's jaw, only to find himself in the grip of a roaring giant, who tossed him head-first into the tender. The engineer, reaching for a wrench as a weapon, found his arm caught in a vise, while Oscar yelled in his face:

"Stop, you fule! You vant to get wrecked?"

Oscar meant a personal wreck, but the engineer thought there might be danger ahead; so, in the parlance of the rail, he shot-gunned the train. The big engine, flung into reverse, threw sparks far above the cab, as the sanded wheels bit into the rails.

The sudden jerk threw Henry and Judge the length of the caboose, where they tangled with Hatton, Stryker and the puzzled conductor. For several moments all of them were too dazed to do anything. Hatton had lost his gun, and Stryker was too stunned to think of one. Henry was sitting on Hatton's six-shooter, but had not realized it yet.

The train was backing up, almost as fast as it had been going ahead, the engine spouting sparks, as Oscar forced the engineer to open up the throttle. They were nearly back to the Scorpion Bend depot when the conductor yelled:

"Look out! Look out! We're going in the ditch!"

Hatton and Stryker were trying to get through the narrow door together, following the frightened conductor, when Henry struck them, knocking them through the doorway. Henry struck the railing, rebounded, and went off the train, followed by Judge, who made a mighty leap, high in the air.

Both men went rolling in the cinders and sage, but Henry saw the caboose leap high, as it cut across the main line, while other cars piled up behind it. Henry had lost Hatton's six-shooter, and as he staggered ahead he saw Hatton and Stryker running past the depot.

Judge was sitting up, panting like an over-heated pup. Henry said:

"Judge, can I—I do anything for you, sir?"

Judge muttered something sour about "only a good embalming job," as Henry headed for the spot beyond the depot where he had left the buckboard and team. Judge came staggering behind him, wheezing loudly. Men were running to the wrecked train, but the sheriff of Tonto was not interested in that.

As quickly as possible he untied the team, ignoring Judge's panted questions, ordered Judge into the seat and climbed in behind him.

"Sh-shall I dud-drive?" panted Judge.

"Hang onto your hat!" snapped Henry. "This is a man's job."

HENRY WHIRLED the team away from the fence, swung them down a short street and onto the road to Wild Horse Valley. People were still running toward the wreck, as the equipage whirled on two wheels and went out of Scorpion Bend in a cloud of dust.

"There's a six-shooter under the cushion!" yelled Henry. "Dig it out—and use it if we are followed!"

"By who?" yelled Judge, digging frantically with one hand, while he clung to the seat with the other.

"By any of the Circle M outfit. If we can reach the grades ahead of them, they'll have a fine time getting past us on that narrow road."

Ignoring ruts and sharp turns, where the buckboard mowed down cactus and mesquite, they reached the grades, and Henry drew down the weary team.

"Go easy," squalled Judge. "One mistake is all anyone ever makes on this grade, Henry. But why hurry? Why did we not stay in Scorpion Bend? Why—why, Oscar and Josephine's marriage—"

"Oscar! That is it, Judge! I saw Oscar running for that train.

Somehow he brought it back. It must have been Oscar. Wild Horse Valley should build a monument to Oscar Johnson."

"Make it a tombstone—if Josephine caught him," Judge choked.

A mile or so for a breathing spell, and again Henry sent the team at a headlong pace around the sharp turns. Mile after mile, while Judge prayed, swore, and talked of just how he wanted to be laid away. But Henry paid no attention, except at times to glance back, where the moonlight silvered the stretches of road behind them.

"There is no one behind us, Henry," said Judge. "Slow down, you moth-eaten puffball of an imitation Jehu!"

"Trusting soul," replied Henry, and slashed the tired horses with the whip, sending them down the last twisting grade to the valley level, where without a word of explanation he swung the team off the road and behind, a screen of mesquite, the tires cutting deep in the hissing sand.

Sitting there behind the winded team they saw two riders gallop past in the moonlight, making hardly a sound on the sandy road. Barely giving them time to pass and disappear, Henry urged the weary team back to the road, and on toward Tonto City.

"Who were they, Henry?" asked Judge wearily.

"It might have been Sandy and Albert—but I don't believe it was."

After a mile or so Henry drove slowly, scanning the barbwire fence along the road, finally drawing up sharp.

"There it is," he said. "The old road to the Circle M. I believe that old gate is only wired shut, Judge. It will cut off several miles."

"But we cannot cross the new railroad," protested Judge. "You're loony!"

"I could cross the Red Sea right now, Judge. Take care of the gate."

Grumbling wearily, Judge managed to open the wire-and-stake gate, and Henry drove through. The road was little used, partly grown over, but that was no obstruction to Henry Harrison Conroy. They reached the railroad at the siding, where they managed to bump over the heavy rails, and onto the road to the Circle M ranch house.

They tied the team to a drift-fence and proceeded on foot to the house, where a light shone dully through the curtains of the main room. Henry had a gun now, as they slowly worked their way to the front porch, which was raised about three feet off the ground. Heavy rose bushes gave them partial concealment, as they crouched there, protected from the moonlight by the side of the house. The window was up nearly a foot from the bottom, and voices were plainly audible.

"A—a woman in there!" whispered Judge. "Listen, Henry."

THEN A man's voice, speaking in shrill, frightened tones, saying: "But I can't do that, Hatton. You know I can't!"

"It's up to you, Eckles," said Hatton's heavy voice. "The sheep train is wrecked—and our scheme is wrecked, too. Blast that fat-nosed sheriff! Just when everything was all set—I should have shot his heart out."

"But what do you want of me—of us?" queried Eckles.

"I want you to write a statement, Eckles. Write that this was yore scheme—to sheep out Wild Horse Valley. Say that Peter Hatton was hired by you to do this job. I've got to be in the clear. After you've written and signed that statement, you are both free."

"Wait a minute," begged Eckles. "You say that the sheriff accused you of murdering Brent and Hart tonight. I didn't do that, Pete. They'll hang you for killing them two cowboys."

"They can't prove anythin', you poor fool. I'll face that charge. But I want them to know that the sheep was yore scheme, and that I only worked for you."

"The ranch is in your name, Pete. It don't work out, I tell you. Why don't we all pull out, before anybody comes? You can't harm Jane Laird. Man, she didn't have anything to do with the deal."

Peter Hatton laughed. "No? Then why did she come here and accuse me of stealing her old man's money—of murderin' him. You know blame well, she did. And she hasn't anythin' to do with it. She knows now who killed Brent and Hart. Turn her loose? You fool—and you call yourself a lawyer."

"But there must be a way out," protested Eckles. "You can't save yourselves by murdering us, Pete."

"I can shut your mouths,' gritted Hatton. "Confound the luck! Just when we had everythin' our own way, too. If I ever get a crack at that sheriff, I'll kill him, if it's the last thing I ever do."

"Why argue, Pete?" queried Stryker nervously. "We never know what minute somebody might come here. I tell yuh, somebody was ahead of us. That wasn't fog over the canyon, it was dust."

"Nobody was ahead of us, Len. Let's settle this thing right now."

"Wait. Let me go out and take a good look, Pete. Yuh can see a long ways on a night like this. I tell yuh, I'm skittish."

"Go ahead," growled Hatton. "Don't stay long."

Henry and Judge crouched low, as the door opened and Stryker came out on the porch. He stood there for several moments. Then he opened the door a trifle and said quietly:

"Pete, there's a couple riders comin'. Might be Hank and Pat—and it might not. Better move them two into the back room, until we're sure."

Stryker closed the door and stood there, almost in reach of the two officers, who did not know what to do, except wait. The two riders came straight to the porch. Stryker stepped out to the edge of the porch, calling to them.

"Hatton?" queried one of the men.

"Hatton's in the house. This is Stryker."

"Oh, yes; this is John Campbell and Bob Keys."

Bob Keys was one of the commissioners.

"Yeah," said Stryker quietly. "Kinda late, ain't yuh, Mr. Campbell?"

"It is a little late, Stryker. But a telegram came for Peter Hatton—a rather queer telegram; so we brought it out to him. Mind if we come in?"

Hatton came to the doorway, as the men came up the steps.

"A telegram for yuh, Pete," said Stryker, his voice tense. "The prosccutin' attorney and the commissioner brought it out to yuh."

"If you don't mind, I'll read it to you," said the lawyer, and in the lighted doorway he read aloud:

PETER HATTON, CIRCLE M. RANCH,
TONTO CITY, ARIZONA
    TRAIN LOAD SHEEP CONSIGNED TO YOU WRECKED HERE TONIGHT SEVERAL CARS SMASHED AND CONTENTS SCATTERED IMPOSSIBLE MOVE FOR TWENTY-FOUR HOURS PLEASE ADVISE BIG SWEDE WHO SAYS HE IS JAILER AT TONTO CITY ARRESTED BY MARSHAL FOR WRECKING TRAIN AND WHIPPING ENGINE CREW BUT HANDCUFFED MARSHAL TO A BUGGY WHEEL AND WENT AWAY WITH THE KEY BELIEVE HE WENT BACK TO TONTO CITY WITH A WOMAN AM WIRING SHERIFF AT TONTO.
                                    BENSON AGENT.

"Well, that's shore funny," said Hatton huskily. "Come in, gents."

"I don't believe that we—"began Campbell.

"Come in!" snapped Hatton, and added: "Before I shoot yuh and drag yuh in."

The door closed behind them. Henry whispered:

"My goodness! Locked the marshal to a buggy wheel. Yes, he would do a thing like that."

"My God, Henry, don't you realize—"

"Sh-h-h-h-h!" warned Henry.

John Campbell was protesting against Hatton's actions, and Bob Keys was expressing indignation in no uncertain terms.

"Shut up, you jugheads!" roared Peter Hatton. "Bring 'em out, Len. Mebbe you folks never met. Miss Laird, gentlemen. She stuck her nose into somethin', and couldn't get it out. Mr. Eckles, the crookedest lawyer in Wyoming, who thought he was smarter than Peter Hatton."

Hatton laughed insanely.

"Shut up, Pete," begged Len Stryker. "They can hear yuh in Tonto."

"Who cares? This is my party—and the guests are here. Don't shiver, Eckles—you'll be plenty warm in a few minutes."

"Pete, there's no use makin' it any worse," pleaded Stryker. "We can tie 'em up and head for the Border. No use of—"

"No use, eh?" snarled Hatton. "This is my blaze of glory, damn yuh! All my life I've schemed and planned to get somethin' for myself. If a man stood in my way, I killed him. I'm close to fifty now—and all I've schemed and planned has been ruined by a red-nosed sheriff who don't know the difference between a sheep and a goat.

"Yeah, we can be safe across the Border—safe and broke, dodgin' every time we see a white man. What's life worth that way? All I've got left is a chance to get even with the people who ruined me—and I'll get even. I'll make Wild Horse Valley date time from the night they ruined Pete Hatton.

"I'll send this place up in smoke—and then I'll get that sheriff. If it hadn't been for him I'd sheep out this whole valley and get rich. I'd be the big man of this range. They'd all come to Peter Hatton."

"But it ain't worth it, Pete," said Stryker. "Stay, if yuh want to, but I'm goin' now."

"You are—are yuh?"

The concussion of Hatton's forty-five rattled the windows, echoed by his insane laugh of derision. Jane Laird screamed. Then the room was silent, broken only by Hatton's chuckle.

"Yeah, you went somewhere, Len," purred Hatton. "I'm still the boss. I'll light a fire that they can see in Tonto City. Mebbe it'll bring the sheriff. That's the idea. Bring him out here and kill him in the light of my fire."

Henry leaned in close to the window.

"My goodness, what an ambition!" he exclaimed loudly.

CHAPTER VIII

FOR A MOMENT there was silence in the house. Then Campbell gasped: "Henry Conroy!" With a roaring curse on his lips Hatton forgot all caution, as he leaped for the door and flung it open, his six-shooter high in his right hand.

Six feet away from him, the big forty-five clutched in both hands, Henry Conroy was shooting swiftly, driving bullet after bullet into the crazed killer, who plunged forward, smashing into the porch-rail, flinging his gun out into the yard.

A moment later, the empty gun dangling in his hand, Henry stumbled into the smoke-hazy room. Horses were galloping into the yard of the ranch house, and Judge yelled:

"Sandy! You are just in time!"

"In time for what?" queried Henry. "Breakfast?"

Sandy Crane and Albert Novelle came in with Judge. Jane Laird and Sam Eckles were tightly bound, but Campbell and Bob Keys were loose. Sandy quickly unbound Jane and Eckles, while Henry leaped over and examined Len Stryker.

The tall cowboy was not dead.

"You—you got Hatton?" he whispered.

"Yes, I believe the gentleman is deceased, Stryker," replied Henry.

"He went crazy. I—I reckon he allus was crazy."

"My God!" exclaimed Campbell. "He was going to burn us all up in this house. The man was criminally insane, Henry. I never realized it. And he blamed you for ruining him. We brought a telegram—"

"I know all about that," nodded Henry. He turned to the white-faced Eckles. "You better tell the truth, Eckles," he warned. "It is the only way you can save your neck."

"I'll talk," quavered Eckles. "Hatton and I looted the Laird and Novelle outfit. It was easy up there, where—they believed us. Hatton killed Novelle. I can't prove it, but he did. I believe he killed Laird, too. Our scheme was to steal everything and move the sheep down here. I bought the Circle M with stolen money. We forged wills, bills-of-sale and everything we needed. It was easy. But I had to do everything in Hatton's name, because I couldn't show in the deals.

"Everything was air-tight—but Jane Laird was suspicious and came here to see Hatton. Novelle wanted an accounting; so he came here, too. I came to warn Hatton and help him get rid of them—but he doublecrossed me and tried to murder me; only his bullet struck my belt-buckle and just knocked me out.

"I was terribly sick, but I managed to walk to Tonto City. I stayed in the sheriff's office, while a man went to get the sheriff—but Hatton and his gang took me away before I could tell what I knew. I can easily prove that the Circle M belongs to Jane Laird and Albert Novelle. Several thousand sheep, too. Some money and bonds. But I want you to understand that I never murdered anybody."

"Which one of Hatton's men was killed at Brent's ranch, Stryker?" asked Henry.

"**BEN WALL.** We didn't dare get a doctor for him. We were buryin' him when that runaway buckboard almost ran over us. Then Hatton got the idea of burnin' him in that old ranch house. When Hatton heard that you had found a corpse in the ashes, we went down there at night and destroyed everythin'."

"Hart had recognized Hatton?"

"That's right. He knew we were sheepmen. He'd have blocked our deal. Hatton shot Brent in yore doorway that night."

"What about that brass shotgun shell at the JP?" queried Judge.

"Oh, that!" grinned Henry. "Why, I saw Bugs Taylor in town yesterday and told him I'd like to have a matchbox like the one he carries. He said he could give me a twelve-gauge shell, but I'd have to go to the Circle M to find a ten."

"What were those telegrams?" queried Stryker weakly.

"Jail-bait," replied Henry. "I knew I could not deliver them—and I felt sure that Hatton would have the station burglarized, trying to discover what they were all about."

"You—you knew all this—and did nothing?" queried Judge. "You fiddled while Tonto City nearly was sheeped out. Dilatory, I would say, sir."

"Just a moment, Judge," said Bob Keys. "Henry's methods worked out just right. I congratulate him. As I said to the board—"

John Campbell cleared his throat raspingly. "I believe we owe a lot to Henry and his organization."

"We certainly do," agreed Keys heartily.

Albert grinned wearily at Jane. "I came here to see you—but you were rather hard to find, Miss Laird. But everything is all right now."

"I hope so," said Jane weakly. "I am still dazed."

"So'm I," said Sandy.

"You always was," smiled Judge. Sandy grew embarrassed, when Jane looked at him. She said:

"Why, you are the man who met me at the train that morning."

"Yes'm, I'm the man; the one you lied to. Why didja say you was Pete Hatton's daughter? If I was pickin' out a father, I'd do better than that."

"Just a foolish whim, I suppose. You were so curious." Jane smiled.

"Listen!" exclaimed Henry. From outside came the sound of

lusty singing; as a roaring voice neared the porch. Not melodious, but loud.

"That vitrified Viking!" exclaimed Judge. "That is his fighting-song."

Oscar Johnson came on the porch and looked at the body of Peter Hatton. "Ay will be dorned!" he snorted. "Somebody beat me to him. Oh, hallo."

He stepped into the room and looked around. Oscar was minus coat and hat, and only a remnant of his wedding shirt fluttered from his mighty shoulders.

"You are late, Oscar," reminded Henry.

"Yah, su-ure," agreed Oscar disgustedly. "Ay olmost had to ride a sheep. But Ay found Free-holey and Ay took his hurse. He's valking back—with a yug in his hand. Are de ship-horders all dead?"

"Everything is under control, Oscar," replied Henry. "Where is Josephine?"

"Yosephine?" gasped Oscar. "Yosephine? Yudas Priest, Ay forgot her!"

"Never mind, Oscar," said John Campbell. "We will put on the biggest wedding ever seen in Wild Horse Valley. Don't you realize what you've done tonight?"

"Ay will," replied Oscar, "as soon as Ay meet Yosephine."

"We will erect a monument to you," said Bob Keys.

"Oh, yah," sighed Oscar. "Yust put little lamb on top. Ay know Yosephine."

Thirty minutes later the cavalcade moved on to Tonto City, while across the old road came the two Mexicans on their slow-moving mules. On the main road they had met Hank Hess and Pat Dolan, the two cowboys from the Circle M who had been in town. They stopped to question Thunder and Lightning, who gave them a weird account of the wreck of the sheep train.

"Yuh can go to the Circle M and tell Pete Hatton that our address is Somewhere in Mexico," Pat Dolan told them, and that was why the Mexes were on their way to the Circle M.

They knocked loudly, but there was no response. The door was unlocked. Fearfully, they entered, calling for Peter Hatton.

"I'm theenking we better go home," quavered Thunder. "Nobody ees here."

Lightning found a match in his pocket, which he scratched on the sole of his boot. On the rough couch was a sheeted figure.

"*Madre de Dios!*" whispered Thunder. "W'at ees eet, Lightning?"

Lightning reached out a trembling left hand and drew aside the sheet. The match fell from his fingers, leaving them in total darkness. From the throat of Thunder Mendoza came a strangled, "Ee-e-ek!"

The next moment they went through that doorway together, tore down what was left of the sagging porch-railing, and leaped into the darkness. The two weary mules lifted their heads and watched the flying figures disappear down the road. It was only about nine miles to the JHC; so why bother with a mule?